*Nabela,*

# THE AWAKENING

*Best wishes
for the New Year!
Yvonne Heidt*

# By the Author

Sometime Yesterday

The Awakening

# THE AWAKENING

*by*
## Yvonne Heidt

2013

# THE AWAKENING

ISBN 13: 978-1-60282-772-1

This Trade Paperback Original Is Published By
Bold Strokes Books, Inc.
P.O. Box 249
Valley Falls, NY 12185

First Edition: January 2013

**Credits**
Editor: Victoria Oldham
Production Design: Stacia Seaman
Cover Design by Sheri (graphicartist2020@hotmail.com)

# Acknowledgments

It takes a small village. I would like to thank mine at Bold Strokes Books. Radclyffe, Victoria, and Cindy, I appreciate your patience and willingness to work with me. Thank you, Connie, for reading my crazy e-mails. The team at BSB is one that I'm very proud to be a part of. A special nod to Ruth, Stacia, Kathi, Toni, and Sandy. Sheri, your covers are outstanding. Also, I would like to thank the authors for including me in your reindeer games. I'm having a blast.

Thank you to my family and friends who have been so amazing through this last year. I wish I had the space to thank you all. It wasn't until I typed your names out that I realized it would take an entire book just to list you. Thank you all for your support and encouragement.

Maralee Lackman for tirelessly promoting my books and holding my hand when I need you to. I have the best BFF in the world.

Stephanie Keeler, my most amazing ninja, thank you for being an awesome beta-reader!

Sheila Powell for answering my questions about the other side.

An amazing friend, Wendy Sailor, crossed over this year. She touched a thousand hearts with her kindness, and I'm going to miss her. I also lost a beloved aunt, Joyce Ansbro. My posse on the other side is getting bigger.

Thank you, Mom and Papa, for your support and love during this challenging year.

Sandy, thank you, sweetheart, for taking care of me and inviting my characters to have dinner with us. There is nowhere on earth I'd rather be than here with you.

For Kerri-Ann & Daniel.

# PROLOGUE

Sunny Skye waited on the wide front porch, dancing nervously from foot to foot and impatiently brushing wild curls out of her eyes. She checked the watch she'd received for her eleventh birthday the week before, and tapped the crystal. "They're late!"

She had been looking forward to this weekend for months. Her father had put together a film crew and invited two additional girls they had picked out of twenty case files to take part in a documentary he was shooting about psychic children. Special kids with extraordinary abilities. Her mother, also gifted, was going to be in it as well. Sunny was beside herself with excitement. She wanted to spend time with other kids who wouldn't think she was crazy whenever she started talking to someone they couldn't see.

A dark sedan pulled into the driveway. "Never mind," she called over her shoulder before running down the stairs.

The rear passenger door opened, and Sunny saw a small girl with red hair pulled into a long ponytail. She was huddled against the backseat and looked as if she might cry. A woman who Sunny assumed was the girl's mother got out of the car, walked past her and up to the house, not bothering to take the girl with her.

"Don't be scared," Sunny said and held out a hand to help her out. "I'm Sunny, and I'm so happy that you could make it."

"My name is Tiffany Curran. I don't like to touch people."

"Oh," Sunny said. "That's right. I forgot." She stepped back from the car to let Tiffany out. "My dad says that you have psychometric abilities. That means you can read people's minds by touching them, right?"

"Sometimes. And when I touch things, I sometimes see what happened there. Like walls and stuff."

"Place memory? That's cool!"

"What do you do?"

Sunny smiled. "I'm an empath and I can hear and talk with ghosts."

Tiffany's light blue eyes widened. "Do you see them?"

"I see them in my mind." Tiffany was staring at her with her mouth open. "What?" Sunny asked.

"Your eyes are two different colors."

"Mom says they were both blue when I was born, and six months later, one of them turned green. Some people think they're creepy."

"I think they're beautiful." Tiffany smiled shyly, flashing two small dimples.

Before Sunny could politely thank her for the compliment, a door slammed behind them. She felt Tiffany startle at the sight of the last girl to arrive. Taller than Sunny, she was dressed in black clothes that hung off her slender frame. The girl glared in their direction from under spiky hair, her dark eyes framed with heavy black liner. She sneered at them, then defiantly took a drag off her cigarette before flicking it into the street.

"Don't ever call me Lacey."

Sunny felt a flash of uncertainty at the anger she heard in her voice but remembered her own manners. "Well, what would you like us to call you?"

"Shade."

Tiffany took a step behind Sunny. "What do you do?"

"Necromancer. I see dead people."

"For reals?" Tiffany's voice squeaked.

Shade laughed. "That line never gets old."

Tiffany looked confused, so Sunny explained. "A necromancer can speak to the dead and interact with their shades." Sunny smiled. "Oh, I get your name now, clever."

"What's a shade?" asked Tiffany.

"Invisible zombies." Shade curled her fingers into claws and moaned dramatically.

Tiffany gave a little squeak and ducked behind Sunny again. Sunny continued to grin, deciding she liked the angry girl despite the dark energy that seemed to be hanging around her. "It's just another name for a ghost."

The van behind Shade peeled away with a screech of tires and sped down the street. Sunny felt a sharp jab of hurt emanate from Shade that didn't match the angry scowl on her face. Sunny's power of empathy continued to be a mystery to her since she didn't fully understand how it was she could feel what others did. She hated it when their emotions didn't match their words or body language. Sunny went with her instinct and stepped closer to Shade.

"Why didn't your mother stay?" Tiffany asked.

"She doesn't care about a stupid movie. She's just happy to get rid of me for the weekend."

"It's not a movie. It's a documentary about special kids who have psychic abilities," Sunny said.

"Whatever." Shade turned away from her and wiped at her face. "It's stupid."

"My mother says I'm cursed and it's the devil inside me." Tiffany blushed and stared at her feet, her hands in her pockets.

"What?" Sunny was shocked. "They are *gifts,* not curses." She felt instantly protective of Tiffany and shot an angry look at the woman talking with Sunny's parents.

"Oh." Tiffany waved a hand. "That's not my mother; it's my aunt Darleen. We didn't tell my mother we were coming. She flat-out refused when she got the invitation, so we lied and said we were going to Portland for the weekend."

Shade chuckled and crossed her skinny arms. "This might not suck."

## CHAPTER ONE

*Fifteen years later*

Something crunched under Sunny's boot, sounding unnaturally loud in the silence as she took another step down the pitch-black hallway. "That was just me," she said for the recorder.

"Um, Sunny?" the voice crackled from the radio on her hip. She unclipped the walkie from her belt. "Go."

"There's movement to your left on video two."

Sunny glanced at the night-vision camera in the corner and spun to her left with her recorder and thermal detector held in front of her. "Hello? Is someone there?" She knew the question was just for the recorder's sake, since she could clearly feel a spirit energy, *other*, as she had called them from childhood. Her body tingled with the familiar sensation of electrical pulses under her skin, raising the hair on her arms slightly.

*Now, that's more like it.* So often when they did investigations in private homes, there was little to no paranormal activity to show for their efforts.

She felt rather than saw a shadow that darted past her. Goose bumps raced along her spine and the temperature dropped. The equipment in her hand confirmed what she already sensed. "EMF spiking at point two, temp reading sixty-seven, now sixty-two, fifty-nine."

She continued to stare through the small camera screen, but she didn't see any additional movement, and when she glanced down at the thermostat, it was once again at base reading of seventy-one, taken at the beginning of the investigation. She set the thermal camera back on the table and called Shade on the radio.

"Sunny to base."

"Yo."

"See anything else on the monitor?"

"That's a negative, but I think I caught it on video."

"Okay." Sunny felt the absence of *other* and called to her third team member. "Tiff?"

"Here."

"What's going on down there?"

"A couple of knocking sounds. Nothing on the thermal to indicate animal presence."

Static pierced Sunny's ears and she held the radio at arm's length. "Tiff?" Concerned, she started toward the basement stairs. She hadn't quite reached the door when a scream pierced the darkness.

Sunny snapped on her flashlight before hitting the landing. She found Tiffany doing her I-hate-spiders-dance at the bottom of the stairs. It was kind of cute actually. Her arms were up in the air, and she wriggled around in a circle before brushing off her skin maniacally. "Damn, Tiff. You scared the hell out of me."

"Check now!"

"Hold still, then." Sunny ran the routine of checking Tiffany's hair, moving down in a smoothing motion. "Shush, it's okay. Calm down."

"You know I hate the basements."

Sunny bit back her laughter. Tiffany really was scared of spiders, unnaturally so. "It was your turn, remember?"

Tiffany shuddered dramatically before Sunny called base. "False alarm."

Shade's laughter seemed to burst through the tiny speaker. "I know. You should have seen the look on her face."

"Laugh it up, funny girl. It's your turn next investigation." Sunny turned her attention to the left, seeing a small movement out of the corner of her eye. "I just saw a shadow duck behind the boxes." She flipped off the light and turned her camera back on. "Hello?"

Sunny didn't care how many investigations she went on, the thrill was there every time she saw, felt, or heard something from the other side. She moved carefully across the concrete floor, making sure not to trip over the usual detritus found in a basement, wondering as she often did why people had so much clutter and why they didn't bother to clean some of it up before they called her team in. Standing still for a few moments, she closed her eyes to listen with her senses but heard only the sound of Tiffany's soft breathing behind her. She'd just taken another tentative step when she was shoved violently from behind. "What the—"

"Oh God, I'm so sorry." Tiffany reached down to help Sunny up from her sprawled position on the ground. "I stepped on a skateboard."

Sunny cupped the elbow she'd landed on, and her hand came away sticky. Great. She was bleeding and it was filthy down here. "S'okay, Tiff." She made the decision to wrap the investigation for the night. "Let's pack it up."

❖

Jordan Lawson stared at the small stack of boxes lined up against the wall in her new apartment, thinking it was a sad state of affairs when thirty-one years of living could be packed up and moved in one small truckload. The meager belongings she'd brought along mocked her, showing her how much the last ten years of her life had actually been lived for her job rather than her home life.

Other than the new bed, couch, and desk she'd had delivered, the apartment in the old brick building was empty. Like her.

Her boot heels echoed off the newly refurbished hardwood floors as she walked to the naked window, reminding her she would have to buy an area rug as well as curtains. Where the hell did someone buy curtains, anyway? Every shithole she'd ever lived in had those ugly gold monstrosities with the white rubber backs, turned gray over time and older than she was. She assumed the lack of window dressing was due to the recent remodel of her apartment. Jordan sighed and cut open the box labeled DESK. She'd just pulled out a stack of manila files when a loud knock at the door startled her into dropping them onto the floor. She hadn't met any of her neighbors yet, and truthfully, it wasn't high on her list of priorities. She didn't want to be bothered, and she sure as shit didn't want anyone coming to borrow anything they had no intention of replacing. Other than the landlord, the only person she'd met in Bremerton so far was the sergeant who'd done her interview after her transfer from Seattle.

Jordan peeked out the security hole; she didn't see anyone but opened the door anyway. The hallway was empty and the door across from hers was shut. Puzzled and a little irked at what she thought might be a prank, she went back to the box she was unpacking.

One of the files lay open and scattered on the floor. The article written by her friend, Katerina Volchosky, on three missing teenagers caught her eye. Jordan ran a finger down the face of one of the girls. The picture of Gina Brayden had been taken when she was still in high school. When Jordan had met the girl, there was little trace left of this innocence caught on film. By that time, she'd been on the street for a year, and months of prostitution and drugs had exacted its toll.

She picked up the poem that Gina had given to her on a piece of dirty notepaper and read it.

*Throwaway girl*
*Curled up in the gutter*
*Dirty and scared*
*What are you crying for?*

*No one here cares*
*What happens to you.*

*Throwaway girl*
*Everything's for sale.*

*Your innocence,*
*Your trust, your body,*
*And your mind.*

*Past, present,*
*And future.*

*Throwaway girl*
*Let me set you straight.*
*You don't need.*
*You can't feel.*
*Forbidden to want.*

*You'll do what I say*
*When I say it.*

*Throwaway girl*
*Shut your mouth.*
*There's a hundred*
*More behind you*
*To take your place.*

*Unwanted, unloved,*
*Forgettable and lost.*

*Throwaway girl*
*Get back in line.*
*You're just doing time*
*On this blood-soaked street.*

The last line still gave Jordan chills. It hurt her to know that someone so young knew so much about pain and violence. Gina reminded her so much of herself at that age.

When she went missing along with two other kids, Jordan had questioned every teenager in the pack that ran together near Pike

Place Market, but she never uncovered a single lead. Gina Brayden disappeared without a trace. Jordan tried not to think of the *if onlys* and carefully put the file into her desk and shut the drawer before standing. New town, new job, and she couldn't save them all. But damn, how she wanted to.

Putting the empty box next to the front door, Jordan decided to call it a night. Tomorrow was her first day at the Bremerton Police Department and the first day back on the job since she'd been shot several months earlier. She hated the thought of having to start over, but it wasn't as though she'd left anything important behind in Seattle.

A memory intruded of brown hair and cold green eyes almost as if to argue with her. She ignored it. She wouldn't give the betraying bitch any more time than she'd already stolen.

Jordan walked into the bathroom to splash cold water on her face and stopped short in the doorway. The bathroom box was sitting in the middle of the white tile floor. She could have sworn she already unpacked it. Yet there it was, a full carton staring back at her, and the medicine cabinet door stood open.

She quickly put the items away, irritated that it was so cold in the small room.

Jordan switched off the overhead light and climbed into her new bed. Her apartment was on the third floor, and the streetlight outside her window illuminated her bedroom with an almost dirty yellow glow. She added blackout curtains to her mental list. She guessed they'd sell those wherever the hell they sold ugly drapes.

She punched the pillow and turned away from the windows to stare at the closed bedroom and closet doors and prepared herself for a restless night. She hated going to sleep in unfamiliar places. She'd learned as a child that the worst dangers came at night. Jordan was on the verge of falling asleep when she heard a loud crash outside the bedroom. She was instantly alert and aware. When she caught herself pulling the comforter up to hide under, she was disgusted at the reaction. What was she doing? She was a cop, not a helpless, terrified child waiting for her junkie mother's latest conquest to find her. Since she'd been shot, the memories seemed to surface at sudden noises. It made her sick that the wall she'd built around the horror of her childhood seemed to be crumbling.

Jordan swore when her feet hit the icy floor. She didn't need to turn on a lamp; she could see perfectly by the sickly light coming in the window.

She heard laughter and a car door slam shut in the parking lot outside. Jordan glanced at the clock and saw that it was three in the morning. Inconsiderate assholes. With a heavy sigh, she threw herself under the covers and pulled them up over her head to block out the light. For good measure, she also pressed the extra pillow over her ear in an attempt to muffle the sound.

❖

The sky was clear and sharp, which was somewhat unusual for Bremerton. This time of the year was usually overcast and gray. Sunny sat in the front seat of the van, bracing her feet on the wide dashboard. Laying her head back on the seat, she closed her eyes and imagined all the remnant energy of the night flying out the window. As far as investigations went, this one was pretty normal. It wasn't all evil, all the time, as some television programs would have people believe.

She opened her eyes again when Shade pulled the van into Tiffany's driveway to drop her off.

Tiffany gathered her purse and opened the side door. "Good night. See you around noon."

Sunny turned to look at her. Tiffany's freckled and fine features appeared washed out in the harsh, overhead light. "I'm sorry about the whole spider and skateboard fiasco."

Sunny smiled. "All part of the job."

Shade waited until the porch light went off before backing out slowly. "I worry about her."

Sunny turned. "Why? Have you seen something?"

"No, not like that." Shade ran her fingers through her choppy brown hair and paused. "Life just seems so hard for her, you know?"

"Is that asshole ex-husband of hers hassling her again?"

"Not that I know of. We could handle that. She just looks so tired all the time."

"Well, we do work odd hours. You know how much energy it takes out of us. Tiffany had three back-to-back healing sessions this afternoon before we left, and you know how much that takes out of her. I tried to get her to reschedule, but she said she needed the money."

"Being a single mom is tough."

It was beyond frustrating that Tiffany wouldn't accept any help. Sunny was comfortable financially, but what good did it do if she couldn't help the people that she loved? The ghost investigations didn't bring in much, and she never took money from people who couldn't afford to pay. It was the individual readings in their own specialties for clients that paid the bills for all three of them. Each felt a personal responsibility to help others with her gifts in her own way. The investigations were an integral part of that. To assist people and spirits on both sides of the veil. They rode in silence for the last few miles, and after Shade stopped the van, she turned to Sunny and put a gentle hand on her leg.

Sunny felt the blast of hormones fill the space between them and winced internally. She loved Shade, she really did, but they'd gone down this road. She knew the best thing to do would be act normal and friendly to defuse the tension. "It's late."

A wicked grin spread on Shade's face. "Want me to stay?"

Sunny heard the hope in her voice before she shut the mental door in her mind. "You can sleep in the guest room."

"Nah, I have a hot date."

"At four a.m.?" Sunny knew that Shade would break that date for her in a second, and it made her sad. She pulled the evidence box from the backseat to bring inside with her, careful not to touch Shade while doing it. Shade pulled her shoulders back.

"Yeah. You know me. Anytime, anyplace."

Sunny did know. Shade's androgynous beauty turned heads all the time, male and female. There was something so edgy about the bad girl with her dark Cleopatra eyes who always wore black leather. "Lucky girl," she said.

Sunny heard the whispered response before she closed the door, but walked away as though she hadn't.

"But she's not you."

❖

Sunny's house was a once-grand Victorian that had been converted into apartments in the sixties and then renovated back into a single residence by her parents in the early eighties. When they remodeled, they turned three of the four bedrooms on the second floor into comfortable sitting rooms for clients and left the tiny kitchenette.

Sunny appreciated the setup. She didn't have to go downstairs to fetch water or tea either for herself or a client. It was also a great place to hide the junk food her mother protested against. Sunny loved the game. She hid cookies and potato chips, and her mother pretended not to notice.

Three years after her father died, her mother retired and turned her client list, and the large house over to Sunny before buying a nearby condominium that overlooked Puget Sound near the ferry terminal. But she hadn't been able to stay away and insisted on being the receptionist for Sunny's new business, Sisters of Spirits. The idea had been born fifteen years previously after she met Shade and Tiffany during the filming of her father's documentary. Sunny thought the abbreviation S.O.S. was clever.

She paused in the spacious foyer. From where she stood, the client reception area was to her left and a sitting room with a large fireplace was on her right. The reception area was a circular wall of bay windows with lush potted foliage and a window seat with colorful cushions. Her mother's pretty carved desk was positioned so she could easily see who was coming and going, and there were even more plants on her desk. In keeping with the house's era, table and floor lamps with their elegant stained-glass shades were present in each room. Sunny always left them on before she left for the evening; she loved coming home to the soft colored light they emitted.

Sunny turned one of them off on her way to the kitchen, passing through the dining room that doubled as a conference room. She trailed a finger across the long, teak table that her mother kept so well polished it looked like glass.

Standing at the small farm sink, she rinsed her travel mug and went up the kitchen staircase. The entire third floor was her private space. The old architecture and antiques mixed with modern furniture formed an eclectic style that Sunny considered reflective of her personality. Crystals shimmered in the windows, and fairies and dragons lived on her shelves alongside her precious books.

When she renovated the bathroom, she tried to keep to the old details of the house, ending up with an antique bathroom with all the modern conveniences. She glanced with longing at the large slipper tub next to a window overlooking the bay. Instead, she conceded to the late hour and opted for the quicker shower.

Sunny laughed when she climbed up into the bed and heard a yowl. "Oh," she said to the pair of Siamese cats. "Excuse me. Did I bother you?"

Isis purred and stretched before butting her head against Sunny's shoulder and toying with her wet braid. Ash couldn't be bothered to move, but she petted the cat anyway and stretched out. "You know, guys, I should get a dog. Then I could have someone meet me at the door when I get home."

## CHAPTER TWO

Jordan woke to the sound of banging on her front door. Three hard knocks in quick succession. Startled at waking in an unfamiliar environment, it took her a second to adjust and remember she was in her new apartment. Maybe she'd imagined the noise. Just as she thought it and checked the clock, the knocks repeated.

Who the hell would be banging on her door at six in the morning? She stalked down the hallway, not bothering to check the security peephole, and swung the door wide. "What?"

The landing was empty. Again. Pissed off, she ran to the railing to look down and catch the punk messing with her. Even with a clear view down, she couldn't see or hear anything.

Jordan turned to go back to her apartment when the front door slammed shut in her face. "Shit!" She tried the knob to find herself locked out, in her skimpy white tank and boy shorts.

The sound of slow, plodding footsteps carried up the stairs. Great, she was, for all purposes, half-naked in a strange environment. No sense in pretending. There was nowhere to hide. She turned to face whoever was coming.

A tall, skinny young man rounded the second flight of stairs carrying some plastic bags, looking down at his rather large feet, which meant he didn't see her standing there until he reached the third stair from the top. He screamed shrilly, throwing his arms up in the air, groceries went flying in all directions. When it appeared that he was going to fall backward, Jordan grabbed his arm and pulled him to the landing. His face turned white and his eyes bugged behind his thick glasses. *My new neighbor, evidently.*

"Jeezus, you scared the crap out of me." He apparently noticed her underwear because he averted his eyes, blinking them almost spastically.

"What are you doing?" asked Jordan.

"Trying to wake up. It's not every day that I come home from work to find a naked woman waiting on my doorstep."

"You ass! I'm not waiting for you. I got locked out of my apartment."

He looked incredulous. "You're the cop? Are you working vice?"

Jordan folded her arms against her chest. "Some punk-ass kid has been pulling knock and dash on my door. I was trying to catch them and my door slammed shut."

He shuffled his feet after stuffing his wayward groceries back in a bag and held out a hand. "Jackson. Steve Jackson."

She shook it. "Jordan Lawson. Get your eyes off my chest, Jackson."

"Right." Steve bent to pick up various bags. His shoulders began shaking and he coughed.

"Are you laughing at me, Steve Jackson?"

He cleared his throat. "No, but I am wondering how you're going to get into your third-floor apartment in your underwear. The landlord lives on the other side of the courtyard."

Jordan's head started to hurt. "I have to get ready for work."

"You have a problem." Steve unlocked his door and ushered her in. "Come on in. We'll call Agnes to unlock the door for you." He handed her a flannel shirt hanging on a grinning skull hook.

She quickly put it on while she followed him into the kitchen. It was an exact reversed replica of her own. Well, except the counters were buried in takeout containers, dirty dishes, and fast-food wrappers. "Maid's day off?"

Steve stood in front of the open refrigerator, a milk carton halfway to his mouth. He blinked behind his glasses. "Huh?"

"Never mind. Phone?"

"Oh, right. It's in on the coffee table." He gestured to the living room.

Jordan stepped through the small dining nook. Dirty clothes draped the couch and floor. A sixty-inch television nearly covered the wall in front of her. Several game consoles lay on the floor in front of it. Books covered every surface in the room, stacked on tables, the stained carpet, and overflowing on the shelves.

"Holy shit!" She tripped over a mound of clothes.

"Sorry about the mess. I don't have much company."

"I can see why," she muttered under her breath. She would wait standing up.

❖

"Well, look who just rolled in." Sunny took a sip of her coffee and glanced at her watch. "At two in the afternoon." She tapped a fingernail against her mug. "Late night?"

Shade stood in the doorway and tried to focus. "My eyes are bleeding," she said, slipping her dark glasses down to peer over the top.

"Oh, they are not."

"Says you. I'm the one looking out of them."

Sunny laughed. "Well, c'mon, tardy girl. Tiffany is already reviewing last night's recordings. I saved the audio for you." She paused. "Since the video would be too hard for your bleeding eyes and all."

Shade gave her a quick salute and headed for the back office on the first floor.

Sunny heard the laughter from her spot in the reception room and was glad for it. Sometimes, the work they did was so shrouded in darkness, or rather other people's perception of it, that laughter was hard-won.

The front door's merry little bell rang, and Aura Skye, Sunny's mother, came through the arched doorway laden down with packages. Today, her toenails were visible through her gladiator sandals and were painted blue. The silver anklets and bracelets she wore rang as she moved closer. Blond hair hung down her back, the same honey shade as Sunny's, only stick straight, a trait that Sunny envied on some days. Sunny smiled when she recognized the patchwork skirt made from her father's old clothes. "What?"

"Nothing, I'm just taking a minute to love and appreciate you."

Her mother's face lit up. "Oh, I love you too, baby. What a good girl you are. Now get out of my chair."

"What did you buy?"

"Stuff. Go to work." She kissed Sunny's cheek and shoved her toward the back.

Sunny went to join her friends in the war room, as Shade called it, much to her mother's dismay.

She stood in the doorway. Shade kicked back in her chair with her long legs stretched out in front of her and her monster headphones in place, listening to the audio to see if they'd caught any electronic voice phenomena. Tiffany was sitting cross-legged on her chair watching the computer screen and night-vision video. Both were totally engrossed in their tasks; neither one looked up at her entrance.

God, she adored them. *Aren't I just full of sentimentality today?* Sunny checked her watch and saw she still had an hour before her first appointment for the day. She started to sit in the third chair, but Tiffany waved her off.

"We've got this."

"Are you sure?"

Tiffany paused the video and nodded. "I've got a good head start, and I can help Shade when I'm finished. You can go get ready for your appointments."

Sunny started to leave, figuring she could get in a bit of meditation time, when Shade sat up suddenly to rewind the recording to listen again, her head cocked to the side. She automatically picked up a pen to mark the time on the notepad and repeated the section of audio, a smile spreading across her face.

"Class A."

Sunny rushed back to her station. Class A EVPs were voices

caught on recordings that could be heard clearly, without any filters or noise reduction. Donning her candy pink headphones, she twirled her finger in the air to gesture another replay. "Go," she said, closing her eyes to focus. She heard herself say, "Won't you please talk to me?"

There was a pause, then, clear as a bell, a child's sweet voice answered, "I'm okay here."

Sunny opened her eyes. "Again."

"I'm okay here."

Familiar chills ran down her spine, something she felt every single time. It was one thing when spirits talked to her telepathically and quite another when she actually heard them, that underwater quality to their voice phenomenon when the frequency was *other.* She felt a tear burn in the corner of her eye. "I don't hear any threat at all. Did either of you sense a child last night?"

"No," Tiffany said. Shade shook her head.

"Me either."

Sunny took her headphones off and set them on the desk. "Good catch." She was excited and wanted to sit and help, but it was Shade who motioned her out this time.

"Go on. We got this. We'll review after your reading."

Sunny was torn but finally nodded and left, her skirt billowing around her legs as she headed up the stairs to the second floor. She opened the door to the room where she would do the reading and took out her abalone shell and white sage stick to sweep the room. Habitually, before and after every reading with a client, she cleansed the air. The whole ritual was beneficial to clearing the room of any lingering energy of previous readings or stubborn *others* who wanted to stay. Sunny never wanted to know anyone's last name or why they booked a reading with her. It was important to Sunny that her integrity never be in question. She didn't ever want to be accused of misleading her clients, or worse, taking advantage of them. Being a medium was part of who she was, not something she did. It was innate to her identity.

She opened the French doors to the small balcony to let the smoke out before relaxing in the wide armchair to meditate.

Emptying her mind of expectations, she asked her spirit guide to protect her and keep her safe during the time she would be open to unfamiliar energy. It was a comforting and necessary formality before meeting with a client.

The bell sounded over the door, bringing her out of her light, self-imposed trance. She heard her mother greet the woman and the sound of nervous laughter. Ah, a first-timer. They were always nervous.

Sunny went downstairs and saw her mother with her arm around the young woman. Offering comfort or reassurance? Probably a little of both. "Hi," she said brightly. "I'm Sunny. It's so nice to meet you."

"Eve." She held out a hand and laughed nervously. "I'm so giddy. I don't know why." Then her eyes filled. "I'm such a mess."

"Would you like a bottle of water? Then we'll go on up."

Her mother went to the kitchen and came back with a cold bottle. "It's okay, dear."

Eve smiled at her over her shoulder as they went upstairs, looking for all the world like she wanted to run back out the door.

Sunny shut the door. "We can sit at the table or in the chairs, whichever you prefer."

"Which is best?" Her uncertainty filled the air laced with a ribbon of fear.

Sunny gestured toward the wide, comfy seats by the window. Her mind's eye perceived the young man holding red roses standing behind the one Eve had chosen.

Grief was heavy and sharp in the room, and she felt her heart contract painfully. Sunny mentally pulled herself back a step and telepathically told the young man to ease up a little because he was hurting her.

Eve was sitting so still, it was almost as if she weren't there at all, but for the emotion that rolled in waves toward Sunny.

"Okay," she said. "This is how it works. I'm not in charge. *Spirit* is. I have a whole speech about not always getting a reading from the person you may want to hear from, but I don't think that applies here, since it's already clear to me what this is about."

Eve sat with her hands clutched tightly in her lap. "Spirit?"

"You could think of them as angels, God energy, or guides. I choose to call the energy *Spirit* or *other,* because for me, the terms cover all of them without all the religious connotations."

Sunny switched on the recorder and stated the date, time, and Eve's name. "Please try to relax." She patted Eve's knee. "Take three deep breaths. In through the nose, out through the mouth. Better?" Sunny smiled.

Eve nodded.

"Okay, there's a man here eager to talk with you. He's showing me a wedding ring to indicate husband? His name starts with a D. Donny or Danny?"

"Donny," Eve whispered hoarsely before covering her face with her hands, and she began to cry. "Is it really him?"

"It's okay. He wants to say he loves you and he's sorry that you hurt so much." Sunny waited for Eve to gather herself a bit. "He wants you to know that it didn't hurt." An image of a car accident flashed in her mind. "He says he was out of his body like that." Sunny snapped her fingers. "And that there was no pain."

Relief showed on Eve's face. "I couldn't bear the thought that he suffered and I wasn't there."

"He's showing me a basketball and he's high-jumping the rim to score through the net. Does this mean anything to you?"

"Oh," Eve said and laughed. "Donny loved to play, but he was so short, he was terrible at it. When he was growing up, he wanted to be a professional ball player."

"Well, he's showing me that he's very good now. Actually, he's showing off."

"That's Donny. It's really him!"

"Okay, now I'm seeing a Ferris wheel and a stuffed pink gorilla."

"Our first date." Fresh tears ran down her cheeks. "Oh God, I miss him so much."

"He wants to tell you that he's okay and not to cry so much. It makes him sad to see you so unhappy." Sunny paused. "He's sorry that he didn't get to say good-bye but that he's with you. He's not gone, just in a different place."

Still choked up, Eve nodded.

Sunny continued. "There's a young woman next to him holding his hand. She looks a lot like him. Sister?"

Eve's eyes widened. "How did you? Never mind, yes. She died very young of leukemia."

"She wants to tell you that she's taking good care of him, okay?"

"Yes."

"She's asking me to tell you that she would like for you to tell their mother that they are together and happy."

"Okay."

Sunny felt some of the emotional grief ease up a little. This was one of the many reasons why she loved her gift. To be able to help those who hurt and offer some comfort. "He says that it was him the other night, but he won't tell me what he did."

Eve's smile was genuine and two red spots appeared on her cheeks. "It's okay. I know what he's talking about."

Sunny let it go. Even in this space, some things were private. "He says to be happy, and that he's always there next to you when you need him. Now he's waving and moving back a little. Do you have any questions?"

"No, I think you covered it. I might think of a thousand later, but I think you covered the most important ones."

"He's blowing you a kiss."

"He's gone?" When Sunny nodded, Eve continued. "Thank you so much. I was so skeptical when I got here. When I told my family I was coming here, they were so free with their opinions and fraud warnings that I almost backed out. It was nothing like they said, and I'm so grateful." She leaned back in her armchair.

"You're very welcome. I'm glad that you came and Donny showed up."

"But you're so good. Don't they always show up?"

Sunny clicked the recorder off. "Thank you, but no, not always.

It depends on the relationship they had here in the physical world. Spirits don't usually lie, and sometimes they say hurtful things that aren't very nice to the people that want to talk to them. People don't always appreciate that the dead might not say what they want to hear."

Eve looked fascinated and leaned forward again. "Do you tell them?"

"Depends on their motive and what their energy tells me. Being an empath, it's very easy for me to know if what they're saying is truly how they feel." Sunny was pleased to see Eve's aura brighten a few degrees. The green heart chakra still had some murky spots, but that would take time. She would give Eve some clearing meditation exercises to do at home to begin healing.

"What do you do if they don't show up at all?"

"I usually refer them to one of my partners, Shade."

"Why?"

"She's the necromancer." When Sunny saw Eve cringe at the word, she patted her hand. "It's nothing like the movies would have you believe. Let me explain." Sunny pulled three polished stones from the decorative bowl on the end table and placed one on the surface.

"This is me. I can see and talk to people who have died, in the here and now. They appear in my mind's eye as they want to, usually coming through as they were in their prime, or the age they feel was the best for them."

Sunny placed another rock to the left of the center one. "This is Tiffany. She perceives people and places as they were in the past by touch, called psychometry, or place memory. Her gift also includes the ability to find imbalances and heal someone's energy."

"That's called Reiki, isn't it?" Eve asked.

"Yes." Sunny smiled at her. "Now." She placed the last rock to the right of center and pointed to it. "This is Shade. She has the gift of precognition, the ability to see events that haven't yet happened. She also has the talent to call spirits who have crossed over, even if they don't want to come."

"That sounds so dangerous." Eve shivered.

Sunny nodded. "She has the darkest ability of all. So you see, each of us balances out with the other, though we overlap in most areas. Past, present, and future."

Sunny didn't tell her of the blood oath they had sworn when they were eleven years old. How they vowed to be there for one another until death did them part. The ceremony had been as dramatic and solemn as three children could imagine. Sunny knew that neither she nor Shade nor Tiffany would ever break that promise.

Eve popped up and gave her a tight hug. "Thank you doesn't seem like enough. I feel as if a huge weight has been lifted."

"It's always enough." Sunny walked her back down the stairs to say good-bye. Eve turned and waved happily before getting into her car.

Sunny wanted to check the progress in the war room, but habit and responsibility had her returning upstairs to clear the room of energy. She thanked her guides before shutting the door.

What would it feel like to love someone like that and not just feel the echoes of another person's emotions? How would she know the love she felt was her own? She shook her head to clear the questions and handed her mother the recording of the session to transcribe.

"She looked much lighter on the way out," her mother said.

"She did."

"That's a good thing, sweetheart."

"I know, Mom. I'm a little melancholy. I'm not sure if it's hers or mine." She smiled at her mother. "I'm sure it will pass."

❖

Jordan hadn't been late after all since the landlady unlocked her door in time for her to get ready and even graciously offered to take the empty boxes to the Dumpster.

When Jordan started to explain the knock and dash activity she'd been having, her neighbor frantically rolled his eyes and ran his forefinger across his throat. Surprised into silence, she simply stared at him until the woman left.

"What was that about?"

"She's very sensitive and scares easily."

"What does that have to do with—" Exasperated, Jordan cut herself short. "Never mind, I have to get ready. I'll bring your shirt back." Jordan shut the door, leaving him standing on the landing, and put her mind on work. Bremerton was a smallish town compared to Seattle. How hard could it be?

She was right. For a first day, this one had gone pretty well. She hadn't butted heads with anyone, which was always a plus, and nothing had instantly made her think the move was a mistake. Jordan didn't see anyone on her way up to her apartment. After unlocking the door, she stood in the hallway and shivered. The thermostat read sixty-nine degrees. She tapped it and turned it up, hoping it wasn't broken. It felt a hell of a lot colder than that.

Jordan went to her bedroom closet and carefully hung up her uniform after storing her service revolver in the metal box on the top shelf. After changing into a long-sleeved flannel shirt and jeans, she resigned herself to a trip to the grocery store. There was no food in the place, and there was no way in hell she was going without coffee again in the morning.

Traveling the staircase again, Jordan wondered what on earth had possessed her to rent a third-floor apartment. Oh yeah, it was either the view of the Manette district or the garden basement apartment on the street side of the building, complete with bars on the windows.

Rush hour on Warren Avenue wouldn't even be considered a blip on Seattle's streets during the same hour. It took only fifteen minutes to get through it and into the grocery store parking lot on the other side of the bridge that connected West and East Bremerton. It was a pleasant change of pace.

Jordan took her time going up and down the aisles. When she moved, she hadn't bothered to pack the food that was left in her nearly empty cupboards. She left the food for the new tenant moving in, along with the takeout menus that overflowed a kitchen drawer.

It was a strange feeling to have such a clean start. Almost like a rebirth after her near-death experience.

Jordan had nothing but time to reflect on her life during her recovery and enforced inactivity. Some days, the loneliness smothered her, and on others, she replayed the betrayal and shooting over and over in her mind until rage boiled in her veins. The doctors had told her she would never walk without difficulty, and Jordan did everything to defy them and their unacceptable predictions, working hard on the physical therapy that kept her from becoming mired in her own emotional chaos.

Jordan filled the rest of her cart, barely noticing what she put in, and got in line. What was it with these grocery stores anyway? Ten checkout aisles were built, but only two were operating at the busiest time of the day. Finally, she loaded up her truck and blasted the radio on the short drive home.

After pulling into her assigned parking place, Jordan opened the hatch on her Ford Explorer and cursed when she realized she'd have to make more than one trip up the three flights of stairs. She'd really have to rethink the whole shopping once a month deal or consider it gym time. She made it to the top of the landing and the door opened behind her. Steve peeked out with his owlish eyes. "Just checking."

"On what?"

"I'll tell you later. Here, do you need some help?"

Before Jordan could refuse, he picked up some of her bags and followed her into her small kitchen.

"Wow," he said. "Clean slate."

Jordan looked at the stark white walls and Spartan counters. In more ways than one, she thought. "Pretty much."

She put away the cans and boxes and grabbed her keys to get the rest, making sure to grab the empty bags to take back to the store on her next trip.

Steve chattered at her all the way down the stairs and through the parking lot to her truck. "See that Toyota?" He pointed. "The blue one? That's mine. So you know when I'm home, in case you need me."

Jordan couldn't think of a single good reason why she might

need the gangly young man, but she didn't want to be rude either. "Uh-huh."

"How was your first day?"

"Fine." She slammed the hatch and pushed her key fob to lock it.

"Don't talk much, do you?"

Jordan kept walking to the entrance of their shared wing, trying to stay a step ahead of him, but he had no trouble keeping up with her and asking questions.

"That's okay," he said. "My mom says that I talk enough for three people."

"Uh-huh," she said over her shoulder as they climbed the stairs and went through the door into her kitchen.

Jordan stopped dead in her tracks, hardly noticing when Steve slammed into her from behind.

Every single cabinet door stood open, and groceries she'd just put away littered the counter and floor.

A strange sound came from Steve's throat. "Dude. I have to go now." He put the bags on the floor where he stood, but before he could turn and run, Jordan spun him around and grabbed him by his lapels, slamming him into the counter.

"Who did this?" she asked between clenched teeth. "What the fuck is going on?"

Steve's eyes rolled in fear and she felt him tremble. "I have no idea."

"Was that your job? To distract me while someone broke in to fuck with me?" *Oh, shit.* She let him go and ran to the closet where she stored her gun. It was still there. Okay, not a robbery. She sprinted back into the kitchen and was surprised to see Steve still standing in it. Logic said he must have been the one to do the knocking. Make fun of the new neighbor to scare her. Well, he had another think coming. But, dammit, he was right behind her when she went downstairs. He never shut up.

"Believe me, Jordan. I didn't do this."

"Who did?" she asked sarcastically. The only explanation that made sense was the previous tenants must still have a key. She would change the locks tomorrow.

"Jordan?"

"What?"

"I have to tell you something."

"Oh, a confession?" She could hear how nasty her voice was and was slightly sorry for it, but she was finding it difficult to find an explanation.

Steve shook his head impatiently. "No."

Jordan felt him watch her as she closed the cabinets, making sure they clicked closed before looking at him.

"This building is haunted."

She certainly hadn't expected him to say that. "Uh-huh, right. Get out."

❖

Sunny sat at the table in her small kitchen and finished the cold pasta salad her mother had left for her. She felt restless tonight and couldn't quite put her finger on why. The house was silent, almost painfully so. She washed her bowl, wiped the spotless counter down, and wandered into the dining room, adjusting the angle of a vase as she passed it. She felt the need to look over her right shoulder, which usually meant something was coming. But what? Her spirit guides were uncharacteristically silent.

After locking the doors on the main floor and continuing to the second, Sunny paused in the turret sitting room to straighten the already razor-sharp edges on her father's books. It had been his favorite room, looking out toward the Warren Avenue Bridge into East Bremerton. Though he'd been gone for many years, Sunny often stood where he stood and watched the streetlights come on in the dusk, joined shortly thereafter by the twinkling of house lights.

She wondered how many lovers were out there. True couples who actually liked each other and shared their lives as joyfully as her parents had. She yearned for that closeness, that easy love that filled her childhood home. Was it so hard to find?

A dark cloud rolled in and blanketed the lights she'd been transfixed by. *Storm's coming.*

She wondered if that was why she was so agitated. When was the last time she'd done a reading for herself? If she had to think about it, then it must have been a long time.

Sunny changed into a long white nightshirt. She crossed over to her sitting area and pulled a wooden box from the top shelf, taking a moment to run her fingers over the ancient symbols she'd carved into it. *Here be Dragons*, she automatically translated. This particular deck of tarot cards her father had given her the week before he died. Even if she knew her father's soul lived on, it still hurt to think of how much she missed him in the physical world. Sunny shuffled her cards and placed her question firmly in her mind. "What's coming?" Isis jumped onto her lap, and she was glad for the company.

She pulled random cards out of the deck and lay them in Celtic cross formation, pausing briefly before turning the first card that represented the significator at this moment, in this case, herself. Expecting to see her usual card, The Empress, she was surprised to see The Fool instead. Number zero in the tarot deck, a major arcana card that in simple terms represented a place between, the pause before a transformation. Interesting, she thought, being that she already sensed impending change. She wasn't sure if it was good or bad yet.

She turned the next card, representing opposing forces to her question. Death. She felt a tingle of apprehension though she knew it didn't have to represent danger, but another change, an end of something to make way for something new. Still, it was moving in opposition to her normal life. The third card she turned, representing helpful forces at this time, was The Wheel. Decisions and balance. She continued and turned the fourth card over, representing present events, Eight of Wands—movement and energy. Air represented in the suit of wands as well as her Libra sign. So far, perfect picture of where she was.

Sunny tapped a fingernail on the card before turning the card in the fifth position, representing her subconscious feelings. The Hermit, another major card and pretty self-explanatory; a space of self-imposed solitude. Sunny needed that state often to decompress.

Next, number six, the card of past influences. Three of Wands, an air card meaning planning and partnership. Sunny smiled. The card clearly meant her business with her friends, Sisters of Spirits.

Card number seven, representing a possible immediate future. She paused and felt a small knot form in her stomach. The Tower. Major card of discord and catastrophe. She knew the illustrations on these cards like the back of her hand, yet she stopped to study the details again. She couldn't remember if she had *ever* pulled this card from the deck for herself. It was a disturbing thought, that everything she'd built could be destroyed, her dreams turned to ashes. Well, she refused to accept that. The card could also be interpreted as out with the old, in with the new, or a shattering of old beliefs. The future wasn't set in stone; this was only a possible scenario. Still, she shivered before straightening her shoulders. Next, number eight, representing her own fears and attitudes, King of Cups, a masculine influence. Sunny felt her throat close a little; it was usually her father's card. However, in this reading, and the position it fell in, she knew it represented emotional upheaval. *Great.*

Turning the ninth card, the one representing family and friends, she held her breath. The people she was close to mattered more than anything else in the world, and this reading was darker than one she'd ever done for herself. She uncovered the Five of Swords. A fire card that indicated arguments, problems, and failure. Sunny tensed. She was almost sorry she'd started the reading, but she would finish it out.

The tenth card, showing the results of thoughts and actions, was the Ten of Swords, another fire card that promised dark times. No wonder she kept looking over her shoulder. She took small comfort in the old adage that forewarned was forearmed.

Just as she was to turn the final card, Isis yowled and jumped onto the desk scattering the cards to the floor before shooting off in another direction, her fur on end. Startled, Sunny called out to the cat. "What was that about?" Only one card landed face up on the floor. The Hanged Man. Suspended activity and challenges to the way she currently lived.

She fought the chill crawling up her spine and picked up the rest of the cards before carefully putting them away. The reading solidified what she already felt, but it raised more questions than it answered. Thunder rolled in the distance, making good on the sky's earlier promise of a storm.

Isis and Ash waited patiently for her on the bed, purring and curled like bookends. Sunny climbed under the comforter and waited for them to settle on either side of her. Then she put the anxiety of the reading aside. Whatever was coming would show up whether she worried about it or not. She'd just have to be ready when it did. She fell asleep just as the first flash of lightning lit the sky outside her bedroom.

❖

Jordan turned over and tried to stop the dream before it started. But her eyelids felt heavy and wouldn't open.

The small girl huddled in a corner in an attempt to make herself disappear. Obnoxious, loud laughter from the living room had woken her. It was Mommy's bad laugh.

She pulled her knees even closer to her chest and closed her eyes tight, clutching her baby koala bear and praying that this time, no one would come into her room to look for her. Oscar's fake fur was a comforting smell against the odor of cigarettes and woodsy scent of alcohol that came from under the door.

Hard rock music pounded against the walls, and she felt her heartbeat speed up to match the drums and bass.

Unaware of time, she held herself still, knowing that movement called attention to you, and that was the last thing she wanted. She couldn't hear her mother anymore, and that was sometimes worse than the bad laughter. She had to go potty. Wary, she clutched Oscar and tiptoed to the closed door. She was nearly there when it swung open and a monster stood in the opening framed by the light in the living room. Red eyes glowed at her from the dark, pinning her in place.

"Well," the voice boomed. "What do we have here?"

She scrunched up her face in fear and felt the pee flow down her legs before the wicked laughter grew in volume as a large hand picked her up by the throat and then tightened.

"No!"

Jordan bolted upright. She fought to get air into her lungs and held her hand over her heart, which was trying to pound its way out of her chest. "Okay, okay. Nightmare. Breathe, Jordan, relax."

Her pulse gradually slowed down, and the phantom grip on her neck lessened so she could breathe easier.

Impatient with herself, she pushed her hair from her face, becoming aware of the perspiration soaking her face and the T-shirt she was wearing. What was with this place, turning hot and cold as if the apartment had a mind of its own?

She went into the bathroom to splash cold water on her face and fought to bury the memories back where they belonged, behind closed doors in her mind.

Like she always did. It was the only way to move forward without losing her mind.

❖

Sunny sat on the porch swing, enjoying the warmth of the sun on her face while listening to the joy of the birds singing in the background.

"Changes are coming."

Sunny turned and looked at her father sitting next to her. She loved these dreams when she could visit with her dad. She was so happy to see him, wearing his familiar Levi's and denim shirt, smelling of his favorite brand of pipe smoke.

She laid her head on his shoulder the way she so often had when he was alive and rocked with him in the happy sunshine.

"Mmm." Then his words penetrated the moment.

"What's coming, Daddy?"

He didn't answer, and when she opened her eyes to look, he was gone, as silently as he'd appeared.

Loneliness gripped her heart like a vise, squeezing so hard she thought her heart might break all over again. "What's coming, Daddy?" she asked again.

The lovely dreamscape suddenly turned dark, and Sunny tried to wake up. A black crow landed on the porch railing and cawed loudly, swiveling his neck until his black eye was looking directly into hers. Sunny was swept into a swirling energy where she spun in circles, aware of only the sensation of falling. After what seemed like an eternity, the vortex collapsed in on itself and she landed on her back in a small dim room. She pulled herself into a sitting position and looked around.

The room smelled of old urine and fear, prickling her skin uncomfortably. She turned and saw the tiny dark-haired toddler curled into a ball in the corner, crying pitifully. Sunny started to crawl toward her when the door swung open and a siren sounded, piercing her eardrums.

Sunny forced herself awake, realizing that the siren in her dream was actually her alarm clock. Who was that child? She took a moment to put the fear away because it wasn't hers; it belonged to the young girl. What did this dream mean?

Sunny became aware of her own pain, remembering her father's warning. But right this second, that didn't seem as important as the feeling of her cheek against his shirt.

Sometimes being psychic just created questions. So many things were up to an individual's interpretation, and waiting for answers could take longer than she liked. She knew from experience she had to trust that more would be revealed as it was needed.

Knowing that the only thing that would pull her mind out of the dream was hard physical exercise, she got up, washed her face, and dressed in yoga gear to go to her basement gym. She grabbed a bottle of water on her way down the stairs and flipped on the radio by the door. Sunny was a firm believer in the whole mind, body, and spirit credo. It was the universal idea that if you took care of all of them and found balance, you would live a fantastic life.

Besides, when she worked out, she didn't have room for anyone else's feelings. Sunny finished stretching and set her treadmill on a steep incline, preparing to do battle with no one but her legs and a heavy bass beat.

# Chapter Three

Jordan took a step back when her landlady screamed.

"That's it! I can't take any more of this."

Any more of what? Jordan thought. She'd simply told Agnes that her thermostat wasn't working properly; she hadn't even told her yet about the god-awful groaning noises the plumbing made in the middle of the night, or the weird knocking at her door. She reevaluated the woman in front of her. Apparently, she'd just woken up, as she was dressed in a thin, old-fashioned housecoat, the kind that snapped up the front. Her Lucille Ball–red hair was in curlers, something Jordan didn't realize women still did in the age of curling irons. Sweat socks much too large for her feet pooled around her ankles. All she needed was a cigarette dangling from her mouth dropping ashes as she spoke to complete the picture of one of Jordan's early foster mothers. She hadn't thought of that woman in years. Well, not until the nightmares came back, anyway.

She was dimly aware of Agnes speaking. "I'm sorry. What did you say?"

Agnes's bony hand patted her arm. "Are you all right, dear? You look a little peaked."

Okay, thought Jordan, she was nothing like the old foster mother. She was certain those words had never fallen out of that woman's mouth, or that she showed one iota of any concern for her. "Um..." *What did I come here for?* "Right. I just wanted to give you this." She handed Agnes a shiny silver key. "I had to change the locks."

Agnes's lower lip trembled, and she looked to be on the verge of tears. "Why?"

Before she could answer, Jordan watched her eyes roll back in her head, and Agnes fainted dead away. She barely caught her before she hit the floor.

Footsteps pounded on the entry stairs and Steve looked down at Agnes. "Now you've done it. I told you not to tell her anything." He helped Jordan, and together, they managed to get Agnes to her couch. The apartment was tidy but smelled of old cigarettes.

"Get her some water." Jordan patted the old woman's face. "Agnes? Wake up now."

Watery blue eyes stared back at her. "What happened?"

"You fainted."

"Here, Grandma," Steve said, handing the water glass to her. "There you go, darling. Drink up."

"Why isn't there whiskey in this glass, boy? I fainted."

*Grandma? Whiskey?* Jordan was confused.

"Crap. I knew I shouldn't have rented her that apartment. Oh, sit down," she snapped at Jordan. "I hate when people hover."

"Why not rent me the apartment?"

"Because it's haunted."

Not this again. Part of Jordan wanted to humor the old lady, but a larger portion didn't want to encourage her delusions, so she said nothing.

Agnes slapped Steve on the hand. "You knew she had problems here?"

He rubbed the spot. "Ow, Grandma. Yes, but I didn't want you to be upset."

Jordan thought of making a quick run for it. This conversation was insane. There was no such thing as ghosts, and that was that. Suddenly, it made sense that her weird neighbor and quirky landlord were related. She slapped her palms on her thighs before standing. "Well, gotta go. Are you sure you're okay?"

"But…"

Jordan backed to the door. "I work swing tonight. Lots to do. See you later." She quickly crossed the courtyard to her own apartment wing. Ghosts? Some people would believe just about anything. There had to be some other explanations for the things keeping her on edge in this new place. She just had to figure out what they were.

❖

"Fucking tweakers."

Jordan looked over at her new partner. Vince looked friendly enough with his boyish good looks and easy manner. He had been very helpful over the last week, making the new partnership and transfer relatively painless. She raised her eyebrows at the venom in his tone.

"Look at him, ass and feet up in the air, digging through that Dumpster." He pulled the cruiser in behind the old station wagon half hidden in the back alley of the department store, blocking it in. They walked silently up to the large green bin until they were close enough to hear mumbling over the rustle of paper and trash from the interior. Vince tapped his flashlight on the metal, and the noise stopped abruptly.

"Police. Come out of there right now with your hands where I can see them."

The feet disappeared into the dark interior before pale hands and a white face appeared.

"What, Officer? I wasn't doing anything."

"Get out."

The man climbed out slowly. His eyes seemed to be bugging out of his skeletal face. He was emaciated, and his clothes hung from his skinny frame.

Jordan could almost see him think of one excuse after another, looking for a way out of his predicament.

Vince kept his flashlight on the man. "Jack."

The man grinned, showing black gaps and jagged teeth. "Hey, Officer Abbot."

"Aren't you on probation?"

The smile disappeared. "Aw, c'mon. I'm not hurting anyone here."

Vince's eyes narrowed. "You know the routine. Hands on the back of the car."

"You're not going to arrest me, are you?"

"Depends on what I find on your person and in your car, Jackie boy."

Jordan pulled evidence bags out of the cruiser. She was certain they would find needles and drugs on this man. You didn't get to look like a walking corpse tweaking through garbage in the middle of the night any other way.

Jack leered at her. "You're new. Want to frisk me instead?"

Swallowing actual bile at the thought, Jordan snapped on her rubber gloves. "Not happening, Romeo."

"What's this?" Vince asked, pulling a full syringe out of Jack's pocket along with a small plastic bag of crystal shards. "Jackie, Jackie," he said, his voice dripping with sarcasm while he continued to empty his pockets of assorted change, buck knife, two large white pills, a little black book, and a melted mini candy bar.

Vince read Jack his rights and put him in the back of the police car while they waited for the tow truck to take the old car. It too had yielded more needles, empty baggies, old computer parts, and garbage bags of clothes.

Jordan radioed the jail advising them of incoming. She looked back at Jack and saw he was out cold and drooling. Vince got in the driver's seat and glanced in the rearview mirror. "Probably been up for days."

Having firsthand experience with junkies, Jordan simply nodded and was silent for the rest of the trip into Port Orchard, memorizing landmarks and the locations that Vince pointed out that were known drug dens and hangouts along the way.

They made two more trips to the jail that night to take in a domestic violence perp and an obnoxious drunk driver. After the paperwork was done near the end of their shift, they drove back to Bremerton.

"So," said Vince. "Do you want to talk about the big pink elephant in the room?"

Surprised, Jordan turned. "What?"

He continued on in his pleasant voice. "Not that it matters to me. I think you're going to prove to be a good partner and that you did the right thing by testifying with Internal Affairs. But you know how the rest of the force feels about IA, and there are rumors about what really went down in that alley."

The treachery still burned in her chest. No, she didn't want to discuss it. "Let 'em fucking talk."

Vince grinned. "Okay, maybe later."

Jordan appreciated him backing off so easily. "Thank you."

"No problem. Good shift. See you on Tuesday."

Jordan got into her own vehicle. The next two days loomed in front of her, and irritation sat on her tense shoulders before she made a conscious effort to relax them. *Rumors, just fucking awesome.* As if the reality of being shot by and betrayed by one of their own wasn't enough dirt to play in.

Now wasn't the time for introspection. *Yeah, right. Like there will ever be a good time.*

Jordan stopped at the red light, looked out her passenger window, and saw a sporadic beam of light bouncing on the top floor of a house that was otherwise dark. She turned the corner, cut her headlights, and spotted a dark van parked in front. Was that a light shining from under the back door? Suspicious, she unclipped her phone from the visor, ready to call it in.

Suddenly, the van's back door swung open, and a tall, dark figure raced to the front door, a trench coat swirling with the speed of travel. The house's door hadn't been locked, and no lights went on in the path of entry, even after the figured darted inside.

Jordan kept watch as the person came back out of the house and returned to the van, setting it rocking slightly in the wake of her entry. The situation looked hinky.

Once again, a flashlight beam cut through the dark windows. Jordan slipped out of her truck and approached the van. She heard someone talking inside and was reaching for the door handle when it opened, nearly catching her in the face. She immediately dropped into fighting stance.

"Who the fuck are you?" a female voice snarled at her.

"Freeze!" yelled Jordan and pointed her gun. The woman, whom she could see clearly now, yelped and dropped what she'd been holding in her right hand and Jordan kicked it away.

"Oh, for Christ's sake, there goes a few hundred dollars in equipment, asshole. What are you doing?"

"I'm going to ask you the same." Jordan held her phone open ready to dial. "It's the middle of the night and this looks pretty suspicious to me." So did the woman. Jordan took in the black fatigues, trench, and black boots she was wearing and combined the sight with choppy hair styled into tufts and dark eyeliner that made her eyes look three times larger than normal.

"I repeat," said the walking Goth billboard, "who are you?"

"Officer Lawson. Mind telling me what you're doing?"

Static sounded from a radio on the woman's hip and Jordan's eyebrows went up.

"Shade? What's taking you so long?"

"Can I get that, Officer?" she asked. "We're not criminals, and please, put that thing away." She motioned to the revolver.

Jordan noted the sarcastic tone but nodded. She kept her gun pointed at her.

The woman shrugged and talked into the radio. "Tiff?"

"Go for Tiffany."

"Officer Friendly here just broke my new EMF meter."

"What? Come again?"

"Just get out here, will you?"

Another woman came out the front door and reached the van just as a sleek, black Lexus pulled in behind it.

The Lexus driver saw her gun and screamed. "I'm calling the police right now!"

"I am the police, lady!" *Jesus, what a farce.*

The woman drew closer. "Where's your identification?"

"It's in my jacket, in the truck," Jordan answered. How had she lost control of this situation so quickly?

The woman stood firm, phone in hand still ready to dial. "Get it, please."

"Don't move, any of you." Jordan lowered her revolver and backed to her truck to get her badge. The last thing she needed was another fiasco that would bring attention to her. She grabbed her leather coat and holstered her gun before flipping her wallet and badge out to show the trio, who stood looking back at her like a small fighting force in their matching black clothes. A black-and-white patrol car pulled around the corner. Great, thought Jordan as it slowed and the officer rolled down his window.

"Problem here? Someone called in an altercation." He directed his light to see the women. "Oh, hey, Sunny."

Jordan watched the woman smile, almost illuminating the rest of the block. "Lars. No, no problem. Sorry about the noise. Just a misunderstanding. This officer was just getting her badge."

He swiveled his attention to Jordan. "Lawson, right?"

Jordan nodded. She recognized him from the squad room.

"These ladies are all right." He laughed. "I can understand why you would be suspicious. Hey, Shade?" he called. "You got all your paperwork in there?"

"Of course."

Lars motioned Jordan over to his window. "They're okay. Local ghost hunters. They'll have permission from the owners to work late at night. They always do." Did she just hear him right? Ghost hunters? Could this situation be any more bizarre?

"They're harmless." He chuckled again. "Have a nice night, ladies." He pulled away, leaving Jordan standing in the middle of the street with the nuts.

Sunny put away her phone and introduced Shade and Tiffany before holding out her hand. "Sunny Skye."

Jordan carefully kept her expression blank and thought it couldn't be the name on the woman's birth certificate.

"Yes, it is," said Tiffany. "Her mother's name is Aura. Her grandmother was—"

Shade popped in. "—Star."

Sunny shushed them. "I'm sure that Officer Lawson here doesn't need my pedigree." Her hand still hung in the air.

That was creepy. Did the one called Tiffany just read her mind? Jordan finally shook Sunny's hand, and startled at the contact. Tiny shocks traveled up her arm, catching her pulse. She felt her heart skip a beat right before a fire began burning in her belly. She immediately let go of Sunny's hand and felt drunk, like she'd been in a bar for hours instead of on duty. She couldn't stop staring at her. Creamy white skin glowed under the yellow light, almost blurring the freckles sprinkled across her nose. She looked into Caribbean blue eyes. No, wait—not blue, green. Sunny's eyes were two different colors, and the otherworldly sight caught her and pulled her under, nearly taking her breath away.

She had to leave. "Okay, sorry about the misunderstanding. Um, be careful." She felt lame before she even finished the sentence. Careful of what? Ghosts that didn't exist?

"See you around, Officer." Shade stood with her arms crossed, her look challenging.

Jordan snapped on her seat belt and pulled away. What the hell was that? Was the granola girl some kind of witch who'd put a spell on her? Not that she believed in witches either, of course. What was it with the people in this town? First her dorky neighbor, then the landlady, now ghost hunters?

An image of Sunny's face fixed in the reflection of her windshield, and Jordan felt a lustful burn between her thighs an instant before the truck cab filled with the scent of summer flowers. She slammed on her brakes. What the hell was going on? She closed her eyes, and when she opened them, the vision was gone.

She opened the windows and let the night air blow out the strange floral scent. Her head cleared and she felt a bit better, though she was still unsettled.

❖

Sunny watched the truck pull away and turn the corner.

"Uh-oh," Tiffany said.

"What?" asked Sunny.

"I saw that little exchange right there. You both lit up like little Christmas trees."

"If you like tight-assed authority figures. Can we get back to work now?" Shade walked to the house without waiting for an answer.

After following Tiffany inside, Sunny locked the door behind them. "Wow. Mrs. Barbieri wasn't kidding, was she? I didn't feel this when I walked through with her earlier."

Her shoulder tingled. It was a telltale sign she was being watched. "I know you're here." She waited for *other* to communicate with her, but the only image in her mind was the police officer who just left. She gave herself a mental shake and focused on the job at hand. "Ready?" They picked up their equipment, turned out the overhead lights, and headed to the area where Mrs. Barbieri had stated the most paranormal activity occurred.

"Barbieri investigation, master bedroom. Shade, Tiffany, and myself, twelve oh one a.m." Sunny paused while they each took a different position. "Readings?"

"Temp seventy-two degrees. Electromagnetic holding at a point one." Tiffany's voice came from near the bed.

"Good. Anyone getting any indications other than something that would show on the electronics?"

"Wild monkey sex, but it's the clients."

Shade laughed, "God, Tiff. They're in their sixties."

Sunny reined back her amusement. "Working here, guys."

"I'm sorry," Tiffany said. "It's very strong energy. Here. Switch places with me."

"I can cut it out of the recording," Shade said.

"Okay. The client stated that the closet door opens and shuts on its own."

"Great," Tiffany said. "Can I have the bed back?"

A floorboard creaked in the hall.

"Did you hear that?"

"Shh." Sunny listened at the door, but her senses insisted that *other* was behind her.

"Sunny?"

"Yes?"

"Orb to your right," Shade said.

"What do your spidey senses say?"

Shade studied the viewfinder. "It just disappeared into the closet."

As soon as she finished her sentence, there was a thump behind the door followed by a noise in the bathroom across the hall.

"What is that?"

"The faucet turned on."

"Crap," Tiffany said. "I hate the really active ones. EMF spiking and bouncing between a point four and five."

"What is your name?" Sunny asked. "Can you tell us why you're still here?"

"Bathroom is clear," Shade called.

Sunny stood in front of the closed closet. "Hello?" Icy cold air seeped around the frame. "Temp?"

"Sixty-four."

Sunny felt energy crackle against her skin, and an image fluttered in her mind then grew stronger. It was an older woman in a blue shirtwaist dress. Her hair was up in a severe bun and her face appeared thin and drawn. When Sunny reached for the knob, the spirit shook her head.

"I've got something," Sunny said. "But she's either shy or afraid." She sat on the floor and remained still in an effort to receive more. "It's okay. Who are you?" The woman showed her an E and R consecutively. "Erma? No?" L and another E. "Erleen? Yes? Okay, Erleen. Why are you here?" The ghost spread her arms then pointed to her chest.

"But it's not your house anymore, dear." Sunny gently smiled telepathically at her.

"What's she doing?" Tiffany asked.

"She's crying."

A loud crash in the kitchen startled Sunny, and the image

wavered. "Did you do that, Erleen?" The image of the woman in her mind looked frightened, shook her head, and abruptly disappeared.

"Shade, what do you feel?"

"Aggressive male energy. Let's go."

"I'm not getting anything," Tiffany said. "It's all that, um…" She paused. "Um, recent stuff that I feel."

"It's okay, Tiff," Shade said. "I got it."

The air in the kitchen was heavy and stifling. They waited, but there were no more noises in the area. Tiffany crossed to the counter and laid her hand on it. "Residual," she said. "I can see an older man, and he's wearing one of those old-time tank tops. He's balding and has a pot belly. He just threw a chair. Wait, it's looping again and I can see a woman cowering on the floor. He's telling her if she ever leaves, he'll find her and kill her."

Sunny heard an audible scream and knew the recorder caught it.

"Still residual," Tiffany said.

"Asshole. Do you want me to call his ghost up?"

"Absolutely not. Poor Erleen is terrified enough. She's been trapped here too long."

Tiffany turned to Shade. "Are you sure he's not still here?"

"I'll go downstairs and check." Shade chuckled. "Do you want to come to the basement with me, little girl?"

"Bite me, Shade."

"All right, you two," Sunny said. "Tiffany, will you come with me to talk to Erleen?"

"Of course."

Sunny grabbed her bag before reentering the bedroom. She lit three white candles before settling on the floor across from Tiffany and holding her hands. Sunny imagined a tiny light and focused on it. Tiffany's energy joined with her own, and the light grew until it was a bright sun.

"Erleen?" Sunny called. "He can't hurt you anymore. Honey, it's time to go home."

The spirit looked longingly at the light through obvious tears, and Sunny felt the desire emanating from her even as she hesitated to go.

"It's okay. Do you still see the people waving? They're waiting for you. Go on. I promise you, it will be all right."

Erleen looked over her shoulder and smiled. The older woman vanished, and in her place stood a much younger woman whose hair fell in soft waves around a lovely face. *Thank you.*

She turned back to the light and took a step. Sunny briefly felt her intense joy before the light went out.

She loved her job.

## CHAPTER FOUR

Jordan nearly spilled her beer when Steve jumped off the couch. "Where's my flag?" he yelled. "What are you, blind?"

Jordan laughed and moved the potato chip bag to safety. "Ain't no flag, son. The Niners are kicking your ass!"

Steve turned, horror clearly visible on his face. "Where's your loyalty?"

Jordan held up her hand. "Hey, born in San Francisco, nineteen seventy-nine."

"Oh," he said. "Now, that's just wrong. Go home."

Jordan raised her eyebrows and tipped her bottle at him before setting it back down on the coffee table. At halftime, the 49ers were a touchdown ahead of the Seahawks, and Steve left to use the bathroom. Jordan looked around the mostly cleaned-up apartment from her perch on the couch. At least he had made an effort.

It was still a far cry from her obsessively clean rooms, but it was comfortable. She reached for her beer, and her hand stopped in midair as she watched the bottle slide four inches to the right. The tiny hairs on the back of her neck prickled, and she pulled back. It must be the condensation on the bottom of the bottle. *Of course.*

Steve returned. "What's wrong with you, traitor?"

Jordan snagged her beer off the table. "Nothing, loser."

They traded insults for a few minutes during the halftime show until Jordan had to use the bathroom herself. She was half-tempted to go across the hall to use her own. Who knew what strange creatures were growing in Steve's?

Feeling a little stupid, she forced herself into his. It wasn't too bad. He'd clearly put some effort in here as well. She liked Steve. He was a good guy. A little annoying, but friendly enough. Every time she tried to push him away, he reminded her he'd seen her underwear. Good thing it was in a little brother way or else she would have kicked his ass already. Jordan stood at the sink to wash her hands. Her right palm tingled and felt hot, but without burning. It had been doing that off and on since the night she met the granola girl and her merry band of flakes. Ghost hunters. Please. Why couldn't she stop thinking about that woman? And why did she feel as if she were missing something important? Irritated with herself, she dried her hands on the small towel in an attempt to wipe off the heat and the memory at the same time.

Sunny received information from her spirit guides early in the morning, and it turned the simple Singer investigation into something much more personal than just a house haunting. After discussing the message with Shade and Tiffany, she decided to bring the information to the Singers on her own. It was a touchy situation and sure to be emotional for the couple.

Hollywood and religious dogma had attached so much fear to the phenomenon of ghosts that the whole psychology of it had to be addressed, and each client brought a different set of beliefs that had to be addressed.

Sunny knew how fortunate she was that her parents were so open to universal energy. She'd never had to contend with any of the religious stigma attached to her psychic abilities. In fact, they were encouraged at all opportunities. Her father had his own gifts and had written several books on paranormal research years before it was fashionable or in vogue. He found a kindred soul in her mother. They were a pioneering force, way ahead of their time in the field, and her father's books were still in print over twenty years later.

Sunny blew an imaginary kiss to her dad before she gathered up the file and her laptop. It was better to go to them on their own home turf, especially after they heard what she was going to say.

She pulled into their driveway, and after noticing that the husband's vehicle was gone, Sunny felt relieved, since his whole demeanor had been one of skepticism, and he'd been angry with the whole investigation to begin with. Her job just got easier because she knew that Mrs. Singer would be much more relaxed and receptive. Her elbow stung as she remembered the tumble she took in the basement. The door opened before she could knock, and she was led to the dining room, where a pretty spread of cookies and coffee was already set up.

Sunny felt trepidation radiating from the woman, but she hoped the feeling would be gone this afternoon.

"I'm so nervous."

Sunny smiled easily. "No need to be. Please sit down and relax."

The woman held a hand to her stomach, and in an instant, Sunny knew she was absolutely doing the right thing.

"I'm sorry that it's taken so long to get back to you and for the last cancellation. My husband…" She trailed off.

Sunny reached for her hand. "It's fine, really. There was a reason for it, and that will become clear while we talk. First, I want to tell you that we did get an EVP."

Mrs. Singer paled. "That's electric voice phenomenon, right?"

"Yes, the recorder can pick up voices that the normal ear usually can't." Sunny made a decision on the spot not to tell her about the shadow movement caught on the video. She knew that it and the voice they caught on the recorder were the same energy. She didn't want to frighten her unnecessarily. "Second, I want to ask if there has been any more activity since we did our investigation."

"Honestly? No. That's when my husband decided it was all in my imagination."

"I'm just going to let you listen to this, and then we'll get started, okay?" Sunny brought the recording up on her laptop and briefly explained the lines showing decibels and frequencies on the graph. "Pay attention to this area right here." She pointed to the screen and highlighted a portion of the bar then pushed play.

*"I'm okay here."*

With her eyes wide as saucers, Mrs. Singer leaned forward to listen to the small voice again. "It's a child!"

Sunny felt the excitement radiate from her client; the feeling was eagerness and not fear. Good, that's what she was hoping for. "Wait. It comes in again in thirty seconds."

*"I'll be seeing you."*

"Does that say 'I see you?'"

Sunny pulled the bar back with her mouse and played it again.

*"I'll be seeing you."*

Now she did feel fear from Mrs. Singer, so she jumped in to put her at ease. To offer the psychic impression that she'd received just this morning. Reaching for her hand again, she talked in a soothing voice. "I want you to relax and listen to me, okay?"

Sunny took a deep breath. Mrs. Singer's reaction could go one of two ways, and she hoped it would be the one that could lead to some comfort. "Mrs. Singer, did you lose a child?"

"Oh, God." She pulled her hands away to cover her mouth. Her grief erupted into keening sobs. "How could you possibly know that?" She swung around in her chair to look at the pretty, but empty, kitchen. "Is he here? Is my baby here?"

Sunny felt her pain stab at her own heart. "No, ma'am." This was the hard part. Sunny felt the loss of that child as if it were her own, and tears stung her eyes while she tried to center herself. Not mine, she reminded herself. This pain didn't belong to her.

"Ma'am?"

Mrs. Singer had rested her head on her arms. It was several moments later when she began talking. "Five years ago, before I met my husband. We were living in Montana with my parents." She steadied a bit and sat back up. "Keith was three years old. It was the middle of winter and he got a cold." Her eyes pleaded with Sunny for understanding. "A stupid cold and we were snowed in, trapped by the blizzard that swept through the state. Oh, we weren't worried, my mother and I; we just did the normal routine that you do when your babies get sick." She looked to the left, as if to a faraway place and a different time. "His temperature started to climb in the middle of the night, and I woke up my father. We couldn't get out, and the nearest hospital was forty miles away on impassable roads. While my parents frantically tried to dig out the truck, my son died in my arms." Tears ran silently down her face. "I felt his little soul leave me."

Fresh grief spilled over her, and then Mrs. Singer straightened. "No one here knows about Keith but me. It was before I met my husband. Oh, he knows about my son; he just wasn't part of my life then, or any part of the pain that you go through when you lose a child." Her eyes almost looked fierce. "You tell yourself that you'll die too. After all, how could someone walk around feeling like a knife is living in your heart and not drop dead from the pain? You think you'll die, pray for it even, but you don't. You wake up, you eat when someone forces you to, and you go to bed. Eventually, you add chores and other activities to your day, but it's never the same, not ever." She stopped and her eyes snapped back to Sunny's. "Oh my God. Was that actually Keith? 'I'm okay here. I'll be seeing you'?"

Sunny nodded and rubbed at the knot in her stomach. "I believe so."

Mrs. Singer got up, pushing her chair back. "I need some water."

Sunny stared at her back. "He has a message for you."

"A message? From my baby boy?" The eagerness in her voice broke Sunny's heart a little more.

Sunny nodded again. Here goes, she thought. "He appeared briefly and he was holding the hand of a small little girl wearing pigtails and indicated she was his sister. He walked forward with her." She let that sink in for a moment. "He says he's happy and showed me pink paint and rollers. At first, I wasn't sure what he meant by that, but then he showed me a crib."

Mrs. Singer slapped the table in shock. "I just found out this morning! Not two hours before you got here. How could you? Never mind." Her face paled.

Sunny watched the disbelief race across her features, and then finally, hope transformed Mrs. Singer's face, and she relaxed a little. Then she went on. "He says he didn't mean to scare you and he wants you to be happy. He flexed his little muscle when he brought the little girl forward, a sign for big brotherly love. He says he is always with you."

"A little girl?"

"Yes."

"Did he say anything else?"

"Not much, but an older gentleman came up behind him and lifted him onto his shoulders. They were both laughing and then they disappeared."

"My grandfather. He always did that to me, lifted me up like that." Mrs. Singer smiled softly. "He always smelled of peppermint and tobacco."

The air shifted in the kitchen and Sunny felt the heavy grief in the room recede. She knew that Mrs. Singer would shed more tears, but she hoped they would be more of a healing nature.

"Thank you," she said. "I don't know how to thank you."

"My pleasure." Sometimes, Sunny didn't know where to put all the emotion after a heavy session like this one. She felt overloaded and wrung out. But she did know that she helped this grieving woman, and that's what her gift was all about. She closed the laptop and stowed it in the leather case. "Do you want the recording?"

Mrs. Singer considered the question for a moment. "No," she said slowly and pointed to her heart. "It's right here. Thank you again."

They walked out to Sunny's car. After she was buckled in, Mrs. Singer leaned in the open window and giggled. "Pink paint? I think I'll go and buy a gallon to sit in the middle of the kitchen table with my husband's favorite dinner."

"That's sounds wonderful. Good luck to you." She let herself be embraced and poured as much positive energy as possible into the hug before heading home.

Sunny got caught up in the shipyard traffic in Gorst, but it didn't bother her. She always figured she was right where she was supposed to be at any given moment. Today, however, her heart ached with emptiness. Was it remnants of Mrs. Singer's loss or was it her own? Her arms ached to hold a baby. To smell a sweet infant's soft skin and kiss the top of a tiny head.

She justified it as an emotional hangover from the session. It wasn't as if she would be pregnant anytime soon herself. It would certainly never happen by accident since she'd never even been with a man. Sunny had known from a very young age she was lesbian. Because she was homeschooled by her parents, it kept peer pressure from her door. Normal school had been out of the question. It was excruciating for Sunny to be around that many people and the emotions that flew around them like small tornados. She'd loved her parents as teachers. Anything that she wanted to learn, her parents provided the means for her to do so. They took field trips and day trips to the library. Learning was easy for her, people were not.

*Look out!*

Sunny heard the voice in her ear and slammed on her brakes, narrowly missing the car in front of her that had stopped suddenly.

"Thanks, Dad." She paid close attention on the rest of the drive and was still shaking when she pulled into her driveway. She'd always had a fear of car accidents. She didn't know why. It wasn't as if she'd been in one, just that she did and she couldn't get a bead on it. She wanted a bath, a long soak in water that would cleanse her, inside and out. Maybe a glass of wine.

Shade came barreling out the door and nearly knocked Sunny over. "Oh, hey. I'm sorry." She reached out to steady her, instinctively drawing her closer.

Sunny was tempted to lean into her warm body. Just for a second, to let someone wrap her up and take care of her. But she really needed to be alone to decompress. Sunny felt selfish but took that moment of comfort from Shade and let her senses fill with Shade's cologne. From the time Shade was a teenager, she'd always worn CK One. There had been so many nights Sunny had lain wrapped in that heady scent. *Uh-oh.*

Reluctantly, she pulled back and forced a smile on her face. What they had was in the past, and she wouldn't lead Shade down a dead end, no matter how lonely she felt. "I'm okay." She felt Shade's concern wash over her and made an effort to brighten. "Where's the fire?"

"It's not important. I can stay here with you." Shade held the door and ushered Sunny inside, hesitantly waiting for her answer.

"No, I'm fine. I'm just going to go upstairs and take a long bath. Thank you for the offer, though." She picked up two pink phone messages off the desk blotter. Thankfully, neither call needed to be returned until the next day. She turned and shooed Shade away. "Carry on."

"Are you sure?"

"Absolutely." Sunny grinned. "Sally?"

"Yep."

"Lucky girl. Go now. I'll see you tomorrow." Sunny locked the door behind Shade when she left. Please let there not be another interruption, she thought. Ash and Isis sat on the second-floor landing waiting for her. Silent sentries, they flanked her on velvet paws all the way to her room and stood at the door to the bathroom until she reemerged, warm and pink, climbed into bed, and quickly fell asleep.

❖

Jordan hated this time of night. When the distractions were quiet and her mind traveled to the past again and again, like a tongue seeking out the sore tooth. She turned on the television simply for the noise and paced her living room. It didn't help much; the walls still felt like they were closing in on her. She froze when the volume suddenly blared on the TV, blasting from the speakers. Jordan grabbed the remote and turned it off.

"What the fuck do you want from me?" she shouted, then immediately felt ridiculous standing in the empty room. Of course, there was nothing there, because there was no such thing as ghosts. Jordan rubbed the goose bumps that prickled the skin on her arms.

Damn thermostat. She didn't care anymore about scaring the landlady; it was *just* a screwed-up thermostat and she wanted it fixed. The building must have defective electricity as well, sending surging power through the electronics.

See? Now she had something to focus her rage on. She grabbed her leather jacket off the back of the chair and her keys from the counter. Jordan stormed out the door, slamming it behind her. She'd had enough.

By the time she got outside, she felt some of her anger ebb away. What the hell was wrong with her? She wasn't going to yell at that sweet old lady. Jordan shoved her hands in her pockets, oriented herself, and began to walk toward the water several blocks away. Wanting—no, needing—some space and distance from everything, including herself. Deep down, she knew that wherever she went, there she was.

There she fucking was.

Jordan wore her badass attitude like a piece of clothing; no one bothered her or even waved. Even the punks outside 7-Eleven gave her a wide berth. They were looking for victims, not another predator.

She turned left at the corner and continued up the hill toward Washington Street and the ferry docks, hoping the ocean would help soothe the ache in her soul. Jordan felt an air of confusion surrounding her, and it was puzzling. She always knew what she wanted and how to get it. Everything outside her apartment was normal and within her control, as it should be. Well, she admitted, except for her run-in with the ghost brigade the other night. Her palm burned and she rubbed it against her jeans absently.

Only a block to go.

❖

Jordan balanced easily on the slippery rocks, stepping carefully until she found a place to sit. She closed her eyes and felt her shoulders relax while she inhaled the salt air. There was serenity to be found here.

She wondered if that was because one of the only happy memories she had was on the beach. Perhaps that was why she always sought it out.

She'd been about six years old and her mother had been in a good mood. Jordan looked back, and as an adult, she knew it must have been because her mother had been flush with enough money and drugs for the day to make her happy.

It was out of character for her mother to take her anywhere, but that day, for whatever reason, she decided to take her to the beach.

Jordan could still see her mother on that sunny day, so pretty in her cut-offs and long-sleeved peasant blouse. Jordan's adult perception also told her the sleeves covered her mother's needle tracks. Rarer still that day was the absence of one of her mother's men to take away attention from Jordan.

They held hands and raced the waves while the seagulls circled with manic energy, screaming and diving for their hot dogs purchased from the beach vendor.

God, she hadn't thought of that day in years. Mostly, she remembered the loneliness and pain. She never knew if her mother's approaching hand would smooth her hair or slap her. More painful was the question that wasn't answered, never knowing why her mother couldn't—or wouldn't—love her. Jordan had tried so hard to be a good girl.

Logically, as an adult, she understood the junkie mentality. There wasn't room in a house full of drugs for love. Before Jordan could stop the slide, she was catapulted into the past, and the memories came at her like a sledgehammer.

Being eleven years old and coming home to the one-bedroom tiny apartment. The ugly drapes were closed like they always were. Stale cigarette smoke and the sour smell of alcohol stung her senses. Her mother's bedroom door was shut, also not unusual. Her mother slept most of the day and stayed up all night.

Jordan put down her backpack and went into the filthy kitchen to find something to eat. She opened the refrigerator even as she asked herself why she bothered, since it was always empty. Today, a shriveled apple and tiny piece of cheese lived in there. She sighed and went to open a cupboard instead, revealing half a loaf of bread and a jar of peanut butter but no jelly. She made a sandwich to eat in front of the tiny television in the living room that also doubled as her bedroom where she slept on the couch. She hated it, people coming and going all hours of the night. The only good thing about it was she was visible to her mother, and the men she ran with didn't bother Jordan. Not like they did when she was younger and she had her own room. She kept the volume low so as not to wake her mother and watched television until it was dark outside, waiting for the bedroom door to open.

Jordan didn't know when she fell asleep, only that when she opened her eyes, the gray light of dawn was coming in around the closed curtains. She was surprised she hadn't heard her mother get up during the night.

The room was chilly and Jordan felt a little weird. She crossed quietly to the closed door.

"Mom?" No answer. Jordan tapped her fingers slightly on the wood. "Mom?"

Jordan's stomach twisted and she felt nauseated, but she turned the knob anyway. Her mother lay on the top of the dirty blankets, her legs crossed in a figure four. Long, blond hair covered her face, and her arms were stretched to the side.

The smell was horrible. Jordan cautiously stepped into the room, ready to duck and run if she needed to. "Mom?"

Her mother didn't move and it was then that Jordan saw the needle hanging from her mother's elbow and pink rubber tubing by her side.

She leaned over carefully and moved the veil of hair, stifling a scream when she saw the vomit caking her mother's cheek and blue lips, and her eyes stared vacantly at the ceiling.

Jordan remembered choking on bile and how she'd run to the bathroom to throw up before she'd cried and rocked for what seemed like hours on the cold tile floor. There was a blurry recollection of finally going to the neighbors to use the phone.

Social services picked her up and took her away from the

house where she'd found her mother dead. It was the last time she'd cried.

The sound of laughter from the boardwalk above her brought Jordan back to the present. The sharp ache of grief in her chest surprised her. Jordan thought she was over that emotion years ago.

She took a deep breath and straightened her shoulders. Okay, enough with the tripping over things she couldn't change. She wasn't that young girl anymore, and hadn't been for a very long time. Jordan had grown up without affection, and in the years since, hadn't felt as if she even needed it. But she had to admit that as she got older, there were a few times her arms ached to hold someone who could love her back. Was she so unlovable?

An ugly voice from the past whispered in her ear. *What have you ever done to deserve love?* Jordan felt her shoulders tense again. Then, out of nowhere and clearer than the first, she heard another, sweeter voice ask, *What have you ever done to* not *deserve it?*

## CHAPTER FIVE

S unny walked her client to the exit. The old woman hugged her close. "See you next month."

Sunny smiled. "You take care, now." She loved this woman who had been a regular for almost five years. She was a lonely widow, and they enjoyed their time together, which was always more social hour than spiritual work.

Sunny's mother was answering the ringing phone, but waved good-bye to their favorite customer enthusiastically from the reception desk.

"S.O.S. How can I help you?" her mother said into the receiver.

As Sunny drew closer, she could hear the hysteria in the caller's voice.

Her mother put the call on speaker so Sunny could hear the conversation.

"We're booked solid for the next two months."

"But it's getting worse every day!" Harsh sobs left the woman almost breathless, and her fear was palpable even over the phone. Her mother pushed a notepad toward her with the caller's name written on it, circled in black ink.

Sunny couldn't stand it. "Agnes? Breathe, please." She talked soothingly to her until small hiccups replaced the crying. Her mother got up from the desk, giving her a seat, and left the room.

"Let's start at the beginning, shall we? I'm Sunny."

"Okay," Agnes said in a tiny voice.

"Uh-huh. Yes, I know the place. Uh-huh." Sunny took notes while listening. "Well, let me talk to my team and I'll get back with you, okay?"

Sunny winced when Agnes started crying again. "I promise. Good-bye now."

Her mother handed her a bottle of water. Her displeasure was obvious in her expression. "If you keep working on your days off, you're going to burn out like I did."

Sunny knew it was concern that had her mother all tied up in knots. When her mother had disappeared into the gray fog, Sunny had experienced it right along with her. She went around the desk and kissed her. "I'm fine. She needs help. The poor woman is terrified. I couldn't get a sense of anything but her fear."

Her mother opened her mouth to speak, but Sunny cut her off. "I'm taking care of myself, getting plenty of sleep. Please stop worrying about me." Her mother nodded and left again.

Sunny stared at the notepad and felt the little hairs on her neck rising to attention.

*Change is coming.*

She found Tiffany in the war room talking on her cell phone while she gathered her purse and sweater. "I don't see how—Yes, of course. I'll be right there." She turned, and Sunny could see the unshed tears in her eyes before she looked at the floor. "I have to go and pick up the baby. It seems the preschool frowns on her"—she made little quote fingers in the air—"overactive imagination."

Sunny crossed the room to comfort her. "What happened this time?"

"Apparently, she was talking with a classmate, and according to the teacher, she told him that his daddy's spirit was in the room with them and said he was sorry about leaving him and his mother alone."

"Uh-oh. Where's his dad?"

"He's a marine stationed overseas. The boy is in hysterics." Tiffany pushed her glasses back. "So he gets mad, tells the teacher, who dragged my daughter to the office, where she is now sitting alone. A feeling I know quite well, and my heart is breaking for her."

"I know, honey." Sunny felt the empathic tears coming on. "Go and get her. Take the rest of the day off and go to the park or something."

Tiffany shook her head. "I have appointments."

"Well, I'll reschedule them for you. Go on." Sunny hugged her.

"Okay, thank you. Sometimes this is all so freaking hard, you know?" Tiffany rushed out of the office, and Sunny heard the bell sound as she left.

Shade's desk was clean, without any of the usual electronic paraphernalia present when she was working. Her computer screen was still dark. Sunny picked up the schedule that her mother placed on each of their desks in the morning and saw that Shade's first appointment wasn't until late in the afternoon. Shade was notorious for sleeping in, usually because she partied so hard.

She pushed the worry away. Shade was a big girl, and Sunny refused to butt into her personal life, even if she saw the path she was going down. She wanted to warn her and help, but Shade refused to listen, putting up mental bars and barriers that even Sunny couldn't get through.

Sunny heard the phone ring in the silence, then went back to reception when her mother called her name. "Yes?"

"Tara called to cancel her reading today. She said something came up with her family and she'd call later to reschedule."

"So I'm free for the rest of the day?"

Her mother checked the book. "No. You have a client coming in ten minutes. After his reading, you're done."

Sunny checked her watch. "Then I'll call Agnes back and go to see her later."

"I don't want you to go alone. I'll go with you."

"Mom, I'm fine. It's just an interview. Could you please call Tiffany's clients and see if you can work them in over the next couple of days?"

Her mother nodded but narrowed her eyes.

The gesture made Sunny smile. "Besides," she said gently, "don't you have that dinner cruise in Seattle planned this evening? You've been looking forward to it for weeks."

"But—"

"No more buts today, please, Mom."

"Okay," her mother said. "But be careful."

"I promise. Have fun." Sunny called Agnes and let her know she could be there in a couple of hours. The woman's gratitude was as easy to read as her fear had been. Something else tugged at her, a sense of eagerness along with an inclination that something important was waiting for her.

Since she was going without her team, she wanted to keep the meeting informal. Just a quick look-see, she told herself. She had plans later that evening to attend an opening at a new art gallery downtown. She heard a clatter of beads, and a blur in the corner of the hall mirror caught her attention. Mazie stood to the side dressed in her flapper costume. She was one of the few souls Sunny allowed herself to actually see in a corporeal form. She decided when she was very young that having mental images and hearing them was enough for her. She got tired of the ones that would just show up unannounced and scare her silly. Over the years, she learned how to set clear boundaries.

"Be careful," the apparition said.

Sunny smiled at her. "You been talking with my mother again, Mazie?"

She received no answer, and the original owner of her house faded. If everyone was warning her today about this job, why was she so excited to get there?

❖

She'd lost her ever-loving mind; that's all there was to it. Jordan looked at the plant sitting on the passenger seat of her truck. She had never bought anything living and green in her life. She was sure of it.

She was a little dazed. There she was, minding her own business in the produce aisle when the smell hit the edge of her conscious. A light summer scent teased her memory and must have caused the temporary insanity, because Jordan impulsively put the plant in her cart.

Now her truck smelled like flowers, for Christ's sake, like a girl's. Jordan winced before picking the pot up and heading to her apartment. Steve opened his door when she unlocked hers, his grandmother appearing like a shadow behind him.

Jordan peered through the leaves and stared back at them. "What?"

Steve snickered. "Flowers?"

His grandmother slapped his arm and shushed him. "They're lovely, dear." She smiled up at Jordan and they followed her into her apartment.

"Come on in," Jordan mumbled.

"Oh, it's cold in here," Agnes said.

Jordan set the plant on the table and turned toward her. "I told you something is wrong with the thermostat in here."

Agnes shivered. "That's what I wanted to talk to you about. I called—" She was interrupted by the sound of Steve's door slamming across the hall. Her face went pale and she looked as if she might faint again. "I called someone to come and help us."

Steve led her to a chair and sat her down. "Here, Grandma, sit. Water?"

Jordan rushed to get her some and put a glass into her trembling hand. "Help us with what, Agnes?"

The door to her bedroom slammed shut with a bang. Agnes shot to her feet and toddled to the front door in her purple high-tops. "I have to go." Steve followed her out, leaving Jordan standing in the kitchen with her mouth open, wondering what the hell was going on. Again.

Old houses meant uneven floors, settling, and noisy pipes in the walls. What was the big deal? Any of those explanations would do.

Jordan checked her watch and decided she had time to wash some clothes. She picked up the basket in her closet and headed to the basement. Each wing in the old brick apartment complex had its own laundry facility. She was pretty sure she'd have it to herself at this time of day. It was one of the reasons why she loved the swing shift. There was time to run errands when everyone else was working, and she could avoid the crowds the weeknights and weekends brought with them. So far, Steve was the only neighbor she'd met, and Jordan hoped she wouldn't have to meet another.

When she opened the heavy metal door to the basement, she was instantly struck by the odor of damp mold overlaid by Pine-Sol. Why did basements always smell? Along either side of the long hall, storage units lined the walls. They looked more like cages with wire fencing and reminded her of the jail. Jordan saw a woman at the end with an industrial mop cleaning the cement floor. The woman was swinging the mop back and forth from side to side. Every third stroke, she stopped to rinse it and do little booty shakes. She never looked up from the task.

Just before Jordan reached the laundry room, the woman saw her, stopped her dancing, and screamed. It startled Jordan into dropping the laundry basket.

"Jeezus. You scared the shit out of me." The woman held a hand to her heart.

"I'm sorry, and right back at you." Jordan noticed the ear buds when the woman took them out to drape around her neck. Jordan hadn't seen them in the dim light, and it explained why the woman hadn't heard her.

The woman laughed nervously and wiped her hands on her worn jeans. "You're new here?"

"Yes, I moved in a couple of weeks ago. Jordan." She shook the woman's hand.

"Lisa. I live over in the east wing. You'll see me around since I clean the place for Agnes."

A rustling sound from behind Jordan had her looking over her shoulder. "What was that?"

Lisa shook her head. "That's why I wear the headphones so loud. It's never quiet in the basement, and I scare myself silly if I don't."

"Mice?" *Great.* That would explain a lot. "Or rats?"

Lisa smiled. "If it makes you feel better to think that, okay. But Agnes has the exterminators in every three months, and we have resident cats. I clean here, remember? And I have never, not in the three years I've lived here, seen any sign of them." She picked up the mop. "Nice meeting you. The laundry is there." Lisa pointed to the blue door. "I'm almost through here, and I'm on a schedule today." She walked back to her bucket. "Watch out for ghosts, Jordan," she said before turning her back and putting her buds back in.

Jordan picked up her basket and went into the room. *What is it with these people and their cryptic warnings?* Ghosts? It had to be rodents.

*Right?*

Still, as Jordan loaded the washer, she was aware of the nerves singing along her spine. The intuition she normally only felt when she was on duty. A child's giggle had her spinning so fast she grabbed the folding table for support. The room was empty and she thought she heard a ball bouncing in the hall. She peered out the door, hoping to see Lisa. Maybe she had a child.

No. The walkway was empty. The only sign that someone had been there were the wet streaks left by the mop. These people were going to drive her crazy, and Jordan had to admit that these days it would be a short trip. Jordan forced herself to take a deep breath and forget about it. She went back upstairs, and while she was waiting for the laundry to finish, she hung the new curtains she'd purchased. She had to admit they made the room homier.

When she gauged enough time had gone by, Jordan returned to the laundry room to switch her clothes to the dryer and flinched when the heavy metal door closed behind her. Her boots echoed on the cement, sounding as if someone was keeping step with her. *Get a grip, Lawson.* She was only nervous because people kept trying to put stupid ideas in her head.

She forced herself to walk at a normal pace and continued to the end of the hallway. The rustling she heard was just her imagination. It was an old building, and the vents were picking up noises from the apartments above and distorting the sounds here. Yes, that was it. Pleased with the explanations, she opened the door and froze.

The room looked like it had been hit with a bomb. Wet clothes were stuck to the wall and floor, the two washers were on their sides, and the dryers were moved away from the wall with their doors open.

As she stood there, a gray T-shirt fell from the ceiling to plop on the wet floor. Jordan bent to grab it, and when she stood, she saw the words written in red on the wall.

*Leave, bitch.*

Somewhere under the rage she felt at the vandalism, the cop in her took over and she pulled out her phone to take pictures of the destruction. It was personal then. Some asshole in the building had a grudge against the police. *Ghosts, my ass.* It wasn't the first time that some lowlife had found out what she did for a living and written things on her truck or door.

Jordan debated calling it in and decided not to. She was still new, and she didn't want to draw attention to herself and invite other cops into her personal life. They'd question the sweet old landlady, who would tell them about ghosts, and Jordan would never live it down. Nope, she wasn't going to go there.

The last picture she took was of a laundry soap container that looked, well, melted was the only explanation she could come up with. Jordan looked around at the mess. She didn't have time to clean it by herself, and she didn't want Agnes to have to come and help. She called Steve instead. He would just have to wake his happy ass up and help her. "'Lo?"

Jordan heard the sleep in his voice. "Come down to the laundry room right now."

"What time is it?"

"You have five minutes before I take these pictures to your grandmother." Jordan snapped her phone shut. She wouldn't really scare Agnes, but she knew that the threat would get him moving faster.

Jordan defiantly put her clothes in the last standing washer and dug out more quarters. There didn't seem to be any damage to them other than the wild, wet party they'd apparently been to in the last hour.

She heard the door slam then approaching footsteps and waited for Steve to enter. What was he doing, she asked herself when she heard the strange snorting noises. Waiting for an invitation? Jordan pulled open the door.

The hall was empty. "Not funny, asshole!" she yelled. There had to be someone hiding in one of the storage cages. It was the only logical explanation.

The metal door clicked, and Steve appeared in the entry, his hair standing up in tufts around his head.

She waited for him to reach her. "Did you see anyone out there?"

"No. What's going on?"

She pushed him into the messy room and handed him her phone.

"Whoa." His face took on a serious tone as he looked at the snapshots and the remaining mess. "When did this happen?"

"Within the last hour. I came down to switch the clothes and found this." She gestured around the room. "I'm so over this shit." She rounded on him. "And don't you dare tell me a ghost did this."

Steve's eyes were wide. "Must be a poltergeist. I've read they can move heavy objects around and throw stuff."

Jordan rolled her eyes at him. "Right. You really need to give that horse a rest. The rest of this mess is all yours, buddy."

"How come I'm in trouble?"

"I have to get ready for my shift," she answered, and quickly shut the door.

Thirty minutes later, Jordan left for work. When she drove out of the back parking lot and past the front of the building, a familiar car caught her attention. Before she could place it and who it belonged to, the light turned green and she drove through it, still steaming over the vandalism.

❖

Sunny parked and grabbed her briefcase before crossing the street. Originally built for officers of the naval shipyard, the old brick building was in a U-shape, the center area filled with grass and border flowers. She could feel the energy of its long history before she even stepped onto the walkway.

An older woman with dyed fire-engine-red hair stood outside the center wing. Sunny delightfully guessed her character by the way she dressed: black leggings, purple Converse high tops, and a Pink Floyd T-shirt. Her mother would love her. She stood and waited with her hands folded at her waist.

A child giggled behind her, and Sunny half turned before realizing it was disembodied and there wouldn't be anyone standing there. She lived and worked with spirit energy every day, right along with her family and friends. Sometimes it was easy for her to forget that not everyone experienced the world as she did. Agnes was scared enough. Sunny refused to add to it by talking with the child. Instead, she tried to tune out the distracting laughter. She wanted to hear Agnes's story before she connected with any of them.

"Thank you so much for coming," Agnes said.

"You're welcome." Sunny smiled and followed her to the second-floor apartment. She laughed out loud when she saw the sign hanging on the door: *I am the manager and I have a gun.*

Agnes led her to the little living room where she had set the coffee table with a delicate tea set and cookies. Her aged hippie style should have clashed with the frilly apartment, but somehow Sunny knew it worked for Agnes. She felt right at home. Sunny pulled out the notes she made during their phone conversation and held up her black recorder. "I'm going to ask you a few questions. Do you mind if I use this?"

"It's not going to end up on the Internet on that YouYube-y thing, is it?"

Sunny was amused at the question. "No, absolutely not. Everything you tell me is in the strictest confidence."

"Okay then." Agnes looked almost disappointed with her answer before she primped her tight curls. "I've never talked with a psychic before." Her eyes watered. "But I can't take this anymore."

Sunny raised her eyebrows. "Do you want to tell me about it?"

# CHAPTER SIX

Sunny left the art gallery and headed to her car, but seconds later, she heard footsteps behind her and tightened her hold on her tiny clutch, quickening her step slightly. This wasn't the best neighborhood at night, and she'd parked on the third floor of the garage. She darted across the dark street, pulled her coat against her body, and headed to the elevator. Because she was distracted, her high heel caught in the street grate and she felt herself fall, almost in slow motion. She knew she was going to hit the ground.

Sunny felt the painful twist in her ankle and cried out as she managed to catch herself just before her face hit the pavement.

The footsteps were running now, coming closer. Sunny tried to right herself so she could see who was coming and prepared herself to scream as loud as she could. But gentle hands touched her back.

"Hey, are you all right?" Jordan asked before helping Sunny turn over so she could sit instead of kneeling on her hands and knees.

Recognition and relief hit Sunny at the same time, and she laughed nervously. "Officer Lawson. I thought you were, well, never mind." Her stomach clenched, and she forgot she'd just tumbled to the ground. It was the first time she'd clearly seen Jordan, who even now was backlit by the streetlight, giving her a dangerous quality.

Sunny had the strange sensation of déjà vu, but it slipped from her mind quickly as her skin buzzed where Jordan touched her. From her current position on the sidewalk, she let her gaze travel from the tips of her black boots up the long legs to slender hips encased in faded blue denim. Jordan's torso was hidden under a well-worn leather jacket, but her shoulders looked broad and suggestively sexy. Raven hair parted on the side and feathered back to taper behind her ears.

"Did you twist your ankle? Here, let me look."

"I'm sorry. What did you say?" Sunny still felt a little disorientated. "Oh, my ankle." The second she said it, pain blossomed under Jordan's tentative touch on her leg.

Another couple approached from the street. "Are you okay here?"

Sunny observed Jordan move protectively in front of her. "I'm fine. Just a little clumsy in these shoes."

"Are you sure?" The man stared suspiciously at Jordan standing over her.

Sunny sensed his genuine concern and she smiled to reassure him. "Really, Officer Lawson here is just going to help me to my car."

"Okay then." He nodded once before leaving.

"Jordan."

Sunny winced and took off her shoes, knowing how awful her ankle was going to feel tomorrow. She should have listened to Isis when she tried to bat the shoe away when she was getting ready earlier. If only her cats could really talk. "Excuse me?"

"Jordan. My name is Jordan." She took Sunny's shoes, then helped her to stand.

Sunny was a little dizzy, but she'd only had one glass of champagne, not enough to even make her tipsy. Jordan smelled of the ocean and sex. It was a heady combination.

She leaned against Jordan and sighed softly; every curve, every limb fit perfectly against her. She caught Jordan's gaze and locked eyes with her, hearing an almost audible click in her mind before her blood warmed, spreading heat through her body. She was finding it difficult to comprehend anything but her pure physical reaction.

She tried to concentrate instead on limping into the elevator, aware of moisture on her thighs. She'd had fantasies of sex in an elevator with a gorgeous stranger before, though a sprained ankle and skinned knees had never figured into them.

Jordan carefully propped her up on the ancient wall. "Floor?"

"Three," Sunny said then swallowed as the elevator jerked before ascending. Her ankle was rapidly showing visible signs of swelling. Her knees and the palms of her hands burned with the impact they'd taken with the fall, and embarrassment began to set in.

"I'm sorry," Jordan said while they hobbled to Sunny's car, "that this time you thought I was the robber."

Sunny laughed. "That was quite the scene, wasn't it?"

Jordan looked amused. "It was."

"I'm right here." Sunny opened her clutch and dropped her keys. "Damn it."

"I'll get them." Jordan bent over to retrieve them, then fisted them. "I'll drive you home."

"Really, it's not necessary."

"It's your right foot, and it doesn't look good."

"I'll be fine."

"All right then," Jordan said, holding the keys at arm's length, "if you can put any weight on that foot, I'll give them back to you."

Sunny made the effort and was mortified at the small whimper that escaped her throat. "But where's your car?" she finally asked.

"I was out walking. My ride is at home. I saw you and wanted to say hi, which was why I was trying to catch up to you. How far do you live?"

"Not far. Down on Washington, by the water."

Jordan helped her to the passenger side and settled her in before pulling out of the garage and heading in the right direction. "Do you want to go the hospital and get your foot x-rayed?"

"No, not just yet. I can wiggle my toes and move it. Ouch. Well, kind of." Sunny could see as well as feel Jordan's concern, and she was touched. "It's an old dance injury," she explained. "It goes out every once in a while, but I just can't resist the pretty high heels." Sunny let out a small sigh. "Though this particular pair is toast now."

"I never could understand the attraction that so many women have to shoes," Jordan said.

"Ah, but can you at least appreciate how they make our legs look?" Sunny raised an eyebrow.

Jordan snickered. "That I can. That I can." She leaned forward and whistled. "Nice house."

Well, that was a quick conversation switch, Sunny thought. "I know, right? Thank you. I grew up in this house."

"Lots of stairs," Jordan said and went around to the passenger side to help her out. Sunny wanted to tell her she'd be fine, she didn't need any help, but she couldn't seem to find her words. "I don't…"

"Help," Jordan said. "I can help."

It was cute, Sunny thought. Neither of them seemed to be capable of full sentences. Her own nerves were wound tight. Cute, hell, she didn't know what needed more attention, her ankle or her obvious lust for Jordan. She took a moment to thank the Universe that she had leather seats because she knew how moist her panties were. Pain shot through her leg when she stood, which made her focus on her injury.

They reached the bottom of the stairs and headed to the entry. Sunny reached for the railing, but Jordan was ahead of her. "Hold on," she said, hooking an arm behind Sunny's knees and lifting her up before carrying her to the door.

Jordan groaned, and Sunny worried she might be too heavy. "Jordan, put me down." Her thighs burned where Jordan's hand was making contact. Three inches higher and she would feel how wet she was for her. Her clit throbbed as hard as her ankle. And damn if the chivalry routine didn't just make her hotter.

"It's easier if I just carry you. Then you're not putting weight on it."

They managed to get through the door without any mishaps. Jordan tilted Sunny sideways to carry her over the threshold without a problem.

Jordan let Sunny slide down her body to stand and shut the door behind her. *Think, Jordan.* She couldn't think straight or keep two thoughts together.

Where was her cop training, her first aid knowledge? Hell, where was her voice? Panic started to rumble through her. The last time she'd been attracted to a woman and followed through, the results had been disastrous. She didn't care to open that door again anytime soon. Jordan forced more cold logic to argue with her body's reaction to Sunny. It was safer that way, no matter how much she suddenly burned for her.

Sunny took off her coat and limped into the parlor to sit and put her foot up.

Jordan felt weird, like the air she was breathing was different or something. Almost like the really good buzz you got after two drinks but lost by the time you hit three or four. Pretty trinkets sparkled on shelves and tables, as did a multitude of different candles. There were crystals in every color, on pedestals, in baskets, and on every surface, but somehow nothing looked cluttered or messy. Jordan had always kept a Spartan place since she moved into her own apartment at the age of eighteen when the foster system cut her loose onto the streets. She considered herself the antithesis to her mother and their early domestic life.

*God. Don't go there now.* She looked back to Sunny, who was looking at her with an odd half smile on her face. What? Had she done something stupid or amusing, or worse, been talking out loud? "Ice!" blurted Jordan. "You need ice." *And I need a cold shower.*

Sunny pointed to the rear of the house. "Kitchen is back there. But I can—"

"No, no. I'll get you some." She fled down the hall and flipped the light on when she reached the room. She didn't think real people lived like this, with immaculate counters with vases and doodads and appliances that could whistle "Dixie" for you. There was a wonderful citrusy smell too.

The stainless steel freezer yielded the best compress ever made—a bag of frozen peas. Jordan used them herself after altercations with violent offenders. No mess. She turned to head back to Sunny, but something darted in front of her, tripping her, and she landed on the kitchen floor flat on her ass.

"What the hell was that?" Something growled to her left. Jordan slowly turned her head and saw a white cat hunched over and hissing at her. There was a yowl on her other side. Great, twins. Cats hated her, but that was okay. She pretty much hated them too. Jordan narrowed her eyes and hissed back.

"What are you doing?" Sunny appeared noiselessly in the doorway.

Jordan felt like an idiot, sitting on the floor and getting caught snarling at her cats. Could this be any more awkward? She didn't think so. She climbed to her feet clumsily and pointed. "The cat tripped me."

Sunny looked at the larger feline. "Isis, Ash." The cats turned large blue eyes toward her. "Jordan is our guest."

The felines blinked slowly, turned in unison, and left the room. *Okay, that was a little creepy.* "You're supposed to be elevating that ankle."

"You sounded like you needed help." Sunny smiled. "Vicious attack cats and all."

Jordan felt her face flush. "Yeah, well." She kept herself from rubbing her aching tailbone. The frozen bag of vegetables hung limp in her hand. "Let's get you get back into a chair."

Before Sunny got halfway down the hall, the front door opened and a woman came rushing in. "What happened?" She bustled Sunny to a chair and glared at Jordan. "Did you do this?"

The intensity of her stare unnerved her a little and she felt pinned. "No. Well, not intentionally."

"Mom, it's not her fault. I tripped in my high heels, that's all. This is Jordan. Jordan, this is my mother, Aura."

"Sorry, Jordan. I'm a little protective of my daughter. Please tell me you weren't going to use *that*?" Aura pointed at the bag of peas hanging limply from Jordan's hand.

Jordan resisted the urge to hide it behind her back. "Um, yes?" She had also planned on getting her hands on Sunny's sexy legs. Her mother showing up was a cold bucket of water on that plan.

Aura took Sunny into the living room, her body language shouting at Jordan that she wasn't needed any longer.

Jordan handed Sunny the bag and pushed her hands into her front pockets. "Well, I guess I'll be going now."

"Let me call you a cab," Sunny said. "It's the least I can do after you drove me home."

Jordan shook her head. "I know where I am. I can walk." She left quickly.

*That was close.* Every nerve ending in her body was on edge. Had she really been thinking about taking Sunny upstairs? Granted, she was stunning and sexy, but she seemed to be so different, she might as well have been on another planet.

Jordan let the night air clear her head.

❖

Sunny stood in the eye of the storm. Ribbons of emotional energy swirled around her in a vortex of emotions until she bent under the weight of them, suffocating in a kaleidoscope of feelings that didn't belong to her.

A hand appeared through the wall of wind to help her up, and she stood face-to-face with Jordan. A smile lit her face an instant before the gale swept her up and tore her from Sunny's grasp. She opened her mouth to scream, but no sound came out.

Sunny became aware of a tapping on her cheek, and she opened her eyes to find Isis two inches from her face, her paw resting against Sunny's cheek. She thought she saw Jordan's face reflected in the cat's eyes, but she blinked and the image faded. Sunny was filled with a yearning so deep and intense, it was painful. She centered herself and controlled her breathing. When she felt steady, she asked her question. *What did this dream mean?* She let her consciousness fly in an attempt to find Jordan's energy.

Nothing. She couldn't see or feel her anywhere. Sunny brought herself back and felt a moment of panic. That had never happened before. Not since her mother taught her how to astral project when she was twelve. She didn't have many opportunities to second-guess herself. Was Jordan's absence in that realm a good or a bad thing? Not being able to see Jordan left Sunny feeling blind. She tried to quiet her doubts, remembering that what you sent out into the world with your vibrations came back to you. What you went looking for with your thoughts was important because it was always what you found. She curled her fingers around her amulet and pulled white light around herself in a circle of protection. Ash padded across the top of the comforter to curl on her other side. What was it about that woman that drew her so? Other than the intense physical attraction, she felt their lives had intersected for a reason, but the darkness surrounding Jordan made her dreams uneasy.

## CHAPTER SEVEN

The early afternoon sun streamed in the front windows, warming Sunny as she stood in front of them, wishing she had time to play outside. The Pacific Northwest had so few of these days. She loved the beautiful area, but all the lush greenery came at a price and that was rain, rain, and more rain.

As if her thoughts were heard, a cloud moved in front of the sun, and Sunny smiled wistfully. Maybe it was time to plan a trip south again, someplace warm with white sandy beaches, blue surf, and red fancy drinks that wore umbrellas. She closed her eyes to imagine herself there, dipping her pink-painted toenails into the water and feeling the sand shift beneath her feet. Hot naked skin covered her, and Jordan's white musk cologne wrapped around her.

Startled, Sunny opened her eyes and felt her stomach sink a little. Where had that come from? She was so disappointed that Jordan hadn't asked to see her again. She knew she hadn't imagined the attraction between them. Hers had been real enough, but maybe she'd projected her own feelings on Jordan. *Isn't that a mortifying thought?* Maybe Jordan had just been trying to help, as any good officer would.

No, Sunny had been able to perceive Jordan's concern when she helped her. But maybe it was just concern, and not the drenching attraction she thought it was.

Then she remembered her failed attempt to find Jordan's energy and finding not even a trace. Why was it when it came to something that Sunny wanted for herself, she ran up against that block that kept her from seeing? It seemed almost unfair.

Her father had once told her it was because in order for Sunny to grow, she had to experience all of life, all the good, bad, and ugly. If she were able to predict her own future, she would have the ability to cherry-pick her experiences and rob herself of events that were necessary to her spiritual and mental growth. She couldn't predict events for those that were close to her either, for the exact same reason. Oh, she could get inklings and flashes of intuition if she tried, but everyone had free will in their lives and had, in one form or another, chosen events in their lives for their own journeys.

It was a major conflict for Sunny when clients came to see her. What to tell them, what to hold back for their own good. She walked a very fine line in those situations, which was why she preferred not to do predictions. It was much easier and less stressful for her to deliver messages from loved ones who had crossed over. As a medium, she was just the middleman, so to speak, for someone else and not the source.

Sunny turned toward the phone a full two seconds before it rang. She gave herself a mental shake. It was time to get back to work.

❖

Jordan eased Sunny to her back on the large bed. Her long hair fanned behind her and her smile was full of delicious promises as she unfastened the tiny buttons on the bodice of her white dress and pulled the fabric open to expose her pale breasts. Jordan's mouth watered before she bent to flick her tongue across a pink nipple before nuzzling it with her lips.

"We have to follow up on this missing person."

Jordan snapped back to the present, disoriented. "What?" Holy shit, she was on shift. What was she doing? Her mind never wandered like that at work.

Vince narrowed his eyes. "Have you heard anything I've said in the last five minutes?"

No, but she wasn't going to admit it. "Missing person. Follow-up."

"Okay, we'll try this again. Mother called last night and filed a report, her daughter hadn't come home after school."

God, how many of those calls had she been on in the last ten years? Too many. Gina Brayden's face came to mind. She hated these cases even as she was drawn to them with the need to help. "Runaway? Boyfriend? Drugs?"

Vince parked the cruiser in the driveway. "Her parents say none of the above, that she's a good girl."

They always were, thought Jordan. Even the ones that were thrown away. She got out of the car, hitched her belt, and looked at a pleasant split-level house. Flowers bloomed along the tidy walkway. The manicured lawn and clean front porch told visitors it was a welcoming house and well cared for. But Jordan knew how deceiving outside appearances could be. Sometimes the best houses held the dirtiest secrets. She'd seen it before. She motioned for Vince to take the lead when the worried mother with red and swollen eyes appeared in the doorway.

She didn't feel good about this, not one little bit. Jordan steeled herself for the interview with the missing girl's tearful parents.

As she drove by the 7-Eleven on her way home, Jordan searched the faces in the shadows instinctually for the missing girl, even though she knew deep down this particular girl wasn't a runaway. There would be no easy resolution to this case. She had a hunch that this one was going to end badly.

She tried not to attach stories to the kids she did see, the ones hanging out on the street at a time normal parents would want them tucked safely in bed. To get personally involved only caused pain, and usually a great deal of it. Jordan lost more runaways than she saved. How many times had she pulled kids off the street and returned them to their parents, only to see them back on the streets two days later? For some of these teens, the streets were safer than their homes. It certainly had been for Jordan when she was growing up.

Gina hadn't been the first missing person she'd been assigned to, but Jordan had gotten so emotionally involved with the runaway that when she appeared to have dropped from the face of the earth, Jordan felt something inside her break and shatter. A piece of her soul was gone, missing the same way the child herself was.

Jordan entered the hall and heard voices in the stairwell. It was after eleven, and most people were usually in bed at that time. She recognized Steve's voice first, then Agnes's, but wasn't close enough yet to make out the third or what they were saying. She rounded the landing and resigned herself to making small talk.

Steve's door shut, and Jordan was relieved to see no one between herself and her apartment. She was tired and hungry, and wanted nothing more than to eat her takeout teriyaki and kick her feet up in private.

The laundry basket with her neatly folded clothes sat in front of her door, reminding her of what happened earlier in the basement. She juggled her food with her keys and kicked the basket into the apartment. She took a quick shower before heating her dinner in the microwave and settling on the couch. She had just flipped the television on and had the first bite to her mouth when she heard the knock on her door.

"Are you flipping kidding me?" Jordan stalked to the door and swung it open. "Seriously? Do you know what time it is?" The words were barely out of her mouth before she was stunned by the sight of Sunny standing in front of her, holding on to the door frame, her eyes glassy. A microsecond later, her eyes rolled back and she swooned. Jordan barely managed to grab her arm before she fell to her knees. Steve rushed out of his apartment.

"What *is* it with you, Jordan?" Steve asked before sweeping Sunny up in his arms and pushing past her into the living room. "Do you kiss them and make them cry too?"

"He's right, dear." Agnes entered and patted her arm. "You made me faint as well."

Jordan followed, then stood next to the couch. Once again, she felt like she'd been dropped into the middle of a play already in progress and she had no idea what her lines were.

"Here she comes. Where's your whiskey?" Agnes asked when Sunny opened her eyes and looked around warily.

Sunny laughed weakly. "Water is fine."

Jordan fled into the kitchen to get some for her. She had been imagining Sunny flat on her back, but this scenario certainly wasn't how she'd got there. When she returned, Sunny was sitting up with Steve and Agnes on either side of her.

"Are you okay?" Jordan handed her the glass and, feeling stupid just standing there, sat on the coffee table. "What happened?"

"You opened the door."

"I usually do that when someone knocks."

"Okay, I was surprised to see you standing there. I didn't know you lived here."

"The sight of me made you faint?" Jordan asked, incredulous. She tried to find her bearings, and answering questions with another question was second nature to her and usually gave her more time to think.

"I did not faint."

Agnes looked back and forth between them. "You two know each other?"

"We've met," Sunny said politely before meeting Jordan's eyes. "Could you both please excuse us?"

"But…" Steve looked puzzled. "What about…"

"Just for a few minutes. If you could wait over at your grandmother's, I'll be along. When Shade and Tiffany get here, just tell them to wait until I get back to start setting up." She smiled and flashed her dimples. "Thank you so much. I appreciate it."

Steve beamed back at her and then stumbled over his big feet on his way to the door, nearly tripping Agnes, who was close behind him. Jordan snickered, then shut the door in his face before he could ask her any questions.

Now what? Jordan thought. Butterflies fluttered in her stomach. In spite of her fierce attraction, she had already made the decision not to seek Sunny out after convincing herself that one, she came from a different planet than she did, and two, she was so far out of her league that Sunny was in another stratosphere from Jordan. She looked around the small apartment and couldn't help but compare it to Sunny's home, filled with rich things and cats. Don't forget the cats, she told herself; you hate cats.

Every single argument flew out the window when Sunny looked at her. Her hair was mussed and her full lips were parted slightly, begging for a kiss. Jordan moved across the carpet toward her. She felt heavy and sluggish, but the need to get to her was almost overwhelming.

She dropped to her knees in front of Sunny and leaned in. She heard Sunny's sharp intake of breath and stopped when their lips were separated by only a few inches.

"Jordan. Stop. I have to tell you something."

"Mmm." *Stop?* Hell no. She was going to take her right here on the couch. Pin her and take what she wanted. She was going to wrap her hands around her delicate throat and squeeze until she begged for her life. And she was going to like it.

"Jordan!"

"What?" Jordan looked down at her hands gripping Sunny's shoulders. Oh my God, what had she just been thinking? Sunny's eyes were wide and she looked frightened. Jordan was mortified and jumped to her feet.

A chair scraped along the linoleum in the dining room and they both jumped.

What was wrong with her? Jordan's ears were ringing and her hands shook. Sunny approached slowly, almost cautiously. Rage bubbled in Jordan's veins and she snapped. "I suppose you're going to tell me that was a ghost."

"Excuse me?" Sunny looked surprised. "What just happened here?"

"Are the Jacksons in on this too?" Jordan began to pace back and forth. "Who put you up to this?" She was livid. The last thing she needed was someone else messing with her head.

"I'm sure I don't know what you're talking about."

"Don't give me that innocent look." She pointed at Sunny. "I want an explanation for all of this right now."

"Agnes called me to come over and investigate the activity here and help her to get rid of it."

Jordan acted as if she hadn't heard her. "What I can't figure out is how you people got into my apartment to move shit around while I was in it."

"You people?"

"How much did that bitch Lynn pay you—all of you—to drive me completely over the edge? And why?"

"Again, Jordan. I don't know—"

"I'm not stupid!"

"I never thought—"

"How much did you take the old lady for? You and your con artist witch buddies."

"That's enough!" Sunny stood and advanced toward her. "I will not stand here and let you insult my friends and their integrity. I will not tolerate it, do you hear me?"

Jordan stopped pacing. As suddenly as it appeared, the anger ebbed and left her feeling foggy and unsure. What had they been arguing about? The last thing she clearly remembered was thinking how pretty she looked. "But—"

"But nothing. I don't owe you any explanations. You've just stood there throwing around accusations about something I have nothing to do with."

Jordan desperately tried to remember what she'd said to piss her off.

"And another thing, Officer Lawson." She spat the title out sarcastically. "Don't flatter yourself. I didn't faint at the sight of you." Sunny turned toward the door. "I fainted because the demon that lives here was standing behind you." She smiled wickedly and slammed the door.

*What did she just say?* Jordan's pulse skipped and she turned to look over her shoulder. *Did she just say demon?* She flashed back to the age of twelve and her first foster parents who forced her to go to church. She could still see the priest, spittle flying from his mouth as he prayed over her for the sins of her mother. She had been terrified of him and the church's vision of hellfire and brimstone reserved just for her kind—children of junkies, who were evil just by association. As if she ever had a choice in the matter, as if she didn't smell the alcohol on his hypocritical breath. Jordan was never good enough for them, and they always found some fault with her—some reason to lock her in her room. They would roll their eyes and beg God for her deliverance from Satan and his minions. She'd been there less than a year when she ran away for the first time. When the state caught up with her, she was sent to a different foster home.

A worse one, where the so-called demon was an-all-too human and particularly sadistic foster brother. Jordan broke herself free of the memory. She was an adult now, and she didn't believe in their evil fairy tales any longer.

A cupboard flew open and slammed shut in the kitchen as if to mock her.

❖

Sunny's adrenaline had her practically flying back to Agnes's apartment. "Just me and my broom," she said out loud to the night. "That's all I need."

She had absolutely no idea what Jordan was talking about, but she had been willing to be patient and try to find out. But to let her tirade include Tiffany and Shade was never going to happen. Not while there was breath left in her body.

She didn't get mad very often, but Jordan had infuriated her and made her say something to intentionally scare her. Who did she think she was anyway? Sunny could practically feel the sparks standing her hair on end. She refused to acknowledge the small guilty teeth that nibbled at her conscience.

Tiffany took one look at her and her eyes widened. "What—"

"Not now. Let's get this party started." Sunny bumped past her and ran straight into Shade, who stopped her.

"Whoa."

Sunny ground her teeth. "I just want to do this and go home. Don't ask me, don't peek into my head, just step away, please." She felt the tears gather behind her eyes and looked down so they wouldn't be seen.

Shade put her hands up in surrender. "Okay."

Tiffany grabbed her arm and pulled her into the bathroom. "Breathe," she said and forced Sunny to sit on the side of the bathtub before placing one palm on her heart and the other on the top of her head.

Sunny felt some of the anger ebb.

"Again," Tiffany ordered. "You know the drill, in through the nose, out through the mouth. Repeat."

Sunny felt the first tear slide down her cheek, then another, but complied. Her throat wanted to close around the lump of frustration and hurt in it. She hated to cry when she was mad. It made her feel weak and vulnerable, even though she knew the process was a cleansing one.

"That's it. Let it go," Tiffany soothed her. "Let it drain down your legs into the floor."

A few moments later, Sunny felt almost normal, if a bit depleted from the experience. "I'm okay now. Thank you."

"Wow, where did you pick up this dark energy?"

Sunny instantly made the connection. If she hadn't been so mad, the entity wouldn't have been able to push her buttons so easily. Which, of course, could be an excellent explanation for Jordan's explosive reaction and strange behavior.

Now that she was calmer, she felt some shame at how she'd blurted to Jordan there was a demon in the apartment. It was against her code of personal honor to use her gift in that way, to scare or harm someone. "Oh, Tiff, I was awful." She covered her face with her hands. "I told her there was a demon in her apartment."

"Who?"

"Jordan."

Tiffany looked confused.

"Hot lady cop from a couple of weeks ago. Officer Lawson."

"Ah."

"I ran into her again the other night."

"And?"

"Tiffany, she confuses me. She brought me home after I twisted my ankle, and I could have sworn there were major sparks. If my mother hadn't shown up, I'm pretty sure we would have followed up on them. I've dreamt of her almost every night, and it's driving me crazy. Anyway, after I did the walk-through of Steve's apartment, the door across from him looked off to me. I was drawn to it even as I felt I should be running. I knocked, Jordan opened the door, and I was so surprised and happy to see her, I didn't feel the wave of darkness until it hit me and I went to my knees."

Tiffany leaned closer. "Then what happened?"

"It all happened so fast. I was sitting on the couch ready to warn her about the entity in the apartment when she dropped to her knees. I thought she was going to kiss me."

"And that pissed you off?"

"No, that's when I realized she didn't look right. Her eyes were a little glazed, and she grabbed me."

Tiffany stiffened. "That bitch hurt you?"

"It wasn't her, Tiff. There's something in that apartment, and it's ugly. It seemed to take control of her. Then something moved a chair and she turned on me, yelling about how we set this up to drive her crazy. She said some horrible things about us and I lost my temper."

Tiffany smiled. "A rare occurrence."

"My emotions are all twisted up. I don't know what Jordan is really feeling, and I hate that I care so much. I mean, really, I've only seen her a couple of times. I have no idea where this is all coming from."

"That surprises me. You usually always know what others are feeling. Why do you think that is?"

A light tap on the door saved Sunny from answering. Shade poked her head in. "Everything okay?"

Sunny soaked up the concern and love in the small space. "Yes, it will be. I just got blindsided by some dark energy in an upstairs apartment. I'm fine now."

Tiffany patted her hand and left her alone with Shade, who pulled her to her feet. "We okay here?"

Sunny met her gaze. "Always." She let Shade drop her arm around her shoulders and lead her to the table where Steve, Agnes, and Tiffany waited. "Sorry about the meltdown."

"It's okay, dear. Do you want some whiskey?"

Sunny let her amusement wash the last of her agitation away and declined the offer.

"Do you want me to set up the equipment?" Shade asked.

Sunny thought about it for a second. "Not just yet. After what just happened upstairs, there's more to this than I was aware of. It's late, and I have a feeling it's going to take more than one trip."

A little moan came from Agnes, and her face went white. "Crap! I was hoping we could just get rid of them."

Sunny hated to disappoint Agnes, but she made the decision to exclude her from the investigation itself. She hadn't anticipated there being so many souls here, and she certainly hadn't expected to run into Jordan or the dark entity in her apartment. It had thrown her off. Sunny realized she'd become too complacent and comfortable, since she'd been able to handle every other client case over the last year with ease. If she had been on top of her game, she wouldn't have been caught unawares by the black energy. This was going to take much more preparation than she'd done this evening, and she was still shaken from the experience itself.

"Agnes?" Sunny said. "Honey, you can't be here when we do our investigation or communicate with the spirits. We're going to have to come back, and I would like for you to be somewhere else, okay?"

"Oh, sweet baby Jesus, thank God! I was trying to be brave, I really was, but this shit scares the hell out of me."

Sunny laughed. "Well, okay then." She was relieved. Sometimes clients argued the point and wanted to be there no matter the consequences, and truthfully, that only put more pressure on her and her team. Steve looked disappointed, and she hastened to reassure him that they could still use his help. She'd seen his electronic setup earlier, and the complex was large enough that he could assist somewhere out of the way.

Tonight, they would cleanse Agnes's apartment, but Sunny knew it was a short-term solution and more for the landlady's peace of mind than to fix the hauntings themselves. She looked over to Tiffany and nodded.

Shade picked up a case of equipment to bring back to the van and left. Tiffany grabbed her large tote bag and unpacked some crystals and loose sage leaves to spread in the corners while Sunny lit her sage stick and burned the whole thing, inviting only positive energy to stay.

"That smells like wacky tobaccy." Agnes looked almost hopeful. "Is it?"

"No, Grandma, it's not marijuana." Steve pinched the bridge of his nose.

"Oh," Agnes said. "Pity."

# Chapter Eight

A piece of loose gravel from the parking lot stuck in the bottom of Jordan's boot, making a horrible screeching sound on the cement of the path to her building. She stopped at the door and kicked her foot against the frame to dislodge it before stepping into the dark foyer. The lightbulb must have burned out. *Yeah, but on all three floors?* The total blackness above showed there were no lights on the landings above her either. She felt along the wall to the staircase and began ascending, a tread for each beat of her heart.

The higher she climbed, the heavier her body felt. She really hated the dark and wished she'd been in uniform because then she would have had her gun and Mag flashlight within reach. She moved as quickly as caution allowed her.

*Jordan.*

The voice whispered directly in her ear, sending cold fingers along her neck. Jordan swung her fist and connected with—nothing. Her throat constricted, and she reached for the revolver she wasn't wearing.

"Who's there?" Her voice sounded strange, muffled in the heavy darkness. She reached the top of the stairs and took the five steps to her front door, fumbling in the dark to get her key into the lock. A high-pitched giggle came from behind her. Jordan startled and dropped the keys. She dropped to her knees and ran her hand along the carpet, panic making her movements jerky. A bead of sweat slid from her forehead, down the side of her face.

"Steve?" She found the keys and quickly stood so she could place her back against the door. "Not funny, asshole." She spun around, unlocked the door, and barreled through it. Jordan reached for the light switch and flipped it. Of course, it didn't work. She hated this place. She really, really did. It might be time to look for somewhere else to live.

Her flashlight was in the bedroom. Keeping her back along the wall, she sidestepped to the doorway. The drapes she'd just hung were open and she adjusted her eyes in the glow of the streetlight. It was so quiet, the hideous buzzing of the vapor bulb pricked at the nerves under her skin.

Jordan stopped and stared. There was someone in her bed. The covers were messy, and a form was clearly outlined under them. She strained her eyes in an attempt to see better until she felt they might pop out of their sockets. She grabbed the flashlight from the nightstand and slid her hand along the long handle until she gripped the widest portion and it became a weapon.

She slowly raised her right arm over her head, ready to beat down the intruder the second there was movement. She hesitated when she saw the long lock of blond hair visible against the contrast of her dark blue sheets. She knew that hair; she'd been fantasizing about it extensively of late. A small white hand peeked out from under the comforter, the nails painted blood red. "Sunny? What are you doing here?"

The fingers on the hand twitched in response, but the body remained still. Jordan set her flashlight down and cautiously peeled back the covers. She moved the curtain of hair hiding the face and screamed.

Terror shot through her nervous system, leaving her body paralyzed and her mouth frozen open.

Her mother's dead face stared back at her.

Jordan's eyes shot open and she found herself sitting upright. Sweat dripped down her back, and she felt the drops that fell from her face puddle between her breasts. The bottom sheet was twisted and damp beneath her. Jordan gulped air and tried to stop her teeth from chattering while she swallowed the bile that rose into her mouth. The clock's red numbers glowed in the room: 3:15. She placed a hand on her forehead, felt the tremors in her fingers. What was happening to her?

## CHAPTER NINE

Sunny looked around in the dark and tried to place the sound that woke her. What time was it? Three fifteen. The witching hour, the time of morning when the veil to the spirit world was the thinnest. The cats still slept soundly beside her. Something felt off to her, but she couldn't put her finger on it.

"Mazie?" she called out in a whisper. "Is that you? We talked about this. You have to let me sleep." Sunny closed her eyes but didn't find any trace of Mazie. Just dreaming, she told herself before shifting to find a comfortable position to go back to sleep. Still, she felt uneasy and her chest hurt. Sunny concentrated on her heart chakra, the center of energy where she felt pain, and cleared her mind of stray thoughts. She imagined an emerald green circle, spinning around and around until a perfect fan of green petals turned clockwise and the pain lessened. Her last thought before falling back to sleep was of a slender blond woman standing by the side of the bed. She said two words and then dissipated into smoke.

*Help her.*

❖

In the morning, Sunny doubled her meditation time and took a saltwater bath to clear any lingering negative energy or stray emotions that didn't belong to her. When she was done, she took her time dressing, choosing a long witchy dress that always made her feel pretty, and chose a silver necklace with a center moonstone. It was her personal favorite for busy days. It helped attract good emotions while protecting her own.

There. That was more like it. She felt more herself than she had for days and smiled at her reflection before leaving the third floor, ready to start her day.

Sunny had three readings this morning, and her clients deserved for her to be in a good, clear space for them.

*What about your needs?* Sunny caught the sharp edge of the question before it could pierce the blue light of protection she'd just placed around her and turned it away.

Sunny smelled her mother before she found her sitting with Shade in the kitchen. She hadn't heard either of them come in. While it was her mother's habit to be here early in the morning, it was never Shade's. "What's up?"

"We've been talking, and I'm worried about you." Her mother's face clearly showed signs of strain, and for the first time since Sunny could remember since her father died, she looked her age. The absence of her charged personality left her a little gray around the edges, as if her internal light were on a dimmer switch.

Sunny's concern brought her immediately to her mother's side. "I'm fine, Mom." The second her hand touched her mother's shoulder, anxiety ran up her arm to settle in her throat. Sunny stepped back from her mother's emotion.

"I can't help it this morning." She took a sip of the tea she'd already brewed. Sunny could see her carefully weighing her words before speaking. "Shade? Why don't you go first?"

Shade cleared her throat. "Okay. I was driving by the other night when Jordan was leaving." She held her hand out. "And before you ask if I stalk much, the answer is no. I've been having really weird dreams lately. It makes me feel better to check on you and Tiff before I go home."

Sunny pulled a chair to the table and sat. She'd better hear what Shade had to say. Her dreams could be prophetic. "What did you see?"

"They started a couple of weeks ago, right after the Barbieri job."

*Right after we met Jordan.* Sunny caught the words that weren't said out loud. Shade's eyes were clear and full of accusation. "Please continue."

"I can't remember all the details, but it always starts with the dark tunnel. I can hear you crying for help somewhere in the darkness. Every time I run toward your screams, the direction shifts. I run and run, and I can't ever find you."

"How awful."

Shade paused and looked at Sunny's mother, who nodded for her to continue. "Last night's was the worst. It started just like the other ones, where I was running and searching, but the screaming cut off." She snapped her fingers. "Just like that, and I was alone in the tunnel. I could hear large wings flapping in the darkness."

Sunny shuddered slightly. She was grateful she didn't have Shade's demons to contend with. "Did you get a message?"

Shade shook her head. "It's like I'm holding my breath, waiting for something to happen."

Sunny didn't know what to say. She was sorry Shade was having these nightmares, but if there was no message, what could she do about it? And why were they here so early to confront her about them? "What did you see?" she finally asked her mother. Sunny was almost certain she didn't want to know the answer, but her mother's dreams and intuition weren't anything to be ignored or shoved aside either. She jumped when her mother's hand hit the table with a loud smack.

"I *can't* see. Anything."

Oh, this is bad, Sunny thought. This is really bad.

❖

Jordan stood in the shower and let the cold water run directly on her face, hoping to wash away her nightmare of the previous night. Now that the door to the memory of her mother's death had been opened, she couldn't seem to close it. Part of her wanted to curl up in the bottom of the tub and cry her heart out, but Jordan refused to give in to that hurt little girl inside her. She ordered herself to pull it together.

Coffee, strong coffee, that's what she needed to clear the cobwebs out of her head. Jordan wrapped a towel around her wet body and padded into the kitchen to make some.

She tried to recall what was going through her mind right before she lost her temper. What on earth had possessed her to verbally attack Sunny like that with no provocation? She recalled wanting to kiss her, but when she tried harder to remember how she got from that feeling to the door slamming in her face, her head began to ache.

She saw Sunny's beautiful face, and then it shifted and morphed into her mother's dead one.

*No!*

What she needed even more than coffee was a distraction. For one of the first times in her adult life, Jordan wanted to seek out the company of another human being.

Fifteen minutes later, she kicked Steve's door with the toe of her boot and held out a steaming mug to him when he answered a minute later.

Steve squinted at her without his glasses, his hair standing up in tufts around his head. Jordan blinked and bit her tongue to keep from laughing when she noticed his Star Wars flannel pants.

"Mmm." He grunted. "Smells good, gimme." He stepped aside so she could enter.

"Morning." Jordan was relieved he wasn't snippy with her; she absolutely would have been if the situation were reversed. *What's that say about me?*

"You on swing tonight?"

Jordan shook her head. "Day shift." Now what? She hadn't thought that far ahead yet. Steve disappeared to get his glasses, then came back to sit with her at the small table.

"Whatssup? What brings you to my man cave this morning?"

Jordan didn't know exactly and thought about running. Why was she here again? Her ears filled with that ringing again and she shook her head.

"Are you here to apologize?"

Her head snapped back. "For what?"

"Look," he said. "I don't know what happened last night with Sunny, but when she got back to Grandma's there was steam coming out her ears. What did you do to her?"

Jordan felt her face flush with shame. "Why? What did she say?"

Steve looked at her thoughtfully. "Not a word."

"Oh." *Why can't I remember?* Pain flared again in her temples.

"Well, whatever. They left without doing anything."

"Ghost hunters," she said. "Give me a break." Her voice sounded far away to her own ears and echoed back to her. She caught snatches of her accusations and a small glimpse of the hurt that had passed over Sunny's face before she left. It was almost like remembering something you did when you were really drunk and regretting it the next day. It made her feel petty and small.

Steve continued to stare at her. "Do you have any other explanations for this, Jordan? These events aren't hallucinations or punks in the building playing tricks. Do you think so little of me that you think I would automatically jump to conclusions? Are you going to sit there with your closed mind or are you going to try and consider the possibility these things are paranormal and help me find some resolution?"

Jordan wanted to be pissed that he'd called her close-minded, she really did, but there was no animosity in his voice or the way he was looking at her. He looked genuinely curious, and she had nothing to fight him about. It was as if he cared about her. She picked at a piece of something hard stuck to the table, and to her horror, the back of her throat began to burn. "But I don't believe in ghosts."

"That makes no difference to them," he said gently. "It doesn't make them less real because you think they aren't there."

"They're just out to take your money," she said and cringed when she heard the childish petulance in her voice.

"Who? The women from S.O.S.? Sunny?" Steve shook his head. "Is that what's got you so upset? You think they're swindlers? Jordan, they didn't charge my grandmother a red penny to be here. She's terrified, and they want to help her."

Why did Jordan find that so hard to believe? There had to be an angle to this whole ghost hunting thing. She just hadn't found it yet.

❖

"I can't see," her mother's anguished voice repeated. "I hear crying, but I can't tell who it is. The spirits are quiet, the crystals are clouded, and the cards won't tell me anything."

"Could you excuse us, please?" Sunny asked.

Shade nodded and headed to the war room.

Sunny could feel her mother's fear. Losing her sixth sense must be like being blind for her. She recalled the Death card she'd turned over last week, and apprehension stung the nerves under her skin. She had been right. Something was coming, it wasn't good, and worse yet, they weren't going to be able to prepare for it. She'd had no idea it would affect her mother and Shade too, though, and anger burned away the cobwebs left by strange dreams and uncertainty about the future.

It wasn't going to do either of them any good to sit and fret over it. Sunny refused to give the fear any of her energy. "We're just going to have to get through it. There must be a reason we can't see it. *Spirit* has never let us down before."

"Except for the day your father died."

Sunny's heart clenched, and she thought back to that day. She had been in a lecture at college when she felt her father die. There was no feeling of foreboding, just the certainty that hit her the moment her father was no longer in this reality. She was leaving her class, pulling her phone out of her backpack when it rang. She knew, just knew, he was gone. His passing from a heart attack left a hole in her soul that would never fully heal.

Sunny had gone back to her room and told Shade, who was also her roommate, what happened

The funeral was a blur. Sunny relied on Tiffany and Shade to hold her up through the ordeal. Her mother insisted she go back to her classes and finish school. The only reason Sunny relented was because Tiffany assured her that she would take care of her mother until she got back. It was when they returned to college that she threw herself into Shade's arms. Sunny had known forever how Shade felt about her, but always kept her at a friendly distance. She adored her and was her best friend. But after her father's death, Sunny convinced herself that it was romantic. She tried to turn her heartbreak into love.

They'd almost killed each other with the intensity of their relationship. Shade's dark side threatened to drown Sunny's light spirit, a clash that left them both exhausted. Sunny's grades began to slip and she lost weight. The dead that surrounded Shade began to appear to her. She was absorbing the necromancer and seeing people as they looked when they died, a gift she never wanted. She preferred seeing them as they wanted to be seen, shimmery around the edges and in the prime of their life. Her empathy threatened to drown her in an ocean of death.

Sunny's father came to visit her one evening when Shade was studying at the library, and she burst into tears. She was mad he left, but so happy to see him again. The emotional roller coaster she'd been on was threatening to derail and crash, to leave her broken in the dirt.

"Why did you leave me?"

"It was my time, sweetheart. I'm good over here. I'm watching over your mother and you."

"But I miss you so much! I didn't even get to say good-bye."

"I know, baby girl, I miss you too. But listen. I came here to tell you something important. You have to let her go."

Sunny was confused. "Who?"

"Shade. She's not for you."

"But I love her." Sunny lifted her chin. "We're soul mates."

"Honey, you know that's not true. You're hurting her more by staying with her. It's not fair, and you're both going to burn to ashes if you don't leave. Your sight is shifting to the dark side, and if you don't leave now, it will assimilate you and take your own abilities."

"I can't hurt her like that, Daddy. It would break her heart."

Her father looked sad. "Each day you wait, it will be harder. Look into your heart, Sunny, and do the right thing for yourself and for Shade."

Sunny cried harder. Now she'd lost her father and her best friend. Sunny felt the static against her cheek and felt her father's feather kiss. "I love you."

"I love you too, Daddy. Please come back." His energy left and Sunny cried for hours.

Later that evening, a boy who had been killed in a horrible car wreck on campus appeared at the end of the bed. He was covered in blood and missing limbs and wanted to talk with her. Sunny realized her father was right. She couldn't do this anymore. Shade's necromancy was overpowering her.

When Shade had come back from the library, Sunny did the right thing and essentially ripped out her heart with careful words. If there had been any other way, she would have taken it. She crushed Shade, and she would feel guilty for it for the rest of her life.

That had been seven years ago. Their relationship as friends eventually survived the fractured aftermath of their painful breakup, and soon after they graduated, Shade moved to Bremerton to become part of the paranormal team Sunny's parents had built.

The sound of her mother stirring her tea brought Sunny back to the present. Why had she gone there? She was so careful to keep that period in her life safely buried. Everyone's emotions were all over the place lately. "Mom, why don't you go home and take the day off? We can manage here."

Her mother looked at her with tearful eyes ringed with dark circles. "I have to be here."

"No, Mom, you need to take care of yourself. You're not okay right now."

She could see that she wanted to argue with her, could sense the reasons why she wouldn't leave. Finally, she looked resigned. "Okay, but if you need me, please call." She pulled Sunny into a bear hug. "Be careful, my baby girl. I can't see what's coming, and that can't be a good thing."

❖

In spite of the worry her mother left in her wake, Sunny's readings went well. By the end of the third one, the kick of energy she'd started the day with was wearing off, and the idea of a nap was sounding better and better. She should get as much rest as she could before returning to Agnes's apartment complex later in the evening.

Jordan. The name slipped into her consciousness and echoed in her heart before Sunny could stop it. She didn't want to open herself to the desire. She felt a flutter in the air next to her and saw the woman from her dream in her mind's eye.

*Help her.*

Sunny felt the spirit's overwhelming grief, and it was too much after her busy day. "Please go away." The woman's eyes filled with tears before she faded away, leaving Sunny alone again.

The bell rang and Sunny looked up from the front desk. As if summoned by her thoughts, Jordan entered the foyer. It was the first time Sunny had seen her in uniform, and the sight of her sent tingles along her inner thighs. "Can I help you?" she asked sweetly while she mentally ordered her hormones to shut up.

Jordan looked uncomfortable and stiff. "Look," she said. "I've come to apologize. I was out of line."

"Yes, you were." Sunny paused. It wasn't in her nature to hold a grudge, nor did she have a problem admitting when she was wrong. She had behaved badly right along with her. "I'm sorry too. I said some things that I shouldn't have."

Jordan's eyes searched hers, but Sunny couldn't perceive

the question she was trying to ask. Why was she so damn hard to read?

*Help her.* The voice whispered in her ear. Sunny pressed her lips together and stubbornly tried to ignore it. She was absolutely *not* going to deliver a psychic message to Jordan.

"I'd like to make it up to you."

"Oh? What did you have in mind?" Her stomach did a tiny flip of anticipation.

"Dinner?"

"Okay, I'll have dinner with you." Jordan was an enigma. Sunny could sense the surface emotions just fine, but the ones that mattered, the true ones inside, were the ones that Sunny couldn't hear or feel.

"Seven okay?"

"Seven is fine. I have a late afternoon appointment with Agnes, so I'll meet you at your apartment after that?"

Jordan smiled and Sunny's breath hitched. She should do that more often; it lit her face.

"Okay." Jordan walked to the door and paused. "Thank you," she said, then shut the door softly behind her.

Shade's heavy steps preceded her entrance into the room. She looked into the corner behind Sunny, tilted her head, and squinted. "Who's the dead lady?"

"Jordan's mother."

❖

Sunny turned to Tiffany and held up two dresses for her inspection. "Which one?"

Tiffany considered the choices. "The flowy blue one says witchy and mysterious, the short red one says I'm sexy and I know it. So just who do you want to be with this woman?"

Since Tiffany nearly spat the last word out, Sunny sat beside her. "I like her, Tiff."

"I know you do, but she upset you, and I can't stand to see you like that."

"It wasn't entirely her fault. I had a part in that as well." She wasn't sure yet what role the entity in Jordan's apartment had played, and she wasn't ready to analyze it.

"She's dark, Sunny. There's something inside her that's twisted and broken, and I don't want you to get hurt."

"She's not broken, Tiff, just deep and guarded. There is something about her, something exciting that I can't immediately read. And that alone makes me want to know her better."

"But—"

"Tiff," Sunny said gently, knowing where her anxiety was coming from. "Not everyone is like your ex. Now, *he* is twisted and broken. I'm sorry that Jordan hits that button for you, but they aren't the same."

Tiffany sighed dramatically. "Touché. Okay then, I'll reserve judgment and hold off making the Voodoo doll until later."

"You didn't really make one, did you?"

"No, but Shade might."

Sunny laughed nervously. As far as she knew, none of them had ever messed with dark magic, but with Shade, one could never be entirely sure what she was up to. "Well, I'll let her know if and when we need one, okay?"

"She's hot," Tiffany said.

"Who? Shade?"

"No, dumbass, Jordan."

And with that smart remark, Sunny knew she could count on Tiffany's support. For a second, she wondered what normal friends did when they didn't always know what the other was thinking or feeling. It had to be easier.

"Jordan is pretty fine, isn't she?" Sunny looked at her dress choices again. "The red one it is."

❖

Agnes answered the door and whistled. "Why are you all dolled up?"

"I have a date after our appointment."

"I'm so nervous. I'm scared of ghosts," Agnes said, wringing her hands.

Sunny smiled to reassure her. "This one isn't bad, and he wants very much for me to give you a message."

The blood drained from Agnes's face even as her eyes grew misty. "Harold? My Harold is here?"

"Actually, the name he's giving me sounds like Thumper."

"Oh, oh." Agnes blushed. "It's what I called him, because—well, never mind. He's been gone for twenty years."

"He says he knows you still talk to him every day."

"You can tell him that I'm still mad too!"

"He says he knows you love him."

"He was my first and only love. There never was another in my life."

"Why is he laughing and showing me a mailman?" Sunny asked.

"Oh, come on, Harold. It was only twice, and love had nothing to do with it." Agnes turned red again. "Did he *watch*?"

Sunny tried not to chuckle and hastened to change the subject. "No, of course not." *Stop it, Harold. I'm not telling her that you did.* "He said he just wanted to keep you honest."

"He always did. My world started and stopped with him. He always made me laugh. Our daughter was so serious all the time, and as she grew older, ashamed of her hippie parents and our past." Agnes paused. "Harold? Did you know that Lucy became a *Republican*?" she whispered the last word.

Sunny fought the urge to laugh. She was charmed by Agnes and pleased that this reading was going so well for her. "There's a tiny woman standing next to him, nodding her head."

"Is she wearing pearls?"

"Yes. Is she your mother?"

"She's standing next to my husband?"

"Yes, but she seems quite content for him to talk."

"I find that hard to believe, since my mother hated Harold and she loved to be the center of attention. She never understood our generation and was horrified when we ran off together." Agnes's eyes seem to be looking to a faraway place, reliving memories from the past.

Sunny patted her hand. "Agnes? Harold is stepping back now, but he wants you to know that he's always close and watching over you and Steve."

"He's leaving so soon? But I have so many things I still want to say."

"He's telling me that he hears you and will be waiting for you when you cross over."

"Oh my God! Is it soon?" Agnes's eyes bugged a little.

Sunny shook her head. "No. Just that he's there. He's laughing again. He's quite the character isn't he? See you later, *chicken little.*"

Tears tracked through the makeup on Agnes's face. "He called me that because for me the sky was always falling. See you, Thumper." She choked up. "I love you."

"See? That wasn't bad at all, was it?" Sunny asked her.

"Thank you, dear. That was the best gift I have ever gotten, aside from my grandson. So are we done here? No more ghosts? Because I can handle it if they're my husband and mother."

Sunny sat back. "Agnes, I have to be honest with you. There are more." She could have lied to make her feel better and said there weren't, but the haunting would continue. So much of her job as a psychic medium was actually being a psychologist, which was why she'd gotten a degree in it. "They don't mean you any harm." She hurried her explanation when Agnes's lower lip began to tremble. "Some of them come because it was a happy place for them when they were alive."

"That's a good thing, right?" Agnes narrowed her eyes. "You said *some.*"

Sunny told her of the harmless children playing in the courtyard.

"Oh, I've heard them, or at least I thought I did."

"They come to knock on doors, run in the hallways, that sort of thing."

"Are they trapped here?"

Sunny shook her head. "Some spirits just like where they are and decide to stay or visit."

Agnes sat up straight. "Well, I can handle that, then. What about the others?"

Sunny thought of the dark entity most prevalent in Jordan's apartment, and refrained from mentioning it. She didn't want to feed Agnes's fear after her positive reading. "The team will be here later tonight, and we'll know more after the investigation. We'll do our best to help clear your building, Agnes. I promise."

❖

Jordan watched Sunny emerge from Agnes's wing across the courtyard and hurried to meet her. She'd just reached the bottom of the stairs when the outer door opened.

"Oh." Sunny held a hand to her heart. "You startled me."

"I'm sorry. I saw you coming." She looked at Sunny's strappy heels. "I wanted to save you the trip. You look amazing."

"Thank you. So do you. Whose car are we taking?"

"If you don't mind, I'll drive."

"Okay, I have a change of clothes in my car. I'll just leave it here and get ready after dinner."

Jordan helped Sunny into her truck. She'd forgotten the investigation. She tried to steer the conversation in a direction she was more comfortable with. "What kind of music do you like?"

"It depends on what kind of mood I'm in. Could be anything from AC/DC to Bach."

*That didn't help.* Jordan pointed to her black case. "Pick one."

Sunny flipped through the sleeves and handed her a Nickelback CD. "This is a good one. I like them."

Jordan's nerves settled a fraction. They had at least one thing in common. She searched for more small talk. "Hey, did you catch the football game on Sunday?"

"Oh, I don't watch television."

Jordan was shocked. "What?"

"I have a little one. I watch the news once in a great while, but it's usually so depressing and violent."

*Now what?* Jordan *lived* in that world. Her GPS told her she'd reached her destination, and she pulled into the parking lot. "I hope the food is good here. I don't know the area yet, but my partner recommended it." Right after he'd high-fived her. She looked over at Sunny and felt awkward. Sunny was beautiful, light, and breezy, and Jordan was, well—*not*.

*What am I doing?*

"This place is excellent. Your partner has good taste." Sunny pulled her shawl around her shoulders.

Jordan ran around to open her door and helped her step down. Sunny's hand was warm in the chilly evening air, and the contact made her almost giddy. The lights on the boats in the marina reflected off the water in the Silverdale Bay.

"The view is amazing here," Sunny said.

Jordan hadn't taken her eyes off Sunny. "Uh-huh." Oh God, what was she going to talk about? This was a mistake, a huge mistake, and Jordan didn't know how she was going to get out of it. All she could do now was pray she didn't make a bigger ass of herself. Jordan had never been on a date like this before. The women in her past were strictly pizza and beer. Sunny was pure champagne and dancing. And, oh shit, she couldn't dance.

While the hostess led them to a table by the back windows, Jordan's gaze couldn't help but land on Sunny's hips and the way the smooth red material clung to her curves. She wanted to reach out and touch. Sunny looked over her shoulder and smiled before licking her lower lip.

The sight of her little pink tongue slammed Jordan between her thighs as if Sunny had stroked her with it.

Sunny folded her shawl over her chair and faced Jordan before sitting. The low neckline of her dress outlined her breasts and gave a delicious hint of cleavage. Red stones set in a delicate silver chain sparkled in the candlelight, distracting and drawing her in at the same time.

The breadstick Jordan held snapped into pieces, bringing her out of the sexual trance. "Is it hot in here?" Jordan pulled at the collar of her shirt.

Sunny turned on her megawatt smile. "Is it?" she asked, then looked at the menu.

Oh yes, Jordan thought. Dinner. How was she going to eat and get through this barbaric ritual when all she wanted to do was slide Sunny onto her back and see what was under that dress?

"Are you okay, Jordan?"

"Huh? Oh yeah, I'm good." She fumbled for her water glass and took a long drink. No, she wasn't. She was a fish out of water and had no idea what came next.

"Am I making you uncomfortable?"

"No." *Yes.* Jordan wished for a hole in the floor so she could drop into it and end this slow torture.

"Okay, I'll go first," Sunny said. "Where are you from originally?"

"I was born in San Francisco, moved up here when I turned eighteen."

"So were my parents," Sunny said excitedly. "Haight-Ashbury district. Was your mother a hippie too?"

*Too close.* "What about you?" Jordan asked quickly, deflecting the conversation away from herself.

"From Seattle, but I was too young to remember the move here to Bremerton. Is your family here as well?"

Jordan shook her head.

"Siblings?" Sunny asked.

Should Jordan tell her of the parade of foster brothers and sisters? "Nope."

"Really, Jordan, you're not letting me get a word in edgewise. I'm finding it impossible to hold my train of thought while you keep interrupting me."

Jordan laughed. "Enough about me; let's talk about you."

Sunny unfolded her napkin and placed it in her lap. "Thank you," she said primly. "I'm an only child too. Did you ever get lonely?"

*Every single moment of every single day.* "Not really."

"My parents didn't give me a chance. Oh, there were times I wished I had a sister to share secrets with and play with, but my mother couldn't have any more children."

The waiter came and took their orders. Jordan was amused at how he stammered slightly when Sunny smiled at him. *I know how you feel, buddy.*

After he left, Jordan jumped in with another question. "What did your parents do for a living?"

"My mother was a dancer before she met my father. He said the first time he saw her at a rally in Golden Gate Park, he knew he was going to marry her. He was a student at the university, and after he graduated, he wrote books on parapsychology. My mother did tarot readings along with being a medium."

"Is that why you do these...investigations?" Jordan asked.

Sunny laughed. "My parents were ghost hunters long before anybody thought it was cool to take it up as a hobby or television entertainment for the masses. In fact, they took a lot of ridicule for their way of life. Until the day my father died, he was on a personal quest to prove that there is life after death."

"Is being psychic something that you learn? I mean, you know, like reading people's body language for responses to the questions being asked?"

"I think that everyone has a sixth sense. How much they retain after being ridiculed for having an overactive imagination and beat over the head with limiting, outdated beliefs when they're young, now that would be a better question. I was four years old the first time I met a spirit. It was the night my maternal grandmother died. I think I was almost ten before I realized that not everyone could."

"You actually see them?"

"In my mind's eye," Sunny answered. "I get images while they talk to me."

"And you think everyone has this ability?"

"Don't you? As a police officer you have that intuition, that gut feeling inside that you know something is going down or you're certain that someone is lying, but you call it instinct, right?"

Jordan nodded. Of course she did, and she'd earned it. It came from living and working on the mean streets, hard won after painful and very real experiences.

Sunny sighed loudly when the waiter brought their food to the table.

"What?" asked Jordan. "Isn't it what you ordered?"

"It's perfect."

"Then what's the matter?"

"I always feel that initial feeling of guilt when I order meat. God, I love it, but it horrified my mother that Dad and I didn't fully convert. I can still hear her voice in my head. Is that *flesh* on your breath, young lady?"

Jordan chuckled. "Vegetarian Nazi?"

"Militant."

Jordan picked at her food. She was finding that watching Sunny eat her steak was more interesting. She had a dreamy look on her face that was almost orgasmic in nature. It set the butterflies in her stomach back in motion.

"What made you decide to become a police officer?"

"Oh, you know, I wanted to save the world, blah, blah." Jordan kept her voice casual. "What made you decide to become a medium?"

Sunny laughed. "I never decided; it's just who I am, who I've always been. When my father died, my mother stopped doing psychic readings. She rambled around in the big house until I graduated from college and came home. She gave the house and business to me before buying a small condo on the waterfront. But she had a hard time staying away, which is why she works as a receptionist. Really, I think it's just to keep an eye on me."

"And your friends?" Jordan was curious where they fit in.

"Shade and Tiffany?" Sunny's face lit up. "We met when my father was doing a documentary on psychic kids when we were eleven. We've been inseparable ever since. It was only natural that they come and work with me."

Jordan wondered what that felt like. Having friends and family in your life who knew you, grew up with you, cared about you for years. The more she learned about the love in Sunny's life, the more alien she felt.

Sunny looked to her right. "Not now. Stop it."

"Stop what?"

"I'm sorry. I wasn't talking to you."

"Who are you speaking to, then?"

"There's a woman here who wants me to give you a message."

"Where?" Jordan looked around the restaurant, behind her chair, and back to Sunny who was still staring at a spot to Jordan's left. "I repeat, where?"

"I didn't want to do this yet. I know it makes you uncomfortable, but this woman wants to talk to you."

"I don't want to do this at all. Ever," Jordan said firmly. She shivered slightly and tore her gaze from Sunny's to stare at her water glass. She had known this was too good to be true.

"It's your mother." Sunny lowered her voice and reached for her hand.

Jordan snapped it back. She hadn't said a word about her mother's death, and she was so not going there. The adult in her immediately dismissed the possibility, even as the child she'd been cried out for an explanation. Jordan searched Sunny's face and didn't see anything but innocence, but that's what they did, right? Played on your feelings to deceive you? As a cop, she'd busted plenty of con artists who were so good they could sell ice to an Eskimo.

Yes, Jordan had seen it all, but for the life of her, she couldn't figure out what it was that Sunny could possibly gain from this. And until she did, she would resist the incredible pull she felt toward her.

They finished their dinner in a terrible, tense silence, broken only by the waiter occasionally coming by to fill their glasses or take their plates. While people around them laughed and joked over their meals, Sunny felt the invisible brick wall Jordan had erected and was sorry for it, but she knew from experience that the spirit wouldn't leave her alone for long. Part of her couldn't understand the resistance. She'd lived her whole life around people who honored her gift and surrounded her with acceptance. People came from all over the state for her help. Sunny didn't know how to react to this stoic skepticism from someone she very much wanted to get to know better. She tried again. "Don't you want—"

"No," Jordan said. "I really don't."

The energy at the table dimmed even further. Jordan signaled for the check and seemed to look everywhere but at Sunny. For all intents and purposes, the lovely dinner date appeared to be over.

Sunny couldn't stand it. She couldn't read what Jordan was feeling, but her body language was taut as a drum. It wasn't a comfortable silence, and it was in her nature to ease tension and anxiety and put people at ease. Jordan motioned for her to lead the way out of the restaurant, and by the time they got to the truck, Sunny was a bag of nerves. "Jordan."

"Sunny." Jordan looked at her with blank eyes.

"What happened back there?" *What can I do to fix it?*

"We had dinner."

*Talking to this woman is like pulling teeth.* "You know what I mean."

Jordan's expression was empty. "I don't understand you. I can't figure out what your game is."

Sunny felt as if she were slapped. "Game? You think I have a game?"

"Yes. No. I don't know."

Sunny saw a brief flash of regret across Jordan's features and her own anger died down a little. "Which is it? Yes, no, or I don't know?"

Jordan didn't answer, and frustration kept Sunny quiet. Should she just let this go and walk away right now? She was genuinely curious but hurt at the same time. "Look," she said. "I can't change who I am or what I do. I really want to get to know you better, but if you think that I'm playing a game, then we have nothing and nowhere to go from here."

The silence drew out, and Sunny forced herself to stay quiet as they drove away from the restaurant.

When they stopped at a light, Jordan looked over at her. "I'm sorry. It's not in *my* nature to trust, okay? Honestly, I don't think you're playing with me. Are you?"

"I'm not toying with you."

"Sunny, why did you go out with me?"

"You asked me to."

"Well, yeah." The corners of Jordan's mouth turned up slightly.

"Is that a smile?"

"Could be."

"All right," Sunny said. "I went out with you because you're insanely attractive and strong, and truthfully..." Should she tell her that she felt their fate was tied together? That for some reason Sunny felt she had to save her? "I couldn't resist the sight of you in your uniform."

Sunny tentatively laid her palm on Jordan's thigh, hoping that the twitch she felt when she made contact was a good thing. Jordan's muscles relaxed and she covered Sunny's hand with her own. "Are we good?"

"I know I am. How about you?"

The suggestive words shot straight through Sunny, and she crossed her legs against the pounding sensation building between her thighs. She deliberately flipped her hair over her shoulder and winked slowly. "Stellar."

Jordan let out a low whistle in a long exhale. "I knew it."

❖

Sunny changed her clothes at Jordan's for the investigation. She would have loved some follow-through on the sexual tension between them, but when they pulled into the parking lot, Shade's van was already there along with Tiffany's car. She ignored Shade's raised eyebrow when she passed her to follow Jordan upstairs.

*Other* energy lingered in the bathroom. She tried to decipher the cause or culprit, but it stayed just out of reach. She couldn't find a trace of the dark entity that was present the first time she was here and finally gave up. One thing she'd learned over the years was that if a spirit didn't want to be seen or contacted, they could be stubborn about it. She shrugged, folded her dress, and put it in her black bag before stepping out dressed and ready for work.

Jordan was a tall silhouette by the window. Sunny jolted at the dark shadow she projected. Something was off. She slowed her step and walked cautiously closer to see her face.

Jordan turned to look at her and her eyes were bright and focused on Sunny like a predator deciding where the kill spot was. Tiny warning bells went off in Sunny's head. "Jordan?" She instinctively kept her voice low and Jordan blinked, looking slightly dazed.

"I'm sorry. What did you say?" Jordan blinked, and the darkness attached to her disappeared.

Sunny wondered if she'd imagined the danger coming from Jordan. Did she wear the bad-girl image so well, then? It scared her a little, even though a part of her wanted to throw herself at Jordan to see where the darkness would take her. She was so damn tired of always making the safe choices. The image of a moth circling a flame came to mind, and she wondered if they knew it would incinerate them, or just found it so damn irresistible to feel the heat boil the blood in their fragile wings that they never saw death coming. Should she be smart about the example and fly away while she still could? Even as she asked herself the question, she knew she would continue to dance around the fire.

"You keep looking at me like that, and you're going to be late." Jordan moved closer, her eyes locked on Sunny's mouth, her breath coming hard.

Sunny mentally snapped her fingers to bring herself out of her reverie. "Like what?"

Jordan took another step until she was inches away, and when her arm circled Sunny's back, a strong static shock leapt from her fingers and Sunny jumped away from her.

"I have to go to Agnes's apartment. The team is waiting for me."

"Fine. I'll walk you to the door."

"Do you want to be part of it?"

Jordan looked at her for a long moment, considering the offer. "Sure, why not?"

❖

Jordan watched Sunny's rear pockets during the short walk over, and she couldn't decide which view she liked best, the dress or the tight black jeans. *Naked would be better than both.* Agnes opened her door, and the fantasy disintegrated in the face of wrinkles and whiskey. As Jordan and Sunny entered, Agnes left for her sister's house across town.

She sat on the couch and ignored the sideways look Shade gave her. She was probably still mad that Jordan caused her to break her equipment the first time they met. Steve unrolled the building's floor plans onto the small dining table, earning him a dimpled smile from Sunny. She seemed to have that effect on everyone. "Okay," Sunny said. "The energy patterns on the property as I see them are in this apartment, which we've already established is Mr. Jackson, and in Jordan and Steve's wing. Do we agree on this?"

Shade nodded. "There are several spirits that are having a party in the courtyard." She tapped the paper with a pencil. "But the strongest energy is here."

"That's my building!" Steve paled. "Our building." He stared at Jordan, who shrugged. She was just there to observe. A picture on the wall caught her attention. A much younger version of Agnes stared back at her, one with long, fiery red hair held back by a beaded headband. She stood next to a young man who was holding a sign that read MAKE LOVE NOT WAR. That must be Mr. Jackson, she thought. She wanted to ask how they knew it was him who was supposedly haunting Agnes's apartment, but it had to be because they knew she was a widow, right? Steve had already told her that Sunny didn't charge them any money. Jordan would try to reserve judgment until all the evidence was in. She owed Sunny that much.

Shade flipped on the monitor set up on the counter, and two camera views appeared, one framing the courtyard, the other Jordan and Steve's third-floor landing.

"What about the basement?" Steve asked, then looked at Jordan. "Didn't you tell her?"

"Tell me what?" asked Sunny.

Steve pointed at Jordan. "She has pictures!"

Four sets of accusing eyes settled on her. "What?" Jordan asked.

Steve held his hand out. "Gimme your phone."

Why did she suddenly feel guilty, as if she'd done something wrong? Okay, she'd play along if it meant that Sunny wouldn't look at her like that. Jordan pulled up the pictures of the mess in the laundry room and handed the phone to Steve, who shoved the little screen at Shade.

Sunny caught Jordan's eye and her eyes still held... disappointment? About what? "Seriously, are you going to try and tell me a ghost did that?" Jordan asked defensively.

Shade scrolled through the pictures, then handed the phone to Sunny. A high electrical humming noise came from the dining room table.

"What's that?" Jordan asked.

"The Mel meter, right, Shade?" Steve nearly jumped up and down with excitement.

"Yes. That's exactly right. It detects when *spirit* interferes with the room's natural energy."

Jordan puzzled over the possibility. There hadn't been anyone near the table when it went off. She stood and crossed the room to look under the table, then waved her hand over and around it. Nothing.

She had just taken two steps from the table when another piece of equipment turned on. White static noise filled the room, putting her on edge instantly. "What is that?"

"Spirit box," Tiffany said. "It rapidly scans radio channels at a high frequency. It's said that entities can manipulate the energy to communicate."

"I've seen those on television," Steve said.

Jordan's skepticism warred with her natural curiosity. "Does it work?"

"Most of the time," Shade answered before turning the volume down. "There's only one problem with it."

"What's that?"

"It wasn't turned on when I set it there."

## CHAPTER TEN

How the hell did she end up in the damn basement alone during the investigation? Oh yeah, that's right. Shade asked if she was chicken when she balked at going down there. Jordan's internal six-year-old responded before her common sense kicked in. Sunny asked her to set up a camera in her apartment and one in the basement corridor, facing the hall to include the laundry room door. When she hesitated, Shade goaded her, and Jordan didn't want to admit she was still unnerved by the washing machine incident. But there wasn't anything to be afraid of, damn it! She was just trying to take it all in and be cautious, that's all. She puffed out her chest, grabbed the camera setup bag, and stalked to her building without looking back. At least it would prove there was nothing down there.

Jordan flipped the fluorescents on and put the tripod where Sunny indicated, making sure to line up the viewfinder with the laundry room.

Just as she turned the camera on, the lights went out. "Hello?" she called out. "Sunny?" No answer. "Quit fucking around. Turn the lights back on. Shade?"

Jordan kept her back against the wall as she sidestepped the length of the hallway, all the while feeling a strange sense of déjà vu. She'd just done this in her nightmare, hadn't she? Her senses heightened in the dark, every noise amplified over her pulse, which pounded in her ears.

There. A small shuffling sound to her left. Jordan froze and kept her breathing shallow in an effort to hear over it. In the dark, she became aware that silence did indeed have a sound; it whooshed in empty space, a static that usually went unheard in a noisy society addicted to electronics.

She felt a small stir in the air that tingled across her skin, and the hair on the back of her neck rose along with goose bumps on her arms and legs.

There. Again. This time to her right. She directed her gaze to look even though she knew she couldn't see anything. Through the inky blackness she thought she saw a shadow dart around the corner. Her imagination must be playing tricks on her. Jordan took another cautious step, then another, working her way to the stairwell and exit. It felt as if she'd been down there forever, but she knew it couldn't have been more than a few minutes. A small breeze circled her, and Jordan caught a trace of flowers in the air.

Just as she registered Sunny's scent, she ran into a warm body. Instinct had Jordan striking out before she could catch herself, but she had enough time to alter the direction of her fist and connected instead with the cement wall. Pain traveled up her arm to her shoulder and she gasped. "Motherfucker."

Sunny cried out in alarm. "Jordan?"

"Uh."

"What are you doing?" Sunny's breath was sweet on her cheek and her hands found Jordan's shoulders. "Are you okay?"

"Just dandy." She cradled her hand against her stomach and hoped she hadn't broken any bones. "Why did you turn off the lights?"

"I thought you did."

"Do you have a flashlight?" Jordan asked.

"It's dead."

"Didn't you check them when you started?"

Sunny chuckled. "Spirits can drain the batteries for energy. It happens to us all the time."

"Okay, here's a stupid question," Jordan said. "What do they do with it?"

A heavy metal door slammed somewhere behind them, causing them both to jump. "Answer your question?" Sunny asked.

Jordan was aware of every square inch of Sunny's body pressed against her, and heat blossomed under her skin at the contact. Fear had jump-started her adrenaline, but Sunny's nearness kept the blood pounding. Without the lights, the darkness that surrounded them acted like a cocoon for Jordan, making it a safe and enclosed space where only their attraction existed instead of their differences. She could do all sorts of interesting things in the dark.

Jordan brushed a kiss over Sunny's mouth. She was totally unprepared for the body rush that slammed through her at the contact. Heat licked her ankles and burned up her legs like a fuse that had been lit to set her core on fire.

She pinned Sunny against the wall, holding her wrists above her head and pressing their bodies tightly together. Sunny's hips pushed forward to meet hers. Jordan kissed her with an explosion of fierce searching, tasting, tongues battling and sucking. The whimpering sounds Sunny made in the back of her throat drove her crazy.

Another door slammed. The lights came on, flickered, and went back off.

"I want to touch you," Sunny said, helpless to move with her wrists still pinned. Instead, she wrapped her legs around Jordan's waist, grinding her center against Jordan.

Sunny thrust her hips instinctively and Jordan matched her. The air was so thick between them, her blood so hot, she found it difficult to breathe.

"Yes," Jordan whispered, nipping at Sunny's bottom lip. She felt the first wave start at her toes and race to her clitoris, igniting her orgasm and setting her nerves on fire. Her back arched and she cried out, tightening her legs around Jordan and riding out the wave of desire.

Jordan released her wrists and Sunny gripped her shoulders for support as she unwrapped her legs from Jordan's waist. Tears prickled the back of her eyes and she didn't know if it was from embarrassment or because it had been so very long since she'd felt her body react this way. Jordan's kiss gentled until she pulled away slightly, panting against her cheek.

Jordan took a step back to put some space between their bodies, but rested her forehead against Sunny's. "I'm so sorry."

*Sorry? For what?* "Why?"

She felt Jordan's hesitation in the dark. "Attacking you that way, here. I don't know, Christ—you smell so good. I didn't even think. Something came over me. I just had to touch you."

Dread trickled into Sunny's chest. Was it even Jordan's impulse? Or had something else forced her to act? She opened her senses and searched for the presence of *other.* A raspy growl pierced the quiet, and the sound fisted in Sunny's stomach, and ice washed over her heated skin.

"What the fuck was that?" Jordan hissed. Sunny felt her turn and knew that Jordan had placed her own body in front of Sunny's protectively.

Before Sunny could answer, boot steps pounded in the stairwell and the metal exit door opened, filling the hall with light. Sunny turned to look at Jordan's face and saw regret in her expression. She'd thrown herself at Jordan, and although this time she'd taken Sunny up on it, she didn't look happy about it.

Shade stood framed in the doorway. "What happened? I've been trying to reach you on the radio. I thought you were going to set the camera up?"

*Oh, sweet Josephine.* She forgot the camera.

"I have to get out of this place." Jordan grabbed Sunny's hand and headed to the exit.

Sunny noticed and felt the pained expression that crossed Shade's face before she quickly masked it. She wished she could help Shade through her jealousy, she really did, and she would give anything not to hurt her again. But their relationship had ended years ago, and she couldn't stop living her life because Shade refused to let her go.

Sunny was tired. The investigation, wandering in a decidedly haunted basement, and her mind-blowing orgasm in the hallway suddenly combined, leaving her exhausted. Her face grew warm and she dropped Jordan's hand. "You go on ahead. We'll be along in a minute."

Jordan looked at her and then at Shade. "Fine." She stomped up the stairs and Sunny felt something inside herself crumble.

❖

When Jordan reached the first floor, she turned left into the parking lot instead of the courtyard. She needed some air and some time to process what just happened. She sifted through the sequence of events in an attempt to find the evidence, but she couldn't get past Sunny's taste on her lips or the way her body reacted when Jordan kissed her.

She was beginning to question her beliefs and it was uncomfortable. Her powerful paradigm of what she thought life was and what was possible started to shift. Jordan hated to feel uncertain about anything.

Her phone vibrated and she pulled it out of her pocket. "Lawson."

"Hey." It was her partner, Vince. "Meet me at the convenience store by your house."

A slight chill washed over her. It was eerily similar to the call she'd received the night she'd been shot, and it instantly made her suspicious. "Why?"

"Our tweaker buddy, Jack, says he has some information on our missing girl."

"On my way." Jordan ran to her truck and sped out of the parking lot.

The convenience store was flanked on one side by an old brick warehouse, and she spotted Vince near the back of it. It wasn't until she got out and approached him that she saw Jack. If anything, he looked worse than the first time she'd met him.

It was clear he was out of drugs. He had that desperate air around him she recognized. It was a state her mother had been in often. She ignored him and turned to Vince. "What do we have?"

"Jackie here says he knows where our M.P. is."

"Let's go, then."

"Well, here's the problem. Jackie says he wants money for the information. His mother is sick and needs medicine."

Jordan looked back at Jack and something in that wheedling, selfish, and *lying* expression caused her to snap. She spun and grabbed his lapels before slamming him into the bricks. "Listen here, you fucking junkie weasel. If you know where this girl is, you better tell us now before I snap your pathetic neck."

Vince put a hand on her arm, but she hardly registered it. "Lawson."

She tightened her grip. "Now give me the address."

Jack's eyes appeared to bug out further, and he frantically looked around for a way out before he slumped. "Okay, okay."

Jordan let go. "Talk."

"There's an abandoned house in the woods behind Riddell Road. I heard a guy bragging about the new flesh they picked up and how much money they were getting for her."

"I know the place," Vince said. "It's a known drug den. We chase them out and board it up and they keep going back."

"How come you didn't tell us sooner?" Jordan asked.

"I just heard about it and saw the flyer posted in the store here."

"And you hoped to get your next fix. God, you disgust me." She turned her back to him and walked a few steps away. Jordan was so mad she was shaking. She heard a rustle of bills and the sound of running footsteps.

"We'll take my car," Vince said. "Call it in."

"Officer?" Jack's voice came from the shadows behind the building. "They're moving her to Seattle tonight. You better hurry." Vince jogged back and handed him some more bills.

Jordan didn't know how much and couldn't care less. She waited impatiently for him to unlock the door while she called dispatch for backup.

Vince jumped into the Charger and they sped to the east side of town. Jordan's adrenaline increased with each block. "My gun is at home."

"I have mine." He flipped open the glove box and handed her a small revolver. "And this one." He turned onto a small dirt road and turned off his lights. Tree branches scraped along the sides of the car.

"We'll have to walk in from here. There's an extra flashlight under the seat, but I don't want them to see us coming. Follow me."

They'd gone approximately a hundred yards when Jordan saw a yellow glow up ahead.

"Oil lamps. I'm surprised they haven't burned the place down yet."

Jordan crept closer and a stick snapped under her feet. She froze and strained to hear. Something crashed up ahead in the bushes, and she heard someone yelling.

"It's the fucking cops!"

Jordan heard at least three more distinct voices. "Freeze!" she yelled. The woods were silent around her. "Police! Come out with your hands up."

Vince stood. "I think they're gone."

When they received no answer, they cautiously made their way to the front porch. Vince motioned for her to go low through the door.

"Clear." Jordan heard Vince in the back of the house. "Ah, Christ."

She sprinted down the hall to the back room where Vince stood looking at the small figure huddled on a filthy mattress and covered with a sheet.

Jordan tried to take it in but was struck with another feeling of synchronicity and the brutal scene from one of her nightmares.

Long, dirty hair covered the girl's face, a pale hand exposed with blood red fingernails. *No. Not again.* She rushed to the bed. "Call an ambulance."

Time slowed to a crawl and all sound faded away until Jordan was aware only of her heart thumping in her chest. She watched her hand reach slowly to move the matted hair while the other reached to pull the dirty sheet away.

Not her mother.

The girl's face was battered and swollen, her lips cracked and bloody. She was naked and obviously beaten. Through the purple bruises on her pale skin, Jordan could see needle marks. "The bastards drugged her." She gently continued to pull away the sheet.

When she saw the pools of old and fresh blood under her hips, she stopped and closed her eyes. Her mind desperately searched for the image on the photograph her parents had given them when this child had been smiling and happy.

She placed two fingers on her throat. After a moment, she felt a very faint pulse. "She's alive!" Jordan knelt on the filthy floor littered with used hypodermic needles and beer cans. Vince ran out to meet the officers arriving on the scene.

"We've got you. You're safe now." She held the girl's hand gently. "We've got you."

The EMTs rushed in and Jordan backed off. After an emotional call to the girl's parents, she told them to meet her at the hospital. Jordan would stay with her on the short ride to Harrison Memorial.

She nodded to Vince before the back doors of the ambulance slammed. The sirens screamed and Jordan wanted to throw up while the medic was attempting to assess the damage of her brutal ordeal. She refused to look away. She would be a silent witness to this girl's pain and the horror she endured.

They pulled into the emergency entrance where a trauma team waited to take the teenager away. They tried to get Jordan to wait outside, but she refused to budge until a front desk nurse approached her to tell her that the parents were waiting to talk to her.

❖

Sunny carried her gear to the van and handed it to Shade. Tiffany waved before pulling out.

She felt hollow, not the normal drained feeling she usually had after an active investigation, but literally empty. It was foreign to her, this ache that she couldn't place or blame on someone else's emotions.

"We done here?" Shade asked before hopping out the back.

Sunny looked to the dark windows of the third-floor apartment. "Yep. We're done here," she answered sadly. Jordan couldn't wait to run away from her and hadn't come to Agnes's apartment to say good-bye. When they went to get the camera from her apartment, it was clear she hadn't even stuck around to see what they were doing. She was gone. Why had she hoped that inviting Jordan to the investigation would change her skepticism about the paranormal? Instead, it appeared that Jordan had chosen to keep her distance. Sunny was at somewhat of a loss because she'd never been in this position before. How could she be the person Jordan wanted if she couldn't read her feelings?

"See you tomorrow, princess."

"What? Oh. See you tomorrow, buddy." She went to her own car and drove home. When she got there, she grabbed the evidence box and took the stairs slowly, feeling like every minute of the day's events weighed on her shoulders. She noticed that Shade had followed her in the van but drove away before she was fully inside. Shade must really be upset, since she usually waited until Sunny was inside with the lights on. It was just another emotional piece in a puzzle weighing her down.

After she locked the box in the safe, Sunny was halfway to the kitchen to get some water when the doorbell rang. It had to be Shade, making sure she was safe after all. She hoped she wouldn't have to make too many excuses because she was too tired to think of them, and she certainly didn't want to discuss Jordan with her.

Sunny turned on the porch light, flipped the dead bolt, and opened the door to find the porch empty.

"Ha, ha. Very funny, Mazie." *Not.*

Ash appeared on the stairs behind her, arched his back, and hissed, viciously baring his sharp fangs. Ten seconds later, Isis came out of the office and immediately took an aggressive stance. The growl that erupted from the tiny cat had every hair on Sunny's body standing at attention, right along with the cats' fur.

*"Pret-ty."*

Sunny heard the raspy voice and fought the urge to shudder. She *hated* it when they followed her home.

"Oh no, you don't," she yelled. "Get out!" She slammed the door and took the red energy from her anger and wove it together with ribbons of white for protection, an old charm her mother had taught her. She wove it tightly around her, closing any gaps with white light, until it encircled her fully. Instantly, the fog she'd been wandering through since her time in the basement lifted some, and she was surprised she hadn't felt the intrusive oppression earlier. Why was that? Sunny finished with the light shield and thrust it through the reopened door. "Out."

The fetid wind that swirled around the door nearly gagged her, but the next breath she took was a clean one. She burned sage anyway, leaving the front door open while she cleansed the area and herself.

When she didn't feel there was any trace remaining, she shut the door and leaned against it. When had her life gotten so complicated?

*Right around the time I met Jordan.* She looked longingly at the bed when she passed it on her way to the bathroom. The encounter with the entity and the effort to throw it out had left her depleted. Sunny wanted nothing more than to drop facedown into the bed and go to sleep, but knew from experience that it would leave her open and vulnerable while she slept.

Her hands shook while she lit the candles and filled the tub with water, but she stayed with her routine, stripped, and threw her clothes down the laundry chute to be washed first thing in the morning.

Sunny sank into the hot water and closed her eyes. She felt the stiffness in her shoulders relax marginally, but her mind insisted on taking her back to the basement and Jordan, which caused a different tension altogether.

The way Jordan had looked at her across the table over dinner...

Was that only last night? It seemed longer than that. Sunny

smiled to herself when she recalled the playful flirting in Jordan's apartment when Sunny changed her clothes.

She remembered her visceral reaction that shut out her inner voice. It was a new and unique feeling to be alone in her head and stop *thinking* all the time and wondering what someone else was feeling. She had no point of reference for the experience.

She replayed her explosive orgasm over and over and the feeling of Jordan's hips thrusting between her thighs. The sensation echoed and Sunny's pulse picked up. *I've got to get out of here.* Jordan's parting words intruded and threw ice water on Sunny's fantasy.

She forced herself to get out of the tub and put on her nightshirt. What she needed tomorrow was a day of reflection. Her friends and mother meant well, but she didn't want any company. Sunny changed the outgoing message on her phone.

"Hi, I hope you're having a nice day. I'm fine but taking a mental health day. Thanks, love you, bye."

She didn't take too many of those, but when she did, barring an emergency, she knew it would be respected. She could sleep in and recharge.

Sunny got into bed and willed herself to clear her mind and energy. It was time to go to that place where her feelings began, to concentrate on that white light in her belly that burned without flame. She shut out the physical world and let the day go.

*Breathe in. Breathe out. Focus on the light.* When her soul began floating and she no longer felt the barrier of her skin, she left her room behind and her spirit flew on the wind of her thoughts, over a cascading waterfall on the wings of an eagle, across the ocean and beyond.

A drum beat to the rhythm of her heart, and Sunny drew nearer to the sound by simply willing it. An old woman sat on a braided rug in front of a small fire and beckoned her to sit across from her. The evidence of a long-lived life was etched into her kind face while her smile radiated love and patience.

"Why do you deny yourself, daughter?"

Sunny felt sorrow well up from her soul, coming from an urge she couldn't vocalize past the lump in her throat. "Jordan doesn't want me as I am."

"You're afraid," the old woman said and stoked the fire.

"I've tried."

"No, daughter, you're using Jordan's emotions as a crutch to gauge whether you should move forward."

The truth of the words stung her skin, and Sunny felt tears drop into the fire where they burst into dancing blue sparks.

"You have to learn to follow your feelings and reach for the things you desire. If you don't ask, the answer is always going to be no. The time is at an end where you can let life just come to you like loose leaves blowing in the wind. Destiny waits for you."

"I thought giving messages to people from their loved ones was my destiny." Sunny was appalled at the trace of bitterness she heard in her voice, here in this sacred place.

The old woman smiled gently at her. "That's only part of who you are, child. The other part is love."

"Where do I start?" Sunny asked.

"You already have." The forest scene shimmered around her, and Sunny felt herself falling sideways. She closed her eyes against the vertigo.

When she landed in a dark room, she opened her eyes to see the little dark-haired girl huddled in the corner. This time, Sunny thought she knew who it was.

# CHAPTER ELEVEN

It was close to four in the morning when Jordan entered her apartment. She flopped on the couch and stretched her legs over the coffee table. A small piece of duct tape caught her eye, and she noted the camera in the corner was gone. She closed her eyes and felt regret knot in her stomach.

*Sunny.* Jordan had never called her last night to tell her what was going on and why she left so suddenly. It was too late to do it now. She really needed a couple of hours of sleep first. She could call when she got up.

Jordan woke suddenly and was instantly alert. When she convinced herself that nothing was amiss in the apartment, she glanced at her watch, surprised to see she'd been out for three hours.

She rose from the couch and stretched her stiff muscles before heading into the kitchen to make coffee. It wasn't until she was done that she looked down and saw the blood on her clothes and dirt encrusted in the knees of her jeans. The nightmare of finding the missing girl replayed in her mind while she stumbled into the shower.

Jordan tried to put it away, but the weight of it made it difficult. Jordan wrapped herself in a towel and went into her bedroom to get dressed.

The rising sun came in her window and something red sparkled on her dresser. Curious, she crossed over and picked up Sunny's necklace. She must have left it there when she changed last night. Jordan recalled how beautiful she had looked over dinner, the red stones glittering against her pale skin.

So pure, so good. Jordan's throat tightened. She wanted Sunny so badly it made her chest ache. And that was before she kissed her. The little moans she made, the way she smelled, her incredible uninhibited response. Jordan had been unable to stop herself from taking more.

The room grew oppressive around her. Jordan took an honest appraisal of the way she lived. There was so much ugly in her life. What could she possibly offer Sunny?

Her bright and positive personality was a direct opposite to Jordan's, and she couldn't find one scrap of evidence that would convince her otherwise. Sunny was too good for her and she knew it.

Knowing that hurt much more than Jordan thought possible. Just once, she wanted to reach out and touch something better. Just once, before she had to crawl back into her dark place in the world. She finished dressing and carefully put Sunny's necklace in her pocket. She decided to walk over. She could use the extra time to remind herself she liked being a loner and didn't need anyone special in her life.

When Jordan reached Sunny's house, all the curtains were closed and she realized she must still be sleeping. It was probably for the best anyway. She would leave her necklace in the mailbox and do the right thing. She would walk away.

She'd just crouched on her knees to slip it through the little metal slot when the door opened and she nearly fell on her ass before catching herself. Sunny stood in front of her wearing a white sports bra and yoga pants that hung low on her hips. "That's it? You weren't going to talk to me?"

Jordan was caught off guard and couldn't find her voice. To her horror, Sunny's eyes filled with tears.

"Why do you keep pushing me away?"

"I don't." Sunny's accusing look reminded her otherwise. "I don't mean to, okay? I thought you were still asleep. Can I come in and explain?" Jordan slipped by her when she stood to the side. Sunny pointed to the sitting room.

"Do you want some coffee?"

"No, I'm good."

"I'll be right back," Sunny said.

The house smelled of her, and Jordan knew that for the rest of her life the scents of summer would remind her of Sunny.

"Okay. I'm ready." Sunny sat across from her. "Where did you disappear to?"

"I went outside for some air and my partner called with a lead on a missing girl. I didn't mean to not let you know. Things just happened so fast."

"Oh."

Sunny was so quiet, Jordan began to feel a little defensive. "It's my job."

"I realize and respect that, but you still haven't answered my question."

Sunny deserved the truth, but the wall Jordan built to protect herself was in the way, right alongside the pride that was stuck in her throat. "I don't want to push you away, Sunny."

"So don't."

Jordan felt torn. The best thing to do was walk away, but the thought of doing so twisted her up inside. "You make me want."

"Is that a bad thing?"

She looked at the floor before answering. "You make me want things I've never had. And yes, that's a bad thing."

"Look at me, Jordan." Sunny leaned closer. "And tell me why."

Jordan felt herself caught up in her gorgeous eyes. The words caught in her throat, forcing her to almost whisper. "Because I can't miss the things I've never had."

Sunny got up and knelt in front of her. "I'm right here, Jordan. You don't have to miss me. Can't you feel this between us? Am I the only one that feels this way?"

Jordan shook her head. "No, I—"

"Then let's see where it takes us." She stood and pulled Jordan to her feet.

Jordan held her breath and tried to remember the argument she had for leaving, but Sunny stepped into her arms and licked her lower lip, and all logical thought dissolved. Jordan felt the blood rush from her head to pound between her thighs, and all thoughts left her completely. She fiercely matched the passionate attack, glad to have Sunny's body back where it seemed to fit so perfectly.

Sunny tugged at her leather jacket, and Jordan drew her mouth away just enough to help her pull it off, letting it lie on the floor where it dropped. Her lips were fused to Sunny's while she was led to the stairs, stopping only long enough to pull in a breath when Sunny stripped off Jordan's T-shirt and her own sports bra.

Jordan made it halfway to the third floor before Sunny dropped onto the stairs, pulling Jordan down on top of her. "Right here."

Jordan didn't hesitate, balancing on the tread below her, and nibbled her way down Sunny's neck to stop and pull the hard nipple between her teeth, kneading the other under her palm.

Sunny whimpered and grabbed Jordan's belt buckle. "Too many clothes. Off."

Jordan dropped her hands to the waistband of Sunny's loose yoga pants, yanking them down in one fluid motion. She moved back a little and was awestruck by the sight. Sunny was perfect. Her face was soft with desire, eyes half-lidded while she looked at Jordan looking at her. Tiny stones glittered at her neck and navel, her hair fanned on the step above her, and with her thighs spread, giving herself to Jordan, she looked like a goddess waiting to be worshipped. The small white triangle of fabric between her thighs was the only obstacle between them.

Jordan kissed the silky fabric, letting her tongue slide over the length of it. The scent of Sunny's pleasure made her mouth water, and the soft flesh quivered under her lips. The frantic pace of the moment was replaced by reverence when she pulled Sunny's panties to the side. "You are so beautiful." She gazed at Sunny's glistening flesh, naked but for a small strip of blond curls.

Jordan blew gently before tasting her, running her tongue slowly along the sensitive skin. Soft, she was so soft, and getting wetter by the second. She continued her unhurried, lapping strokes until Sunny's hips twitched and her steady moans became little bird cries in her throat. Jordan sucked the hot flesh between her lips, increasing the motion until all of Sunny's sex slid in and out of her mouth.

"Jordan!" Sunny's hips bucked and her sweet juices ran freely to cover Jordan's chin and puddle on the stair beneath her ass. "That feels so good. Please, Jordan, I need you inside me."

Jordan complied, lifting her mouth just enough to enter her with two fingers. Sunny gasped. "Yes, oh, yes, I'm going to come."

Jordan stroked her center, and every time Sunny's walls tightened around her fingers, she felt her own sex clench in response and she heard her own muffled moans vibrate against Sunny's clit. Jordan's tight pants rode almost painfully between her legs, and she rocked against the friction, never losing her rhythm between her hand and her tongue.

Jordan tore her eyes away from Sunny's sex to look at her, and the sight of Sunny kneading her own breasts shot straight to Jordan's clit. Sunny cried out again, soaking her with her orgasm, and Jordan pressed her face tightly against her, drinking it greedily. She didn't want to miss a single drop. Her own orgasm exploded and she moaned against Sunny's wetness, driving her fingers deeper into Sunny as the waves of pleasure rocked her own body.

Jordan pulled her weight to the side and tried to catch her breath.

Sunny started laughing. Jordan was instantly worried.

"What's funny?"

"Oh, that was *wonderful*." She pulled Jordan up for a kiss. "Mmm. My ass has rug burns."

"God, I'm sorry."

"Why are you always sorry, Jordan?"

"Taking you on the stairs like that." Jordan stood.

Sunny giggled. "Help me up."

"Are you laughing at me?"

"Absolutely not. Jordan, we have to talk."

Here comes the kiss-off, Jordan thought. "I'll go."

"What?" Sunny searched her gaze. "Upstairs, Jordan. I was going to say we need to talk upstairs." She smiled. "We almost made it." She took Jordan's hand, leading her to the bedroom.

"My shirt," Jordan protested.

"You won't need it." Sunny sidestepped Ash, who darted under the bed. "What's wrong with you?"

Crap. Jordan forgot about the cats. "He's not going to answer you, is he?"

Sunny patted the bed next to her. "Nope. Not so you would understand anyway."

A breeze blew past Jordan, and she saw Sunny's eyes widen before she fell back as if struck. Jordan rushed to her side. "Are you okay? What just happened?" She pulled Sunny's trembling body closer. Her skin was ice cold.

Sunny's teeth chattered. "I forgot about the sha-shadows."

"What?"

"I was so-so wrapped up in what we were do-doing. I didn't protect myself." Sunny burrowed closer to Jordan.

"Protect against what?" Jordan looked over her shoulder. "There's nothing here."

"Jordan, sit." Sunny's color began coming back. "You have some serious dark energy attached to you."

"Not this again." Jordan was conflicted. She was drawn to Sunny as she'd never been drawn to another human being. Their chemistry was mind-blowing, and her skin still burned from the insane sex they'd just had on the stairs. But she was still insisting on bringing this witchy stuff into the conversation.

"Hey! Did you just roll your eyes at me?" A hurt expression crossed Sunny's face.

A sharp burst of pain blazed across Jordan's back and she arched. "Ow, Jesus!"

Ash perched on the bed, his hair on end, puffed up twice his normal size. He hissed at her, showing his sharp little fangs. "Fucker scratched me."

Isis joined him on the bed and growled, her tail twitching behind her as she crouched, ready to pounce.

"Stop it right now," Sunny snapped. "I'm so sorry. I've never seen them act this way before." She clapped her hands together to get their attention.

Isis immediately dropped her stalking stance, but Ash's eyes darted around the room as if he were watching an invisible bouncing ball. "Bad kitty."

*Bad kitty?* Her back was on fire from his claws. This was a pissed-off wild animal at the moment. *Kitty, my ass.*

Ash hissed one last time before dropping off the bed and racing from the room.

"Come with me," Sunny said, guiding Jordan to the bathroom. "Sit here." She pointed at the vanity stool.

From her vantage point in front of the mirror, Jordan watched Sunny move around the room, gathering things, completely unself-conscious in her nude state.

"We're going to have to work on your cat skills," Sunny said.

Jordan winced at the sting of alcohol cleansing the scratches. "What?" The moment felt a little surreal. The cat had attacked *her*, and Sunny was walking around as if she hadn't been close to fainting. As if she hadn't been spread wide for Jordan's attention on the stairs a few minutes before that. Jordan's nipples hardened and her skin heated at Sunny's gentle touch. The pain on her back receded and was replaced with a flush where Sunny's skin made contact with hers.

Jordan met her gaze in the mirror and Sunny's eyes smoldered with lust. Jordan felt as if she had to brace herself against the intensity. Her heart rate sped up and pounded in her chest when she focused on Sunny's tongue a fraction of an inch from her neck, and when it made contact, she felt a hammer of desire slam between her legs. She was sure the pounding that she heard was her own pulse until Sunny moved away from her.

"Crap."

Dazed, Jordan shook her head to clear it. The noise was from downstairs. Sunny put on a robe hanging on the back of the door.

"It's my mother." She cocked her head to the side. "And Shade. I'll be right back."

Jordan sat for a moment and tried to reason with herself. Why was it she could never quite find her footing when she was with Sunny? Her constant companions of reason and logic were nowhere to be found. It was a little disconcerting, as they were two of the qualities she was proud of and relied on the most in her life.

Shouting voices floated to the third floor, and Jordan stood before she realized she was half-naked and remembered her bra on the stairs. *Oh no.*

Jordan didn't stop to think about the implications, she just grabbed the remaining robe that was on the hook and flew out the door.

❖

"I was washing dishes when I felt danger surrounding you." Sunny's mother almost suffocated her in a bear hug, then shook her before enveloping her again. "I thought I heard you screaming."

"Mom." Sunny kept her voice even and tried not to soak up her mother's panic. "Mom, please, you're hurting me."

As soon as she let her go, Shade grabbed her, and the fear Sunny felt emanating from her unnerved her. Shade was never scared. Where was this urgency they felt coming from? Sure, she felt a dark energy and it had slapped her, but it wasn't still here.

Was it? Jordan's presence in the house muffled her sense of *other.*

"Stop it, please," she said. "I need to breathe." Sunny took a couple of steps back and looked at Jordan thundering down the stairs with a wild look in her eyes. She didn't stop until she reached Sunny and stood in front of her, pushing her back between her body and the wall. The aggressive posture shouldn't have made Sunny thrill inside. But it did.

Jordan must have heard shouts and raced down to protect her. Sunny looked over Jordan's shoulder and saw the look on Shade's face. *Uh-oh.*

"Everybody calm down." Sunny stepped out from behind Jordan, stopping her when she would have moved with her.

Thick emotion flew around the room, overwhelming her, and she sank to the floor. The trembling started in her hands and her body began to shake. She hadn't had a panic attack in years, not since she'd learned how to protect herself from other people's chaos.

Sunny's breathing labored and she struggled to breathe, but the air around her was dwindling. Her mother immediately laid her hands on her back and lent her energy, pushing positive healing light toward her lungs. Warmth washed over her, and she felt lighter when the panic began to subside. She became aware of Shade and Jordan crouched on either side of her but quickly shut them out. She needed to concentrate.

Sunny spotted a swatch of black a foot away on the floor. Jordan's leather jacket lay where she'd dropped it earlier. *Focus.* She recalled the smell and then forced herself to count the teeth in the zipper. *Breathe.*

*Twenty-seven, twenty-eight.* Sunny became aware of the wood floor under her and sank back into her body. She took her first full pain-free breath, then another before the nausea cramps hit and she covered her mouth and staggered for the bathroom with her mother directly on her heels. They disappeared inside, and Sunny's mother closed the door firmly behind them.

Jordan tensed to go after them, but Shade body-blocked her, pushing her back a step. "Haven't you done enough?"

The question stunned Jordan. "What are you talking about?"

Shade narrowed her eyes and Jordan felt the animalistic fight for territory exuding from her.

Jordan held up a hand, keeping her temper in check. "Wait a minute—"

"No, you wait a minute, cop. This is your fault."

"I didn't do—what did you say?" How had she gone from offense to defense so quickly? She straightened to defend herself and paused, feeling stupid in the girly robe. She was so out of her element.

Shade picked up her shirt and jacket and threw them at her. "Are you really that dense?" She pointed to a spot behind Jordan. "You showed up here with *them*?"

"Who? What the fuck are you talking about?"

"Don't you *get* it? It's you. It's your nightmares and ghosts. You're hurting Sunny and you need to leave. Take your dark shit with you." Shade picked up her keys from the entry table. "I'll drive you home."

Jordan turned her back to Shade and pulled on her shirt. "Not going to happen." The sound of Sunny retching had Jordan turning toward the hall.

Shade grabbed her elbow and Jordan wrenched it away and moved into her personal space to meet her eye to eye.

"Are you really going to throw down here?" Shade held her ground, matching Jordan's stance and forcing her words between clenched teeth. "And with her mother in the house?"

Jordan's adrenaline screamed yes, but Shade's words penetrated the anger. "No."

"You can quit the Amazon routine. I'm not scared of you," Shade said. "I eat breakfast with demons. A pissed-off cop doesn't even put a hitch in my stride."

Didn't that sound like a challenge, Jordan thought before hearing the word cop. She was acting completely irrational and she knew it. But for the life of her, she couldn't think of an appropriate response to that last statement. "Whatever."

"Let's go."

"Not until I talk to her." Jordan spun and walked to the bathroom. She knocked and opened the door a crack. Sunny lay curled on the floor with her head in her mother's lap. "Hey. Are you okay?" she asked.

Sunny opened her eyes to look at her, then lunged to heave again in the toilet. Jordan felt helpless. There wasn't room for her to go help since her mother huddled over Sunny protectively.

"Jordan, please go home," Aura said. "Please. She's not going to get better unless you do."

"But—" The violence of the retching that caused Sunny to choke is what swayed her. "I don't understand."

Aura made eye contact with her, and the top of Jordan's scalp went numb. "I know you don't." The hard lines in her face softened slightly. "Go home, Jordan. I'll tell her you said good-bye. She needs to sleep. Call her tomorrow and I'm sure she'll explain."

Jordan didn't want a ride home, especially from Shade, but she had questions she knew she needed the answers to. Just as she knew when she got back to work, she would be running Shade through the system.

❖

Sunny nested in her comforter with Ash and Isis next to her, neither cat showing any signs of their strange behavior from earlier. Her mother came in with a cup of tea and set it on the nightstand before crawling onto the bed.

"Better?"

"Hmm." Though the panic attack had passed, it left her drained. Her mother had taken away the headache and the darkness, just as she had so many times before. And while it comforted her, for the first time, Sunny felt like a child and didn't want to. There was something missing here, some piece she hadn't seen before. Her mind swam with vague questions but none solidified enough to articulate.

Sunny had always been confident with her gifts and her place in the world. But this was twice now she'd been caught unprepared by dark, unfamiliar energy. Jordan's face came to her mind's eye. Beautiful, dangerous, edgy, sexy Jordan.

*Mine!*

Sunny almost dropped her tea when she heard the deep voice and growl in her head but was aware enough to slam down a protective wall around herself. *Not if I can help it.*

Her mother shifted on the bed. "What was that?" Sunny paused to check her surroundings, but there was no trace of the intrusive *other* voice. She relaxed marginally. Her mother's concern filled the space between them. "What's been going on here? Please don't shut me out when I can help you."

Sunny was surprised her mother didn't know the details, but was grateful at the same time. It was uncomfortable to think her mother might peek into her very personal space. Sunny was glad to know she was strong enough to hold the wall to keep her privacy. Especially from her mother.

"Mom, do you remember when I was little and first told you I could hear things other people couldn't?"

"Of course. You weren't even three years old yet."

"You and Daddy always believed me."

"Why wouldn't we? I'd seen spirits my entire life."

Sunny patted her hand. "I had a wonderful childhood, full of magic and acceptance. Thank you."

Her mother smiled. "Thank you for being such an amazing daughter. But what brought this on?"

"Jordan's mother showed up after I met her. She keeps asking me to help her."

"But that's not who attacked you."

"No, it isn't. But I'd like to know what did. It feels like it wants to harm me and keep me from Jordan." Sunny paused. "And don't tell me to back away from her. I'm not going to. Tell me how to deal with it."

"Your father and I wanted to protect you. We never wanted you to deal with the dark energies."

"I do know that, Mom. But I can't depend on you to protect me all the time. It's not fair to either of us. This entity actually struck me physically, and for a second, I felt an unfamiliar energy. It felt odd but powerful at the same time. I could clearly see the color purple intertwining with my light, but then a dark cloud obliterated the lights."

"Sex energy," her mother said. "Jordan's shadows meeting with your energy. That worries me."

"Mom, how come that never happened with Shade? I mean, we had some powerful experiences and I don't ever recall this feeling."

Her mother sighed. "Shade soaked it up for you, keeping your light separate from her darkness." She smiled sadly. "It's one of the reasons you wouldn't work as a couple. It was so taxing on her."

"I didn't ask her to protect me."

"I know you didn't, honey. But the people who love us can't help but do so. We were so apt in naming you Sunny. It's your nature and personality. The light simply radiates from you, sending out a beacon for miles around."

Sunny closed her eyes. Had she really been that ignorant? That the people around her took care of all the dirty work for her? She was appalled. "I have to learn how to take care of myself. We'll start with this. What is in the darkness that threatens me?"

Her mother was quiet, but Sunny waited patiently for the answer.

"Jordan's nightmares."

❖

The ride to her apartment had taken less than five minutes, and Jordan was still waiting for Shade to talk. The fog hadn't lifted and still surrounded the city, making it seem much later than it actually was. Irritation nibbled at her nerves. "Listen—"

"No," Shade said and turned sideways to face her. "You listen. Sunny's special."

Jordan felt a stab of jealousy just hearing the words and was uncomfortable. It wasn't an emotion she was familiar with and she ground her teeth. "And?"

"We protect her."

"I'm not trying to hurt her. And isn't who Sunny chooses to spend time with, I don't know, maybe her business?"

"Look. I'm not saying that you mean to, but I'm telling you that you *are* causing her pain. She has an amazing gift, one that makes people feel better just for being in the same room with her, you know?"

Jordan didn't know about others; she only knew that she was drawn to her. She mentally switched herself into work mode as if she were listening to a confession. She was good at that, shutting her feelings down into a tiny compartment so she could see a situation clearly. Jordan nodded shortly to signal Shade to continue but had already made up her mind that her reasons to keep Jordan away were entirely personal and nothing to do with any woo-woo excuses.

"You're only partially right," Shade said.

Jordan shifted in her seat. She hadn't said anything out loud.

"I've known Sunny since we were eleven years old. When I met her and her family, they changed my life." She paused. "I was almost exactly where you were at that age."

Jordan was immediately suspicious. How could she know where she'd been at any age? "You don't know anything about me." She tried to stare Shade down. "Nothing at all."

"You see? That's the problem with you. You don't get it. You don't understand."

Jordan had no clue what she was talking about. The conversation made no sense whatsoever to her. Nothing had seemed normal since she moved to Bremerton. Her emotions were all messed up, and she couldn't think of the questions she wanted to ask. That never happened. Where was the cop in her and where were all her questions?

Shade continued. "You have yourself shut up in this black-and-white world and refuse to acknowledge there's shit you don't know about. Stuff is going on all around you, Jordan, that you don't perceive, and you're held prisoner by your skepticism because of it."

"This conversation is so fucking off the wall. I don't know what you're trying to pull here."

"I know. And until you do? Until you admit you know nothing about what we do and get rid of this garbage you carry around with you, you need to stay away from Sunny. She doesn't work with the dark energy, and you just keep shoving her against it, where she's blind."

"I—" Jordan found herself still at a loss for words, and comprehension stayed just out of her reach.

"Just because you don't see it doesn't mean it's not there."

Jordan twitched hearing the phrase for the second time. Steve had told her the same thing.

"Look, I have to go," Shade said.

Jordan stood at the curb while the van drove away. She startled and turned when a man laughed in her ear, but there was no one else around. She was alone in front of the building.

The hair rose on the back of her neck. She really hated all this creepy shit.

# CHAPTER TWELVE

Jordan got to work early and plopped down at her desk where she began typing commands into the computer. When she found what she was looking for, she studied the screen then laughed out loud when she read the name at the top. Lacey Stewart. It conjured an image of a frilly girly-girl, and Shade's persona couldn't be any further from it if she tried.

She felt a small twinge of guilt. Shade hadn't done anything to break the law, that she knew of anyway, and nothing that would warrant the background check. No, Jordan's motive was pure jealousy and she knew it.

She'd tossed and turned for most of the night and argued with herself. She remembered her resolve to walk away from Sunny because of how very different they were, but that thought was pushed aside by the sight of her glorious naked body on the stairs and her taste against her lips. She tried to find explanations for what Sunny called paranormal activity, both from the basement and in Sunny's bedroom, but her mind refused to come up with any. Shade's strange behavior and warnings rang in her ears right before the disembodied laughter in her ear. Then the whole process would start over again, looping and replaying from the beginning.

It left her awake half the night. Jordan had been unable to shut her mind off and go to sleep.

The plumbing in the walls banging at odd intervals didn't help either.

When she woke, she was groggy but determined to find

answers. She was insanely curious to find out what Shade meant last night when she said she'd been where Jordan had. How could she possibly know anything? Jordan's own record wasn't available to the public, and there were no references about her childhood that could be found in her online history that Shade would have access to.

Jordan skimmed the report, finding no major arrests or warrants except a criminal trespassing charge that was dismissed three years ago. She had to smile when she saw Sunny's name as a known accomplice. She was sure this was the result from one of their investigations.

A few clicks opened the sealed juvenile record. Jordan didn't know why people thought that sealing the record would have any bearing at all, since they were easily accessed and the information openly available to be used against someone in the right circumstances.

Runaway, petty shoplifting, loitering. Wait. Here was a stint in Western State Mental Hospital, where her mother left her at the age of sixteen. She cross-checked Shade's mother and found several arrests for solicitation and drug dealing. Crap, thought Jordan, she didn't want to sympathize with her.

"What are you doing?" Vince came up behind her and Jordan quickly closed the file.

"Nothing."

He raised an eyebrow but, thankfully, didn't ask any further questions. "Let's go to work."

❖

Sunny stared at the phone in reception willing it to ring when Tiffany walked in. The closer she got, the worse she looked, and Sunny felt pulses of frustration laced with sadness. For being such an amazing healer, Tiffany had a difficult time applying her gift to herself.

"Oh, honey," Sunny said. "Rough day yesterday?" She rose to go to her, but Tiffany held out a hand to stop her.

"Not right now, please. If I get sympathy, I'll start all over again."

"What happened?"

"Two words," Tiffany said over her shoulder on her way to the kitchen. "My mother."

Sunny debated whether she should leave her alone as she had asked or follow her. After two seconds, she hurried after her. "Do you want to talk about it?"

"Not really."

Sunny hated that she looked so defeated but said nothing while she stood next to her.

"You got laid." Tiffany smirked at her, changing the subject.

"God, Tiff. Way to get the attention off you."

"You also had another panic attack." She put a gentle hand on Sunny's shoulder and closed her eyes for a moment. "There's just a tiny imbalance left."

"Mom stayed with me."

"What I wouldn't give for a mother like yours. No, wait. I don't want to get started. Let's get back to the sex."

Sunny smiled. "Love to, Tiff. But I have a client in about—" She was going say two minutes, but the bell on the door interrupted her. "Are you going to be okay?"

"I will be. Now go. You can throw me a bone later, okay?"

"Deal."

The woman waiting at the front desk stood ramrod straight, her arms held closely to her sides, her shoulders back. Sunny felt the dark defensive wall before she even reached her. Great, that's just what she needed, a skeptical client who would fight her at every turn. Readings were so much easier when clients were open. She forced a smile. "Good morning. I'm Sunny. Can I get you anything? Coffee, tea, water?"

The woman looked at her and stuck out her hand. "Hannah, and no, I'm good. Let's get this over with."

Sunny fought the urge to wipe her palm on her skirt. *Awesome, she's mean too.* "Okay. The reading room is on the second floor. Follow me, please." She felt the woman's eyes boring holes between her shoulder blades, so instead she directed her attention to the staircase, flashing on the image of Jordan between her legs. *No, don't go there. Now's not the time to think about it.*

She directed Hannah to the door and took water for herself before sitting across from her at the small round table her client chose. No comfort for Hannah, she thought. Sunny would have preferred to curl up on the soft chairs, but it was always the client's choice.

The agitation bubbling in the air across from her was seeping into her system already. Sunny took a deep breath to center herself and put on her fake smile. "Shall we get started?"

"I don't know why I'm here. I don't believe in this crap."

Sunny paused and heard a male voice. Ah, she thought. The woman's husband.

*I don't know why she's here either because I don't want to talk to the bitch.*

Sunny kept her face neutral but showed her amusement to the spirit telepathically.

*I couldn't stand talking to her when I was alive. Why the hell would I want to talk to her now?*

Sunny did something she'd never done in her career. Instead of beginning the reading and asking the man's spirit for details to give to her client for validation, she stood up for herself. "Then why *are* you here?"

Hannah pulled back in her chair, looking shocked at the retort.

*Ha! That's it, Blondie, give it to her. She's desperate for details on the money accounts that I hid from her. I wouldn't tell her anyway, even if she begged.*

Sunny waited for Hannah to answer. She wasn't going to justify what she did for this woman, or try to convince her. When Hannah narrowed her eyes, her anger came through clearly, almost striking Sunny like a poisoned dart. And that was the tipping point for her. She didn't have time for people like this anymore. She'd had enough. "Look, I'm not going to waste your time or mine." *Or your husband's.* That felt good. "I'll be happy to refund your money downstairs." She stood then walked to the door. "I'll just show you out."

Hannah's face turned red, but she gathered her coat and purse before stalking past her into the hallway.

The man's spirit showed her a dozen roses, but Sunny knew they weren't for his wife; they were for her. She could hear his hooting laughter follow her to reception where Sunny handed the woman a check.

"I'm telling all my friends and acquaintances about what a farce this is."

"Oh, please do," Sunny said sweetly. "I wouldn't want to waste their time either. Have a nice day."

After she left, Sunny checked her schedule and saw she had a couple of hours before her next appointment. Her mother probably wouldn't come in today after staying up so late with her last night. She knew she would have stayed awake and watched over her even while she slept.

Although she should have felt a kind of hangover from the previous day's events, she wasn't tired at all. In fact, she felt energized. She returned to the second floor to cleanse it of Hannah's negative energy. She felt taller somehow after shutting her down the way she did. It felt so good; she made a decision to do it more often.

Another hour passed and the phone still hadn't rung. Why wasn't Jordan calling her? Her newfound confidence slipped a little, then reasserted itself. Why was she waiting for her to call anyway? She punched in Jordan's number, happily anticipating hearing her voice. When it went to voice mail, she remembered, in great detail, the psychic and panic attacks she'd had in front of Jordan, and, deeply embarrassed, she didn't leave a message. She didn't feel quite so invincible. No wonder she wasn't calling her.

Jordan had clearly said she hadn't wanted anything to do with the paranormal. Sunny had nothing in her past to gauge this experience by. She wasn't innocent by any means when it came to sex. She'd had lovers. But always, she'd been able to discern their feelings for her and was able to act accordingly to keep from being hurt. There was always that little part of her that observed instead of engaged. Sunny knew the difference between the women who wanted her for the way she looked, and the groupies who wanted her to be all psychic, all the time. Like the stockbroker she'd dated who wanted predictions for her portfolio two weeks after they started dating.

The detached part of her always knew when to walk away. She felt completely different with Jordan. Not being able to read her emotionally left Sunny open to her own feelings. There were no protective barriers between them, and she felt vulnerable in a way she'd never been before.

The bell rang and Shade walked in. "How are you feeling?"

"Better, thank you. How was Jordan last night? What did she say when you took her home?" *Does she want to see me anymore?*

Shade hesitated and Sunny jumped in. "Truth, please. Don't mollycoddle me."

Shade took off her coat. "Sunny, you have to be careful, she—"

"No, don't warn me off. Let's talk about this." Sunny noted Shade's stiff shoulders but steeled her nerve before softening her voice. "Honey, we've both dated other people over the last seven years."

"I know."

"Shade, look at me." Sunny would give anything in the world to take away the pain that radiated from her. "You have to let this go."

"But I love you." Shade sat across from her.

"I know you do. And I love you too."

"But—"

"But you're my very best friend in the world."

Shade winced and Sunny's heart cracked. It was almost like breaking up with her all over again. "Why does Jordan feel so different for you compared to the other women I've dated? Why are your walls up again?"

"Because you're different with her, and I don't want you to get hurt."

"How am I different with her, Shade? I don't get the feeling she wants to hurt me." Sunny thought of the way Jordan kissed her, then stopped before she put the image in Shade's mind.

"I've already seen the two of you together. Jordan's an open book, and she doesn't have your blocks."

"Oh. Why are you doing this to yourself?"

"I guess there's that part of me that always hoped you'd come back to me."

"Shade." Sunny didn't want to feel responsible for her feelings.

"Let me finish, please. The dancer, the stockbroker, the librarian, the schoolteacher, they were all just company, you know?"

"Hey, you make it sound…" Sunny felt her face flush with heat.

"You didn't love them, Sunny. I could see you with them, and it hurt, but they weren't any real threat to me."

"I don't love Jordan," Sunny said automatically. *Did she?*

"You're *this* close. I know." Shade held her fingers an inch apart. "She lives in the dark, a place I know well because I live there too. But she didn't just fall into it; she grew up there, and she doesn't understand it yet, not the way I do. Jordan has things attached to her that want to destroy you."

Sunny remembered the psychic attack, but the fear was negated by the image of being in Jordan's arms. "But—"

"You can't fix her. You should stop trying to."

"But that's the thing, Shade. I can't read her. When I'm around her, all I perceive are my own feelings. That's never happened before."

"Which is how you got attacked, and that's even worse. I can still hear you screaming in my dreams, and it's killing me."

"That's not fair. You know I would never do that to you on purpose. You have to pull back, for both of our sakes."

"I don't know how."

"Please try." Sunny knelt in front of her. "I can't stand to see you hurting and know that I'm responsible for it. I feel your pain."

"I know, and I'm sorry."

*Why not me?* The anguish in Shade's telepathic question threatened to crush her, but Sunny laid her head on Shade's knee and felt the hand that smoothed her hair. She gathered all the love in her heart for Shade and radiated it outward. Light pressed against the dark, rolling with the energy of Shade's emotional pain as Sunny tried to soothe her.

"I want you to be happy." Shade's voice broke a little. "Even if it's not with me."

"I know how much that costs you. And I want that for you too."

They sat that way for a long time, until the bell over the door rang.

Jordan walked in and stopped in the doorway. She looked at her then at Shade. Sunny didn't have to read her to know how she was feeling. The anger was written clearly in her expression. She opened her mouth but walked right back out the door before she said anything, slamming it behind her.

❖

Jordan got back in her truck and left, disappointment crushing her. She'd been excited to see Sunny's number on her phone earlier, but she'd been in the middle of a briefing and unable to answer.

When she walked in to see her wrapped around Shade's legs, all she could remember was how Shade tried to warn her off the night before. Anger and jealousy warred for space in her soul. So, was Sunny's panic attack the previous night real? Or did she have it because she'd been caught with Jordan and wanted to deflect Shade's anger? The memory she'd efficiently kept behind a closed door and dubbed The Last Great Betrayal escaped and began to play. She'd answered the summons to Vice, racking her brain on why they'd be calling her in. Like a movie where she was the main character, she saw herself walking down the ugly green hallway in full uniform.

She knocked, then entered the small conference room where Detective Lynn Cody motioned for her to sit. Though she preferred to stand, Jordan took a seat at the long table.

"Officer Lawson, thank you for coming."

"Ma'am." Jordan watched her shut the door, and it was hard not to stare. The trim black suit hugged every curve of her body, her jacket casually unbuttoned to show a pretty chemise under it.

"It's been brought to our attention that you've been hanging around Pike Place Market and asking a lot of questions." She smiled pleasantly at Jordan.

"I've been working on a missing runaway's case."

The detective glanced at the file in front of her and tapped it with a long, painted fingernail. "In civilian clothes."

What was this really about? Jordan wondered. "On my own time, yes." She kept her voice even.

"I commend your dedication, Lawson, and it will be so noted in your file. However, we currently have undercover officers working on a case in that particular area that doesn't concern your department. You understand, then, that it could create problems in our investigation?"

Jordan was sitting forward to argue when Lynn licked her lips slowly, a blatant invitation.

At least, Jordan had thought it was. In retrospect, she tried to cut herself a break. She had never been so thoroughly manipulated or seduced by a woman before. Up until then, her relationships were pretty straightforward pickups. Women who hadn't known she was a cop, and if they had would have run the other way. Women who lived on the edge of society, the kind who kept dark secrets and wanted a real relationship about as much as she did. She remembered always living in a half world. Work was clear. She was sure of herself and what she stood for there. She was strong and quick-witted, and could handle herself on the street, but emotionally and on her own time, she went back again and again to the type of people she'd grown up with. To that gray, in-between place where you never knew what a person would do or what direction they would turn, and most of them were only one stupid decision away from prison time.

By the time she'd met Lynn, Jordan hadn't been with anyone in a couple of months, and the attention had been flattering. She pretended to agree with the necessity of being careful never to be seen in public, keeping her relationship with a superior officer a secret. That part was easy since Jordan was used to keeping things to herself. She had no friends or family to talk to, and her solitary life made living in the shadows easy.

Eventually, she began to trust Lynn, and if pressed, might have even said she loved her.

Right up until the night she'd left her for dead in a downtown alley, shot with her own firearm.

Jordan was saved from having to remember her wound and grueling recovery by pulling into her parking lot. Back to the present. Christ, she couldn't recall the drive home. Where had she been again?

Sunny's house. Where she'd found her wrapped around Shade, kneeling at her feet like a supplicant. And why did that seem to hurt more than being shot and left for dead? She slammed her front door open and the cold slapped at her. She punched the thermostat and snarled at it before entering her living room and stopping in her tracks.

It was trashed.

❖

Sunny had jumped to her feet to chase after Jordan, but she was too late. Her truck had already pulled away and turned the corner. She grabbed her keys and yelled for Shade to reschedule her appointment.

She pulled into the guest spot next to Jordan's and got out. Her stomach was in knots. She hated it when people thought badly of her, and the last person she wanted to hurt was Jordan. She knew she hadn't done anything wrong, but felt guilty anyway, knowing how it must have looked. Sunny took off her heels so she could climb the stairs quickly and knocked on the door.

"Jordan?" She knocked again. "Please let me explain."

The lock clicked and Jordan appeared with a faraway look in her eyes that worried Sunny. "Jordan?" She laid a hand on her arm and felt a jolt of dark energy, but she was prepared for it this time, and pushed her way into the room.

Masculine laughter sounded from the bedroom "Not this time, asshole," Sunny said before surrounding herself with blue light. "Leave now. Go away." The heaviness in the air subsided a little and Jordan shook her head, looking confused.

"Sunny?"

"Look out!" Sunny pushed her out of the way when a glass flew out of the kitchen doorway and shattered against the wall next to her head.

"Hey, I heard the commotion," Steve said from the open doorway. He stopped and the smile fell from his face. "Whoa. What happened in here?"

Sunny rummaged in her purse. "Take her next door to your place." She handed him her cell phone. "Call Shade and tell her I need her immediately. She'll know why."

"Fuck that," Jordan said. "I don't need her here." Despite the refusal, she didn't resist when Steve backed out of the room, pulling her with him.

Sunny sighed, hearing the petulance in her voice. "I know, darling. You don't need anyone, do you?" After they left, she opened a small jar and poured salt along her path to the door and in front of the entrance before crossing the threshold. She was also careful to sprinkle some in front of Steve's apartment. There was no way in hell she was getting sucker-punched again. When she was done, she sat next to Jordan on the couch.

She looked around the room. Steve had listened when she told him the other night that negative energy thrived on dirt and chaos. Other than random stacks of books, his apartment was spotless. Good.

"Honey, talk to me. What happened?"

Jordan was pale and didn't respond.

"Here's some water." Steve handed Sunny a glass. "What's wrong with her?"

"Some kind of oppression." She answered automatically, forgetting he wasn't a member of her team. She swore when she felt his fear spike in the room. "Stop it! That's not helping. They feed on fear. Let's just call it shock, okay? Better yet, why don't you go to your grandmother's?"

Steve shook his head. "No, I want to help her."

Sunny was just about to compliment his bravery when there was pounding at the front door and he screamed like a girl. "It's Shade." She bit her lip to keep from laughing. "Could you let her in?"

"Right." His face turned bright red and he coughed. "Sorry."

Shade appeared with a black bag and Steve cleared the table by sweeping his arm across it, knocking books to the floor.

"Right on. That's how I clean too," Shade said before she knelt in front of Sunny and Jordan. "Wow, I can feel her buzzing from two feet away."

Jordan's face was blank and she didn't twitch when Shade snapped her fingers in front of her face. She slowly turned her head to look at her with a sinister smile, one that Sunny was sure belonged to the dark entity attached to her. "Jordan!" Sunny shouted at her. "Come back."

"Fuck this." Shade took the water glass Steve held and threw the contents in Jordan's face.

"What the—" Jordan blinked, sputtered, and then lunged at Shade.

Sunny shot between them before Jordan's body made contact and wrestled her back on the couch.

"Hey, now," Steve said. "Is that necessary?"

"Shade, back away." Sunny lay on top of Jordan, pinning her in place. "Shh. I got you," she whispered to her an inch from her face. "Look at me. That's it, right here. Look in my eyes. It's okay now."

Jordan slowly stopped struggling. A few moments later, Sunny saw her eyes focus on her and she smiled gently. "All right now?"

"Fine." Her voice was tight and clipped, and the look in her eyes told Sunny she still wasn't fully present. But at least she didn't look ready to kill.

"I'm going to get up now, okay?"

Jordan nodded curtly.

Sunny lifted herself in increments, ready to pounce again if Jordan showed any additional signs of violence. Though she had to admit, the water in the face routine would have pissed her off as well.

Jordan's attention shifted to Shade, who stood with her hands on her hips, almost daring her to say something. They stared at each other, neither one backing down, and the atmosphere became electric with their fight for dominance.

"Shade? Could you please go and clear Jordan's apartment?" Sunny held her breath until she finally huffed and left, taking her black bag with her.

"What's she going to do?" Steve asked.

Sunny noted his pale face. "She's going to kick some ass, hopefully." She turned to Jordan, whose body language still radiated with rage. How would she get through to her? Really get through to Jordan's true self, the part that lived inside her wounded soul? Should she even try? Her heart immediately answered that question. Something in Jordan called to her, reaching places deeper than she'd ever known existed. She wasn't going to give up on her.

She wished she could touch Jordan's emotions, but she had so many blocks and walls. Sunny was frustrated she couldn't see what the clear and best responses were to make it easier to get past them. "Hi," she finally said. "Remember me?"

"Mine."

"Steve, could you excuse us, please? Lock the door on your way out."

He stammered and grabbed his jacket "Well, I'm going to Grandma's if you need me."

Steve left and Sunny's pulse raced and raw lust speared her, shoving her caution aside in a swift attack.

Jordan flipped her onto the couch and covered her with her own body. At Sunny's cry of surprise over the lightning-quick move, Jordan smiled.

"I want you," she said, grinding her hips against her.

Sunny's body responded to the aggressiveness, surprising her with her own animalistic response, and she stopped thinking altogether and went into a sexual haze, a place where only sensation mattered, a place where her body knew what it needed and wanted and had no inhibitions about how it accepted what felt good. Tiny warning bells rang in the back of her mind, but her body refused to let her heed them. Instead, she parted her knees to give Jordan more room. Sunny felt cold air against her breasts when Jordan pulled her shirt up and unhooked her bra.

"You are so damn soft," Jordan whispered against her skin. "So beautiful. So mine."

The words shot to Sunny's center. The need to have Jordan possess and be inside her was a fierce one. Sunny almost felt she might faint from it. She stood on the razor's edge of fear and excitement and reveled in it.

Jordan moaned and Sunny's back arched in response. She couldn't get close enough to her. Sunny's lust was red in her mind, wrapping her in ribbons of purple energy that popped along her nerve endings, electrifying her skin.

A tiny voice inside her cried out. What if she lost herself this time and couldn't come back?

The sensation of Jordan ripping her panties and smoothly entering her left her with no doubts, no inhibitions, and no reservations. Sunny gave herself to the sensation, bucking against Jordan's long fingers, drawing them deeper and harder into herself. She had no words, just sighs and cries of pleasure.

Jordan growled low in her throat and it set Sunny on fire. She twisted and arched through her orgasm until her body shuddered with the effort and Sunny had to remind herself how to breathe. She felt raw and new at the same time.

The feeling was so intense, she almost couldn't contain it. Sunny felt tears slip from her eyes, and she shuddered. The only sound in the room was their own heavy breathing.

Jordan came out of it first. What had she been thinking? She vaguely recalled the overwhelming need to fuck her, to mark her as belonging to her. To punish her for finding her in Shade's lap. She was mortified at what she'd done, and even more so at how much she liked it.

Sunny's shirt was under her arms, her bra pulled down to show red teeth marks where Jordan had nipped at tender skin. Her skirt crumpled at her waist, her little white panties shoved to the side, baring her pink, swollen flesh. Purple bruises were beginning to form on her white thighs. Jordan covered her face with her hands, hiding her shame.

"Don't you dare apologize again."

"What?" Jordan looked up, waiting for something scathing, something hard and hurtful.

"I see what you're doing to yourself." Sunny fixed her clothes and sat cross-legged in front of her.

Jordan wondered if confusion was just a part of being around Sunny. She obviously had no control when she was near. She covered her face again, unable to face Sunny's sweet nature in the face of her own demented behavior.

Sunny tugged on her hands, forcing Jordan to drop them from her face. "I have never had an experience like this."

"Of course not! You should be in a canopied bed with rose petals scattered around your precious body, not attacked and taken like an animal on the couch." Where had those words come from? The flowers and four-poster bed image? *I have finally lost my fucking mind.*

Sunny glanced over Jordan's shoulder at the front door. "Shade's in the hallway. I have to talk with her. Then, if all is well at your place, we'll finish this."

*Finish it?* Jordan's head raced with possible scenarios, visions of spells, hexes, or worse, Sunny never letting her near her again. She rose to her feet and guiltily helped Sunny stand. She didn't understand why she'd had the uncontrollable urge to take her like she did, but even if Sunny hated her for it, Jordan felt the need to stand behind Sunny at the door and give Shade a very clear signal as to whom she belonged.

The rage came rolling back up her spine the second she saw Shade, who returned her glare unflinchingly. Jordan knew Shade wasn't scared of her, and the fierce, unspoken challenge in Shade's eyes thrilled her in a primal place.

Shade looked away and focused on Sunny. When her features softened, Jordan wanted to punch her. She felt an invisible hand grab her by the back of the neck and squeeze. Incredibly, at the spectral contact, Jordan's temper began to cool. When she got hold of her emotions and felt calmer, the hand released her.

*Now, that was spooky.* Jordan forced herself to concentrate on what they were saying. Spooky or not, she was glad she no longer felt like throttling Shade.

"So it's all clear now?" Sunny asked.

"For the most part."

"What the fuck does that mean, exactly?" Jordan's voice was as cold as she could manage.

Sunny's back went stiff. *Uh-oh.* Jordan hadn't meant to piss Sunny off with her remark. She'd thrown it at Shade without thinking about the fact that Sunny would take it personally too.

"You'd do better to be thanking Shade right now."

"For what?"

"Never mind. I'm going to walk her to the van."

"Are you coming back?" Jordan hoped the desperation in her gut didn't come through in her voice.

"Yes. Wait here."

Jordan stood at the top of the landing, straining to hear what they were saying, but couldn't make anything out. She ran to Steve's living room, cleaned up the spilled water, and picked up Sunny's purse.

Jordan held it to her chest, giving herself hope. She would come back for that at least.

What could she do to fix the chaos her behavior caused? Where had this quicksand come from that she constantly found herself stuck in? Nothing was familiar; she was insecure and lost in an alternate world where she knew nothing of the native customs.

She locked Steve's door, entered her apartment, and set Sunny's purse down before grabbing the broom to sweep up the broken glass. The windows were open, allowing a small breeze to feather in, and just under it, Jordan smelled smoke. It must be part of Shade's witch ritual.

*What's taking her so long?* Jordan went into her bedroom to look out over the parking lot. From her high vantage point, she saw the van and Sunny still talking with Shade through the driver's side window. She laid her forehead against the cool glass. Sunny's hair was a mass of tangles, reminding Jordan how she'd just treated her as if she were a twenty-dollar whore. There was no seduction involved, no candlelight and dinner, no soft words or gentle kisses.

How could she expect Sunny to want her after treating her like that? Jordan began to wonder if she were capable of love. Maybe her mother's lack of it and her indifference had poisoned her ability to hold on to something pure and good.

Jordan realized that she would eventually bring Sunny down to her level. She would have to let her go before something worse happened and she tainted her somehow.

The thought made the hollow ache in her soul grow.

Sunny turned away from the van and faced the building, her gaze unerringly finding Jordan's. God help her, she didn't want to let her go.

When Jordan heard the front door open, she stepped away from the window and into the hall.

"Where's my purse?"

"Are you leaving?"

"Do you want me to?"

"No."

"Then I'm going to get cleaned up," Sunny said. "You know."

"Okay. Yeah, good. Right." Jordan returned to the bedroom and sat on the bed. She couldn't understand why Sunny didn't cut and run when she had the chance.

"I don't know what came over me over there. I have never done anything remotely like that," Sunny said. "I got caught up in a vortex of the energy around you. But I'm not ashamed of it."

Jordan looked up when she heard her voice from the door. "Why did you come back?"

"Because I see you."

"I see you too. You're standing right in front of me. But I don't see how that's an answer."

"I'll be honest with you, Jordan. I'm not sure why, but there's something about you that I want very much. However, I'm going to make something very clear. I will not tolerate the nasty remarks and attitudes toward my friends. I want to explore this"—she gestured to Jordan then herself—"whatever it is. But hear this—it will never be at the expense of the people that I love."

"Was Shade your lover?"

"Yes. A very long time ago, and I'm only going to explain this once. I've known Shade since I was eleven years old. She's my family, my best friend. She's loyal, kind, and brave. She doesn't deserve your attitude, and I mean that. There is no competition between the two of you but what's in your head. Shade loves me and wants the best for me, and you haven't exactly shown yourself to be that yet."

"I repeat, then why are you here?"

Sunny sat next to her. "Haven't you ever been friends with any of your exes?"

"No."

"Why?"

"Because the last woman I thought I loved shot me and left me in an alley to die."

"Oh."

Jordan could see that her words took Sunny by surprise.

"Tell me. No, wait. Come here first." Sunny scooted to the headboard and leaned against it. When Jordan was next to her, she held her hand. "Okay, now."

"The department psychiatrist they made me see didn't hold my hand."

Sunny laughed. "Was that a joke? Did I just hear you make a joke?"

Jordan smiled. "I love your laugh."

"Laughter heals. Now tell me a story, Jordan."

"Where do you want me to start?" Jordan was nervous and hesitant. Surely, if Sunny knew her life story she would run. *Isn't that what's best?* That would make this easier. Jordan didn't want to be the one to hurt her. It would be better if Sunny walked away from her. Jordan was used to that.

"We'll start with the shooting first, since that's the bomb you just dropped."

"I was working in downtown Seattle when three runaways came up missing. Kids I had gotten to know. No one seemed to care that they were gone without a trace."

"But you did," Sunny said.

"I identified with them for a lot of reasons that I don't want to go into at the moment."

"Okay, we don't have to go there right now."

*Or ever.* "So I started to go down to the streets on my own time. The department noticed. More specifically, Detective Lynn Cody noticed. Anyway, she asked me to back off the search and said that my questions were hindering a current undercover operation. I couldn't see how doing my job would hurt hers, but she was a superior officer and I agreed even though I knew I would continue looking for them."

Jordan paused. This was where it hurt to remember. Hindsight always provided a clearer picture, and she felt stupid for the way she'd been manipulated so easily.

"Did you find them?"

Jordan shook her head. "No. Lynn asked me out. I was so distracted by the way she treated me that all my free time from then on was wrapped around her."

"How did she treat you, Jordan?"

"Like I was special and worth something."

"Because you are."

Jordan ignored the remark. It had all been a lie. "She insisted on keeping our relationship a secret. I was naïve enough to believe it was because she wasn't out as a lesbian. For the next few months, I thought I was in love with her. I did everything I thought she wanted and considered myself lucky that I'd found somebody to care about. Then one night, I got a text from a confidential informant that there was a major drug deal going down. I called Lynn and asked if she knew about it. She said she didn't and that she would meet me at the location with backup.

"I didn't think twice about going into that alley. I found a place that I could see from and hunkered down to wait for the players to show up. I remember thinking how good the other cops were because I didn't see or sense any of them around me. Thirty minutes after I got there, I noticed a man at the front of the alley. He looked both ways before he slid into the shadows and started toward where I was hiding. He sat on his large duffel bag next to several garbage cans, but didn't notice me watching him from three feet away. He was a creepy little man and he kept laughing and muttering to himself."

Jordan caressed Sunny's hair, enjoying the softness under her hand as the ugly memory tore at her. "Another fifteen, twenty minutes passed and my legs were cramping, but I didn't dare move and draw attention to myself. I held still until two figures approached from the street. I heard one of them order the man to bring it out. The voice was female, and I recall thinking it sounded familiar, but I couldn't place it. I drew my weapon and waited until the man brought them the duffel and reached for the smaller case they put in front of him. I assumed it was the money. I didn't have time to think, and I had absolute faith that I had backup, so I stood up and yelled for them to freeze. Creepy man spun around and drew his weapon and fired. I shot back and hit him and he fell. My ears were still ringing when I felt cold steel press into my cheek." Jordan would never forget that moment. She could still feel the muzzle against her skin. "Lynn ordered me to give up my weapon, and I was so shocked I couldn't move. Then she told me I should have minded my own business and stayed out of the way."

"How horrible!" Sunny said. "What did you do?"

"Instinct had me fighting, but I was still trying to comprehend that the woman I'd kissed just that morning was trying to kill me. During the struggle, I slammed into a garbage can and she pulled the trigger as I was falling."

"You poor thing."

"She left me there next to the dead drug dealer. I suppose she thought I would bleed to death."

"But you didn't."

"No, I didn't. I lost consciousness, and when I woke up, I was in the hospital."

"Wait a minute. I think I remember something about this," Sunny said.

"I thought you didn't watch the news."

"I just recall seeing part of a press conference about internal investigation and a trial. This was about two years ago?"

Jordan nodded. "A little less."

"Who found you?"

"One of the detectives in her division had gone to IA when he found out they were taking money and bribes. Lynn and two of her officers had been under surveillance for months. He was on the late shift that night and overheard them talking about the shooting." Jordan was certain that if IA hadn't been following the case, she would have been dead, completely tied up in a neat box with a bright ribbon and labeled fall guy.

"Where were you hit?"

"In the hip."

Sunny's eyes were wet.

"Don't feel sorry for me," Jordan said. "Please. I don't need your pity."

"I would choose the word 'compassion' instead."

"Same thing." Jordan was a survivor, and no matter what you called it, both terms made her feel weak.

The bedroom door slammed shut. Jordan looked at Sunny. "Uneven floors and walls. Happens all the time."

"Is that truly what you tell yourself? After all you've seen and heard?"

Jordan closed her eyes. "I believe that you believe it's paranormal."

"Don't patronize me!"

"Okay, Sunny. How did the door just slam then?"

"You did it."

"What? That makes no sense!" Jordan snatched her hand away.

"Okay, let's break it down. We're still going through the evidence from our investigation here, but I can tell you, most of the poltergeist activity in this building is centered here in your apartment. More often than not, it's a psychic phenomenon and attached to a person who's going through emotional, physical, or psychological events that make them feel like they're losing control, which causes bursts of subconscious energy that have the ability to move objects."

"Let's just say I can suspend disbelief for a second. I wasn't trying to move anything. I've never done it before. And I certainly didn't choose to aim that flying glass at my head earlier."

"That you know of. Emotions have *power*, Jordan, actual, measurable energy. And you telling me about your trauma makes a good point. There are thousands of cases that document people developing psychic abilities after events of this nature. In addition to those studies, this is what I believe. If someone lives in grief, hate, or depression long enough, a part of their spirit forms offshoots. Those fragments become shadows. If you give them enough negative energy, they grow and manifest into separate entities, shadows that attach to you—that hold you in that dark place. And they can have their own strength, enough of it to move objects telekinetically. I'm not saying that it's the only answer here. It's obvious to me there was another entity here, a negative one, that invited itself and rode right in on the back of your anger. It's using your energy. You didn't see yourself, Jordan, or the look in your eyes."

"You're talking possession now."

"Of a sort. I would call it oppressed instead."

Jordan didn't know how to answer. The idea was one she couldn't begin to fathom. She shook her head. "Then why did you let me fuck you, Sunny? If you thought I was possessed?" Jordan heard the sarcasm in her voice but held firm.

Sunny winced. "Honestly? I was caught up in your need at first. I let you because I wanted to show you that it's you I care about.

Then you lit up something inside me and I lost control. The same way I did on the stairs. But I don't want you to think that it's just sex, okay? There are so many things about you that I like. It's your smile, the way you look at me. I think about you all the time since I've met you. I wonder what you're doing and if you're going to call me so I can see you again. When I'm around you, I feel myself. You don't know what a gift that is."

"Try me." Sunny felt all those things? Jordan felt panic building in her chest. She couldn't possibly live up to who Sunny thought she was.

"Most of the time, I feel like I'm standing in a busy airport. There is noise, color, and traces of other people's emotions surrounding me. I can't help but feel it; it's who I am. But I feel like I ride a roller coaster all day, every day, and it's exhausting. You bring me blessed silence."

"Right along with my shadows that hurt you."

"We can deal with those. Let me help you heal. I can teach you how to see good in the world."

*There is nothing good here.* How could she make Sunny understand that? "Have you ever considered that I don't want to see it? I have seen more human suffering than you could imagine. The horrible atrocities that people are capable of. I see these things in Technicolor, every night before I go to sleep. I can't afford to *feel*. In order to be good at what I do, I have to be able to turn my feelings off, or risk drowning in them."

"So you won't even attempt anything that I know would help you."

"No. I don't want you to save me, Sunny." *And I don't want to hurt you anymore.*

"Then I guess we're done here." Sunny moved slowly and deliberately away from her, and Jordan stayed put, watching her leave the room but not making a move to stop her.

Jordan heard the front door close and closed her eyes.

*Please don't go.*

## CHAPTER THIRTEEN

Jordan flipped through channels on the television. Why was it that she couldn't find a damn thing to watch when she had five hundred of them?

Nothing had held her attention for more than a few seconds since Sunny walked out the door over a week ago. Jordan had wanted to run after her but was scared. She wanted to tell her she'd believe in anything she wanted her to if only she would stay.

But Jordan hadn't begged for anything since she was a small child. It never worked. The pain always came anyway.

She tried to focus on the screen again. *Great, another commercial.* Jordan turned it off and threw the remote.

There was a knock on the door and she ignored it. Steve had come by every day for a week. At least she thought it was him. She never answered it.

"Jordan, I know you're in there. Open the door."

She looked down at the ratty sweats she'd been wearing for two days. *Nope. Not doing it.*

"I'm not leaving this time." He pounded again.

"Go away! I'll call the cops," she yelled.

"You are the cops, dumbass. Answer the damn door."

Jordan gave in and stomped down the hall.

"God, you look like shit," Steve said. He pushed past her into the apartment. He stopped and looked around. "It looks like mine used to. What's the matter with you? Are you sick?" He began picking up dirty dishes and half-empty fast food wrappers.

"I don't need a fucking maid."

He looked at her. "No, but I'm sure you could use a friend."

The concern in his voice made Jordan feel small.

"We've been worried. You don't answer the door or your phone."

"I don't want anyone to care." It only hurt in the long run.

"Why?" Steve finished clearing the table. "Sit and talk to me."

She'd rather stick a needle in her eye but sat anyway.

"Did something happen at work?"

"No." She was just going through the motions there. She did her job, period. Work was something that she used to love and that used to be the most important thing in her life. But each day brought more ugliness, and she had begun to dread putting on her uniform.

"Do you want to tell me what happened when Sunny was here last?"

"No."

"Then tell me what happened to make you look like an abandoned dog waiting to be kicked."

Jordan shook her head. "I can't."

"Can't or won't?"

"Please leave it alone." Jordan expected him to get up and leave, but he didn't. Instead, he made small talk and tried to draw her out. She wasn't hearing what he was saying, but she did appreciate the sound of his voice. It was almost comforting.

"They're coming this afternoon with the results of the investigation."

Jordan felt her heart skip but tried to act casual. "Oh?"

"We're supposed to meet over at Grandma's in an hour." When Jordan didn't reply, he sighed. "Look. You need to get out. We can go out for a beer or something when they leave."

"Are you asking me on a date?"

Steve laughed. "I probably should. I've already seen you half-naked."

"Shut up, Jackson."

"Are you going to come hear what the team found? And don't

give me that crap anymore about how you don't believe in ghosts. You're smarter than that."

*Am I?*

Steve rose from his chair. "Jordan, give it a chance." He patted her shoulder awkwardly. "And take a shower. You stink."

Jordan chuckled. "But you're ugly."

"See? Don't you feel better?"

"Go away now."

As soon as Steve left, Jordan went into the bathroom. He was right. She looked horrible. Purple bruises ringed her eyes and her hair stuck out in odd angles. She lifted her arm and sniffed. She did smell. She met her own eyes in the mirror. She had two choices. She could continue to wallow in self-pity or she could take that chance and see Sunny.

She threw back the shower curtain and turned on the water.

❖

Jordan stood on the landing an hour later and smoothed her tucked shirt. She was nervous but hopeful. Sunny was just on the other side of that door and she couldn't wait to see her. She needed to apologize and wanted to see her smile. She wanted to wrap her arms around her and be surrounded by her sweet fragrance.

She wanted a chance to love her. The weird shit in her apartment had stopped. The rage she felt, the feeling of "oppression," as Sunny called it, had completely gone. Whatever kick-ass thing Shade had done in her apartment had worked. Whether she believed in the paranormal or not, that could only be a good thing.

Jordan took a deep breath and knocked. Agnes answered. "Oh, it's good to see you, dear. Go on in. I'm skipping this part. I've learned what I needed to know, and quite frankly, it scares the shit out of me." Agnes hugged her briefly before pushing her into the small foyer.

Tiffany sat at the head of the table with Steve to her left. Jordan scanned the room, nearly frantic. Where was she?

"Tiffany was just going to start," Steve said.

Jordan looked at her. Tiffany's cheeks turned pink and she looked away.

"Sunny and Shade had appointments. I'm afraid it's just me."

Jordan felt flattened under her disappointment. Sunny didn't even want to be in the same room with her. She wanted to slap herself for expecting anything different. But hadn't this been what she wanted in the first place? To push her away so she couldn't hurt her?

How come doing the right thing hurt so badly?

Tiffany cleared her throat. "Shall we get started?"

Jordan thought about leaving but decided to stay and listen. Then she could put all of this away and behind her and get back to normal. It made her sad to realize that until this moment, she hadn't realized what a crappy place it was to be.

"We have some interesting evidence from our investigation. It was very active that night, and we all had personal experiences and psychic impressions. First off, we caught slamming doors on the recorder in the basement." She pushed Play.

Jordan's attention sparked when she heard the metal crash, and she recalled the first time she kissed Sunny. Thirty seconds later, she heard it again and remembered how she fit between Sunny's thighs.

"But," Tiffany continued, "we didn't get any video. The camera's battery shut down."

Jordan felt her cheeks heat. She wouldn't have needed to see the video anyway. The memory of what she'd experienced that night was permanently embedded in her consciousness. It was compelling physical evidence. In spite of her reservations, she wanted to hear more.

"The next thing we caught was this, also in the basement." Tiffany clicked her mouse.

"Is that a growl?" Steve paled. "That sounds wicked and absolutely terrifying."

Jordan's hair prickled on her arms. The sound was eerie. Hell, she hadn't expected this. She'd been so wrapped up in Sunny and her own refusal to believe in the paranormal that she hadn't been paying any real attention to what was going on. She had been so sure that there were logical explanations for everything.

When she heard the laughter of small children, she startled. "Where was that?" she asked.

"The courtyard."

"Are they trapped here?" Steve asked.

"No. They talked with Sunny and told her they came to visit their grandfather, who used to live here. They didn't die here, but he did."

"Which apartment?"

Tiffany tapped the blueprint. "Here. In this building."

"Is he still here?"

"We didn't catch any trace of the grandfather. But that's not unusual. Just because someone has the ability to communicate with spirits doesn't mean that they all step forward to do so."

"What about the washing machines?" Steve asked.

"That episode appears to be connected with this next piece of evidence."

Tiffany clicked again. "This is the camera in Jordan's apartment. We didn't actually go in there to do a reading on the space because Jordan was gone, but it picked up some interesting audio."

*Get out, bitch.*

"Are you fucking kidding me?" Steve jumped out of his chair. "I'm moving." He pointed at Jordan. "You are too."

"It's not done yet," Tiffany said. "Listen."

*Kill her.*

Jordan chilled to the bone. "Is there more?"

"More? You want more? We should go now," he said.

"Steve, I want you to listen, okay?" Tiffany spoke in a soothing tone. "It's gone now. Shade took care of it last week, remember?"

"What did she do?"

"What Shade does best. She kicked some ass. We don't ask her for many details."

"What the hell is it?" Jordan asked.

"After the investigation, we combed through the tapes and

video, then I did some research." Tiffany pulled out a folder from the stack. "I went to the library and found a newspaper article from nineteen fifty-four. Apparently, there was a murder-suicide in your apartment. According to the reporter, they found evidence suggesting the man was responsible for at least four other deaths. All five women were raped and strangled."

"Jesus," Jordan said. "What am I supposed to do with that?"

"How come we didn't know that? I mean, we didn't have any problems in that apartment before."

"We can't know for sure. The entity didn't interact with us at the time. It could be that the recent remodel after the last tenant left woke it up, or the entity connected with Jordan for whatever reason. It could be a little of both."

That dark voice felt connected to her? The thought was terrifying. Was that what Sunny was dealing with when she was around Jordan? She remembered her aggressive behavior toward her and felt mortified. It was all too much to take in.

She did know one thing. She was far too dangerous to be close to. Especially around Sunny.

Jordan got up and left without saying a word.

❖

Sunny loaded her bag into the van and shut the door. Tonight's investigation had been booked two months ago by the new owners of a dilapidated hotel. It had been a while since the team had worked such a large building, and she was excited to get going.

Jordan's truck pulled up and parked across the street. Sunny tried to ignore the butterflies. What was it with Jordan and the push-me pull-you routine? Sunny didn't want to keep justifying who and what she was anymore. It was exhausting her both spiritually and mentally. She'd spent restless nights since walking out of Jordan's apartment thinking about Jordan's hot skin against her own. She'd even cried at the feeling of emptiness inside when she realized they'd never be together. But she wasn't going to give up who she was or deny her gift because Jordan refused to believe in anything outside her closed mind. *Then why is she here?* Sunny motioned to Shade and Tiffany that she'd be right back.

The driver's window rolled down as she approached it. Determined to keep her cool, she sent her senses outward automatically, but hit the brick wall. Again. When she reached the truck, she let out a small cry of dismay. Jordan's cheekbone was purple and swollen. "Jordan, what happened to you?" Sunny forgot her resolution to stay detached and cupped her cheek gently.

"You should see the other guy."

"What? Never mind, get out of the truck." Jordan stepped out and looked embarrassed. Sunny held her for a second before stepping away. "I only have a few minutes, but I want to hear about this."

"What did you do to me?" Jordan looked defeated and lost. "I can't think, I can't eat, and sleep is impossible. I can't do anything."

"How is that my fault, Jordan?"

"I'm almost positive it's all your talk about feelings and personal demons."

"What happened?"

"This morning, I went to work and we got a tip on the kidnappers and rapists who hurt that girl. I got to the location and another unit already apprehended them, but they weren't cuffed yet. One of the fucking punks had the nerve to ask why we were arresting him because the bitch liked what they did to her. Something inside me snapped. I actually felt it rip through me like a freight train. How dare he think he had the right to break her like that, as if she were nothing and didn't matter?" Jordan's voice cracked. "So, long story short, I beat the shit out of him and ended up on suspension."

"What do you want me to do?"

"Take it away."

"What, Jordan? Take what away?"

"The shadows."

Sunny was hurt. Jordan hadn't come to apologize or ask for another chance. If she had said she missed her first or asked, instead of demanding she take them away, she would have been glad to help her. "I don't have time right now. Make an appointment."

"What? Wait. Where are you going?"

"Hamilton Hotel in Seattle."

Jordan's eyes widened. "You absolutely can't go there."

"Excuse me?" Sunny asked. She felt her temper start to rise.

"I mean, it's dangerous. It's full of junkies and it's a major gang hideout."

"The new owners called us. It's been cleared out and it's under renovation." Sunny folded her arms across her chest and stood her ground. "It's *my* job."

"I said no. You can't go."

"I'm most certain that I can. And I don't recall asking for your permission, or needing it, for that matter." Who the hell did she think she was ordering her like a child? "I'm pretty sure we're still done here."

Jordan grabbed her elbow when she tried to walk away.

"You're hurting me. Let go."

"I'm sorry." She immediately loosened her grip. "Let me go with you. I know the neighborhood."

Sunny shook her head. "Why on earth would you want to do that, Jordan? Why would you ask to go on an investigation? You don't believe in ghosts, remember? You're so close-minded, you'll only hamper what it is I have to do, and I don't have time to babysit a skeptic."

"I can protect you," Jordan said.

"Really? Because from where I'm standing, the only thing I've needed protection from lately is you."

"But—"

"No buts, Jordan. I've opened myself up to negative energy several times, yet you *refuse* to deal with the shadows that keep us apart. I don't know whether it's ignorance on your part or fear that keeps you from believing in me, but every time you negate what I feel or believe, you break a piece of my heart. I'm not going to let you hurt me anymore."

Sunny held her tears in check on the way back to the van. She had to keep it together for the job ahead, but she knew she would cry later.

❖

Jordan wanted to run after Sunny, but the van was pulling away from the curb. The conversation hadn't gone at all like she'd hoped. She tripped over her words, and nothing she wanted to say came out. But that didn't really matter did it? The last thing she wanted to do was hurt her. She would have to follow her instead. Jordan couldn't erase the pain she'd caused her, but she would protect her from the very real characters and criminals that she knew trolled the neighborhood she was headed to.

Jordan jumped back in her truck. She'd have to drive around to Seattle. It would take her extra time, but there was nowhere for her to hide on the ferry.

The gas light turned red, and Jordan swore before detouring to get more. She pushed the speed limit for the next hour in a race to get there before Sunny.

It was still light out when she exited the freeway and took a shortcut to the hotel. She knew these streets like the back of her hand. Garbage littered the alleys, and the powerful smell of old garbage and stale beer made her close her window.

Jordan parked a couple of blocks away, then jogged to the building. She needn't have worried after all; new cyclone fences surrounded the property. Had it been so long, then? She searched her memory and felt a little shaky when she realized that she'd been shot only a few blocks away. So much had happened over the last year and a half.

"Jordan, is that you?"

The question startled her. She turned toward the man in the shadows beside the Dumpster. Her stomach tensed before she recognized him. "Liam?"

"How have you been?"

Jordan relaxed and held out her hand for him to shake. He was one of the few fellow officers who had showed support during the ugly internal investigation.

"I heard you were patrolling Bremerton on the other side of the water. What the hell are you doing back here?"

"Oh, you know," Jordan said vaguely and pointed to the hotel.

"Are you moonlighting for the security detail?" Liam looked surprised. "I hadn't heard."

Jordan grasped at the explanation and nodded slightly. She wasn't lying—exactly. She hadn't been hired but came to protect Sunny. She wasn't above playing semantics to accomplish that goal. "I'm late. Where do I check in?"

"They're setting up in the lobby. I can radio you in."

"No, thanks," she said quickly. "Maybe I can sneak in the back?" She was disgusted at her wheedling tone, but would gladly lose a little dignity at this point.

Liam chuckled and winked, producing a key to the gate. "I never saw you."

"Thanks, I owe you one."

❖

Sunny followed Shade, Tiffany, and the owners on their second tour of the hotel while intermittently checking her clipboard. "Okay, you said there was activity in the lobby. Has anything happened since we last talked?"

Eric Whitman glanced at his partner, Frank Story. "You can see how much progress has been made in this area."

Construction debris littered the lobby of the once-grand hotel. Tools, sawdust, empty boxes, and fast food wrappers were strewn around half-finished projects. It looked the same to Sunny. "I'll have to take your word for it."

Frank laughed. "Eric has great vision. But me? Not so much."

"I can see it," Tiffany said. "How it was, I mean. Chestnut wood, brass mirrors, glass chandeliers. It's quite lovely."

Eric nodded. "And it will be again."

"If we can keep a construction crew on site," Frank muttered. "They keep quitting. We're already hiring them out of Olympia."

"What are they saying?"

"You know, the usual. Somebody is watching them, moving their equipment and tools, tapping them on the shoulders, whispers in the ear. That sort of stuff."

"Have you experienced any of this?"

"I have," Eric said. "But the weird thing is that I don't feel threatened at all."

Sunny smiled and tilted her head. "It's because you talk to them."

"How do you know that?" He looked surprised.

"We'll get into that later. How about you, Frank? Any experiences lately?"

"Sometimes it's stronger than others." He pointed to the staircase. "But just last week, I actually saw someone coming down them. I knew it wasn't Eric because I knew he was in our fifth-floor apartment."

"This place is huge," said Shade. "What made you decide to take it on? It must be costing you a fortune."

"More," Eric said. "Thank baby Jesus for Microsoft stock."

"And Google," Frank added.

"Let's get back to the apparition. Did you see what he was wearing?"

"Top hat, turn-of-the-century suit, cane—oh, and a black mustache."

Sunny wrote Frank's description in her notes. It matched the dapper gentleman currently leaning against the banister watching them. Sunny reined in her senses and he vanished from her mind's eye. She jotted the time in the margin.

The group started at the top of the hotel and worked their way down. Frank and Eric took the time to describe each of their personal encounters and those they heard secondhand. So far, the third floor showed the most activity.

The first and second floors and the basement were all still

undergoing major renovation and continued to hold an abandoned feeling. Eric wouldn't enter the basement at all, preferring instead to wait in the cavernous kitchen, and no amount of persuasion could convince him to join them.

"Those used to be the servants' quarters over there that we have plans to turn into a state-of-the-art gym and spa. The last contractor had workers down here who claimed they heard crying and knocking in the walls, whispers, et cetera."

"Have you?"

"I try not to come down here and never at night. But yes, I hear strange noises." Frank led them to another large area with pipes sticking out of the walls. "Laundry facilities." He held up a hand. "And the plumbers quit too. One of them said a pipe wrench flew across the room and stuck in the drywall." Sunny continued to write while he talked.

Frank hesitated in front of the boiler room. "I hate it in here."

"I don't blame you," Shade said.

He looked at her, clearly nervous. "I've heard unholy screaming coming from that room. Forgive me for not going in." He backed away a few paces.

Shade turned to Sunny. "There are energy traces. Do you want me to look right now?"

Sunny shook her head. "No. Not right now. The clients are scared enough. Tiff?"

Tiffany reached out but stopped short of actually touching the door. "It's—no, not without protection."

Sunny could sense *other* trying to get her attention and closed her wall tighter. God, this place was full of unhappy spirits.

❖

Jordan hugged the wall. If the door opened, she was ready to jump behind the furnace. Something tickled her nose, and she hoped she wasn't going to sneeze.

She had just finished searching the basement for vagrants when she'd heard the group coming down the stairs. She ducked into the only room that looked like a hiding space, barely shutting the door behind her before they turned the corner.

There were no transients or junkies lurking in the shadows, and Jordan was glad for it because she had no idea what she would have done if there were. She was on suspension, lied about being security, and to top it off, was in possession of an unregistered firearm. What the hell was she thinking? The sound of voices grew fainter as the group moved away. Jordan let out a sigh of relief and counted to fifty before she crept out of the boiler room.

❖

Sunny spread the floor plan on the reception desk they had set up as command central and marked where she wanted cameras placed.

Eric handed her the keys to the building. "We're going to the Hilton. Here's our cell numbers. Security is outside patrolling, but other than that, we aren't expecting anyone tonight." A look of concern crossed his face. "Are you girls going to be okay?"

"Maybe we should stay, Eric. We could—"

"We're fine," Shade interrupted. "It's not our first rodeo." She smiled to soften the harsh tone of her refusal. "Go on. Get out of here."

"We got a hot tub," Eric said.

"And booked a midnight massage with margaritas."

"Yee-haw!" Tiffany knuckle-bumped Frank.

"We'll see you in the morning," Sunny said, shooing them to the entry. After she locked the glass door, she waved to the officer standing by the fence before returning to Tiffany and Shade to finish their game plan for the night. The building was much too large to work out of the back of the van, and Sunny wanted them all together on this investigation anyway.

By the time they were done, three screens held twelve camera views, and fourteen recorders were feeding into command central.

"It looks like we're setting up for a small war. Sometimes I don't know why we do all of this. It's not as if we can't tell them what's going on without the electronics." Tiffany tucked in an earpiece.

"Hey!" Shade protested. "Don't be dissing my toys."

"Dad always set up stuff like this for my mother before every walk-through. So many people didn't believe them and they wanted some kind of proof. Something tangible to back up what my mother told them. And people who can't see the other side will always believe what they see as scientific proof. I shudder to think what the three of us would have gone through back then."

Tiffany nodded. "Yeah, but your family has always had a psychic in each generation. My gift came from the devil himself. Just ask my mother."

"No, thanks," said Shade. "I don't know where mine came from either."

"True. Well, are we ready?"

They held hands in a circle, completing a ring of mind, body, and spirit along with a representation of past, present, and future. Together, they formed a double trinity of power. Sunny silently asked her guides for protection and guidance for the night ahead.

❖

Jordan peered through the banister on the second floor. The yellow glow of the small lamp on the desk gave Sunny a halo around her hair, and Jordan longed to touch it, to smooth the curly tresses between her fingers while she kissed her. Cup her face and tell her she loved her. Squeeze her throat until she begged for her life. *What?*

Sunny and Tiffany headed to the stairs. Shade sat at the desk and slipped on her monster headphones. Jordan backed away on her knees, stood, and quietly headed for the back stairwell.

"Hey, Sunny?" Shade called out. "Movement and shadow figure running on the second floor."

"Got it." Sunny stood on the landing. "Go ahead and head to the fifth, Tiff. I'll go to the second."

"Are you sure?"

"Yes. Start with an EVP session in the owner's apartment. I'll be there in a few."

*Oh, shit.* Jordan forgot the cameras. The metal door she was headed to would make too much noise in the silence. *Think.* Where could she hide? She felt along the wall and tried the first knob she came to. Thankfully, it turned and she entered quietly, praying the hinges wouldn't squeak.

Jordan dropped onto the dusty floor to peek under it. She could see the beam of Sunny's small flashlight coming closer. Her heart raced loudly in her ears, making her wonder if it could be heard from the hall outside.

She didn't have a reason to hide anymore. There were no threats in the building. She'd checked it thoroughly, keeping one step ahead of the group. So why was she lying behind a closed door on a dirty floor?

The light stopped and Jordan held her breath while she slowly got to her feet and pressed her back against the wall.

The knob turned. What should she do? Continue to hide or scare the shit out of Sunny? *Awkward.*

Jordan felt a sharp pain on her ass when she leaned against a protruding nail. "Ouch." She froze, mortified that she hadn't been able to stop the exclamation. The door swung open and the handle hit her in the stomach, forcing the air from her lungs.

"Who's there?" Sunny whispered.

The jig was up; she was flat-out busted. "It's me."

"What?"

The beam of light hit Jordan directly in the face.

"What are you *doing* here?"

"Protecting you?"

They stared at each other. Jordan was the first to look away. Sunny sighed heavily and closed her eyes. "You followed me?"

"It seemed like an excellent idea at the time."

"How did you get past security?"

"I know one of the guards." Jordan hesitated. "And I lied."

Sunny fought her amusement. She wanted to be angry, but

Jordan was so cute standing there like a small child, shifting from foot to foot. She supposed the dirt that covered her was from hiding. "You stalked me to Seattle?"

"Well, when you put it that way. Um, yes. Sunny?"

"Yes?"

"Could you shine the light back here? I think I stabbed myself in the ass on a nail."

"You're hurt? Let me see?" Sunny set her recorder and camera on the floor before radioing Shade. "Mark the time on that shadow. It was Jordan."

"Come again?"

"Jordan's here."

The radio crackled and Tiffany snickered. "Guess you'll be more than a few minutes."

"Stand by," Sunny said, then clipped the radio back on her belt. "You," she said to Jordan. "Hands in the air, up against the wall, and spread 'em." She felt a surge of sexual power when Jordan turned slowly and placed her elbows and forearms against the wall.

"It burns," Jordan said.

"I'll bet." Sunny stared at the hard buttocks in front of her and ran her hands against the denim. "There are no holes in your jeans. God, Jordan, is that a gun?"

"Sorry." Jordan pulled it out of her waistband and set it on the floor, pointing away from them, and turned back again.

"Drop them."

Jordan looked over her shoulder. "What? Here?"

Sunny chuckled. "I have to see." The muscles in her thighs tingled when she heard Jordan unbuckle her belt and lower her pants a few inches. "Which side? Never mind, I see it." Two angry red welts raised on the white skin about an inch apart. She moved the light behind the door to check the wall. Nothing stuck out. No screws or nails, no torn pipes. It was smooth. She looked back at the marks.

"Poor baby," Sunny said before blowing on them softly. The muscles in Jordan's ass tensed, and Sunny put down the flashlight and held Jordan's hips before kissing the welts. What was it about

Jordan that had her lusting like a cat in heat every time she got near her?

"Sunny! There's a black mass outside the room you're in, and it's getting bigger. Get the hell out of there!" Shade's voice shouted through the radio, instantly shattering the moment.

"Later," she whispered to Jordan. As soon as she stepped away from her, she felt calm and clear. She grabbed the radio and turned on her recorder. "Go."

"It's still there. Get the fuck out."

Jordan fastened her belt and stood ready to open the door. "It's freezing."

After putting the recorder in the camera bracket, Sunny filmed the temperature gauge quickly dropping. "Get the EMF detector out of my lower pocket."

Jordan held it out and Sunny pointed the camera at the needle rapidly spiking up and down, then into the red.

"What is it?"

"The ghost that pinched your ass."

Sunny turned and continued to scan the room, making notes of the readings.

"Aw, come on." Jordan could think of a dozen explanations, but would rather focus on the kiss.

"What's your name?" Sunny asked the space in front of them.

Jordan strained her ears but didn't hear anything. She felt sort of silly.

"Why are you still here? Can you talk into the red light here on my recorder?"

Jordan jumped when a soft knock came from the other side of the door. She grabbed Sunny's radio. "Shade, who the fuck is outside this door?"

"It's gone now."

Jordan whipped the door open and turned on her flashlight. The hall was empty, and she was furious. Messing with somebody's head like that was just fucked up. She raced to the lobby and stopped next to Shade. "What was that?"

"Jordan, sit down." Sunny came up from behind and put a hand on her shoulder. "Shade, please rewind the footage to show her."

"Tiff to base. Are you guys going to leave me up here all night?"

Shade stood. "I'm on my way. Hang tight." She bumped Jordan's hip on her way around the desk. Jordan opened her mouth to say something to her, but Sunny gently nudged her to the chair, working the mouse on one of the screens.

"Watch," she said.

"But—"

"Jordan. Please shut up."

She recognized that tone. It was the one Sunny used right before she cut to the bone with her one-line zingers and walked off. Jordan wanted to protest, she wanted to call bullshit, but she wanted Sunny to stay more than she wanted to argue. It took effort, but she kept quiet.

Sunny pushed the Play button and watched the screen intently. "There." She pointed. "See it?"

Jordan didn't see anything. "No."

"It's right there!" Sunny was excited and rewound it again. "Watch closely. You'll see this dark spot right here." She tapped the screen. "It gets larger and starts to pulsate."

"I don't see anything. No, wait. Are you talking about the blurry spot there?"

"Yes! Look at it move. Look! You can see it walk away and go into the wall over there." She blew up the frame and followed the figure with her fingernail.

While Jordan tried to process what her eyes were telling her, a movement on another screen caught her attention. Shocked, she watched a silver pot in the kitchen shimmy sideways and fall off the shelf.

Sunny danced in place, her voice high and excited. "Activity in the kitchen. We got it on tape!"

She didn't understand why Sunny sounded so glad about something so creepy. Jordan was freaked out. How could she fight something she couldn't see? It wasn't tangible. She couldn't shoot it. "Why do you sound so happy about it?"

"It's for the client's validation. More important, it's proof. It's something to be shown to skeptics who refuse to believe in the paranormal."

"Like me," Jordan finished for her. "This isn't normal, Sunny."

"Who gets to define normal? The government, who tells you only what they want you to know to keep you scared, and worse—compliant? Or how about the churches and the religious sects that shove their beliefs down other people's throats, saying their way is the only way? Maybe it's the mainstream scientists who refuse to open themselves to the possibility that maybe, just maybe, they're wrong about some things and won't even consider the endless clues that are right in front of their faces. You have to ask yourself—where do your beliefs about the world come from?"

Jordan thought for a moment. She was tired of feeling *wrong*. But could she, just for a moment, let go of her rigid beliefs, or at least give them a rest? How would she even begin? Jordan closed her burning eyes and tried to take it in. Sunny's cool hand cupped her cheek and she leaned into it.

"Let me help you."

Jordan wanted her to, and she hoped like hell it wasn't too late.

## Chapter Fourteen

The radio squawked. "Shade to Sunny."

"Go."

"Could you come to the third floor, please? Now."

"On my way." Sunny looked thoughtfully at Jordan. "Could you watch the monitors?" She really didn't want to leave her alone but decided from where she stood, it was best for her. Especially since there was activity and she didn't want to worry about how Jordan would react. She was working and her clients deserved her thoroughness.

Jordan looked relieved and tilted the chair against the wall. "What do you want me to do?"

"Just watch them. If you see anything unusual, mark the time and camera number that shows in the corner and write it on the pad in front of you."

"Okay."

"Are you all right, Jordan?"

"Fine, go ahead. I'll play base."

Sunny was glad to see the attentive look on her face as she turned to her assigned job. "Here's my radio."

"No, you need it."

"Shade and Tiff are upstairs. They each have one." Jordan refused again. "Okay then. Yell really loud if you need me." Sunny headed toward the stairs, taking care not to trip on any of the orange cords or construction supplies.

Shade and Tiffany waited on the landing. "What's happening?" Sunny asked.

"Room three three three."

"Power number. What did you see?"

"That's just it," Shade said. "Nothing. I can feel a wall of energy, but it's weirdly blank. I can't get any further." She shrugged.

"Tiff?"

"Me too. I touched the wall and my hand is tingling like crazy, but it's not showing me any history."

The air shifted around Sunny. "Temp?" She held her night vision camera and focused on the door. She twitched when the EMF detector started to squeal while Tiffany swept the hall with it and then steadied herself.

"Sixty-seven and dropping," said Shade. "Sixty-three, fifty-nine, fifty-two."

"Whatever it is, it's big, bad, and powerful. EMF holding at four point two," Tiffany said.

"Okay. Ready?" Shade turned the knob and the door swung open.

❖

Jordan watched the trio, noticing how fluidly they worked together, their movements appearing almost choreographed. She was reminded of the way cops went in on a raid. Sunny went high, Shade low, and Tiffany entered when the others were clear.

Something rattled to her left and she took her eyes off the screen to look. When she glanced back, the hall was empty and she swore. "Damn it." Now she wished she'd taken the radio. She studied the monitor. At least she would be able to see an intruder. A flesh-and-blood one, anyway. But even as she thought it, Jordan couldn't find it as easy to dismiss the possibility of ghosts as she'd done in the past. Tendrils of doubt snaked their way through her, and it pissed her off that she could no longer ignore the possibilities. Her confidence slipped sideways to play with the sanity she lost.

Sunny was beautiful and smart, and Jordan couldn't make herself believe she was capable of any duplicity at all, and now that she'd seen this setup and the way Sunny appeared to be in her element with it, Jordan couldn't convince herself it was any kind of scam. Jordan hated, really hated, to admit she was wrong. But once she saw the facts, she had to. She realized she was one of those people Sunny was talking about, the ones who needed to see electronic proof to believe. It made more sense now, and she focused again on the monitors in front of her.

Movement on camera three, the kitchen again, caught her attention. A utensil swung independent of the others hanging on an overhead rack. Goose bumps raced over her arms, but she dutifully noted the time in the margin.

Jordan was nervous. What were they doing up there? Was Sunny okay?

A large crash in the area had Jordan leaping to her feet and pulling her gun in a fluid motion to hold it out in front of her as she swept the room. Why the hell did they have to keep it so dark? She couldn't see a damn thing. She reached for her Mag light and braced it over her wrist before moving in the direction of the noise. It might be a ghost, but just in case, she wasn't going to be caught by surprise.

❖

"My batteries are dead again."

Shade reached into her cargo pocket and handed a pack to Tiffany.

"Again? We're going through them like water," said Sunny. "Where's your spares?"

"I used them already when I was upstairs."

Sunny heard a high-pitched scream but couldn't tell if it was only in her head or audible. "Did you hear that?"

"Yes," Shade said. "But she's still not showing herself."

Sunny turned the camera toward Tiffany, who wiped her palms

against her jeans, then placed her palm on the wall and closed her eyes.

"It's vibrating a little, but I'm not getting any images."

"Okay," said Sunny. "Why are you hiding from us? We're not here to hurt you." The red light on her camera signaled that her battery was going dead as well. "Damn it." She quickly replaced it. "Are you draining all our power?" She already knew the answer. She was stalling until she could flip the camera on again. "Are you hurt?"

"Sunny?" Shade interrupted.

"What happened to you?"

"Sunny. Look."

She spun with the camera. There, in the corner by the far nightstand, was an orb that held itself in place, pulsating in midair. She heard the clicking of Tiffany's camera taking still shots. Sometimes, when they blew up the pictures, there were faces in the light. Though she could physically see the light energy, she had yet to get any psychic interaction.

"Will you talk to me?" Sadness crushed down on Sunny's shoulders before she heard the voice.

*Hurt.*

❖

Jordan heard another crash ahead of her. The sound was definitely coming from the basement area. Though the evidence of paranormal activity was becoming more valid, the cop in her didn't want to dismiss the idea of an actual intruder. She kept her back close to the wall as she inched toward the stairs and descended slowly. The dank smell assaulted her and she tried not to breathe through her nose. Was it that bad when she was down here earlier? She was reminded of the dark alley she'd been shot in when she lay in the filth, bleeding to death, and the thought disoriented her for a second. Lynn's cruel expression right before she pulled the trigger flashed before her eyes. The stab of betrayal and genuine hurt she'd felt an instant before the white-hot pain in her hip exploded. Lynn's derisive tone while she dismissed her as garbage, unworthy and unwanted. *Grab the money and the dope. Leave the trash here.*

Jordan blinked and found herself outside the boiler room. "No, I am not garbage!" she said to the memory.

*Go to your room, you whiny brat.*

Jordan could almost feel the pinch of her mother's fingers dragging her to the room that she would lock her in while she sold herself to pay the bills and feed her voracious habit. Suddenly, she felt very small. She was three years old and terrified. Footsteps pounded down the hall, and Jordan slid down the wall and sat, unable to stop the vicious memories from assaulting her senses, dragging her into a past she thought she'd escaped.

❖

In her mind's eye, Sunny saw the female spirit shimmer. Loose curls appeared and framed a young, heart-shaped face. "Hello," she said. "What's your name?"

*I'm lost.*

"Who are you?" Sunny glanced at Shade who shook her head. She still wasn't picking up anything. "How did you die?" Sunny opened herself a little more in an attempt to hear her better. The spirit stood still, obviously crying, but mute. "I can't help you if you don't communicate with me."

The letter *F* flashed, then an *R*, *A*, and *N*, consecutively.

"Francine?"

A soft sigh was audible and Sunny took it for assent. "Did you die here, Francine?"

*I'm lost.*

Sunny closed her eyes to better read the image. In the process, she dropped another piece of concentration that held her protective shield, and Francine began to show her the last few minutes of her life.

In a semi-trance, Sunny dictated what she saw for the recorder. "It's hot, so damn hot. She's showing me one of those summer Seattle days that no one is ever prepared for. The windows are open, and she's standing in front of them, fanning herself. She's waiting, but it doesn't feel like any kind of happy anticipation. It feels more like dread."

Sunny held a hand to her heart. "She's lost someone important. Heartache, loss. She feels dirty. I guess that's the best way to describe it. Wait. Someone's knocking on the door. Now she feels like she wants to throw up." Sunny's stomach cramped and she forced herself to swallow the saliva that flooded the back of her throat.

"Sunny, pull back," Shade said and grabbed her arm tightly.

Though she heard her voice, Sunny was too deep in Francine's memory to respond, and she felt herself go deeper before the rest of the explanation came. The woman had lost her husband in a logging accident and, being unable to support herself, she moved to the city where, desperate to survive, she'd had to resort to prostitution.

Sunny watched as Francine walked to the door, twitching when the pounding started on the wood. She turned the knob, opened it, and looked into the dead eyes of her killer.

The man smelled foul with whiskey and unwashed body sweat, and she felt the bile rise again. There was no small talk; he just pushed his way in and grabbed her before kicking the door shut behind him.

❖

*Jordan, you filthy girl. You wet the bed again. Get up! Christ, it stinks in here.*

"Mama, I tried to get up and go, but the door was locked and then the bad man came in."

*Quit your lying, you little bitch. I swear I don't know why I had you. You're a liar and nothing but a pain in my ass. All you do is whine and leave me messes to clean up.*

Jordan tried to make herself smaller, wishing she could disappear in the face of her mother's tirade.

*Answer me!*

The slap rocked her head back into the wall and thrust Jordan back to the present. She couldn't tell if the burning on her cheek was from the memory or from the punch she'd taken earlier. She waited until she felt steady enough to stand.

Should she find out what the loud banging was behind the boiler room door or go back upstairs? She knew she was being a coward, but she tried again to convince herself it was some punk-ass kid who slipped by security. She needed it to be something she could fight, something afraid of the power of guns and the law.

But she really didn't believe it. The old, familiar explanations weren't working, and they sounded hollow even to her jaded mind. She held still, shaken and unsure what step she should take next. There was safety in numbers, right? Trusting others was something she'd made sure she never needed to do, and she'd always been able to take care of herself. But now, in a dark, smelly basement where guns and logic both failed her, she realized she might not have a choice.

If she took that first step back down the hallway, it was just as good as admitting defeat. But, her heart argued, if she took that route, it led to the one thing she cared about now. It would take her back to Sunny.

Which way? Further into the bowels of the basement, or into the light where Sunny was? Jordan took a deep breath and ran.

❖

Sunny backed up in the room until her knees hit the bed and she fell onto it, her petticoats tangled around her legs and the man's rotten breath blowing in her face.

*Wait. Not me. Francine. This happened to Francine.*

A dirty hand closed on her breast, twisting it painfully until Sunny gasped. She heard material ripping and her heart skipped a beat. "No! Stop it, Francine. Show me. Don't make me relive it, please!"

The heavy weight lifted from her body, and Shade pulled her into a sitting position, holding on to her to share the connection. "Me, Francine. Show me," Shade said.

Sunny tried to speak past the lump of horror in her throat, but gave up. The bed lowered next to her where Tiffany sat to lay hands on her. She felt Francine's spirit turn her attention to Shade and she breathed deeply, letting the connection go.

"Whoa." Tiffany leaned into her and Sunny pulled the healing energy closer until she felt some of the tension in her body ease. "She's strong."

"It's him," Shade said. "He's the dominant force in here." Shade took her hands off Sunny's back, and she knew it was because Shade had connected with the murderer himself and didn't want to share the menacing energy with her and Tiffany. Shade moved away from them.

Sunny always worried when Shade took on the negative aspects of a haunting. She knew that it cost her, but she always went into the dark willingly and managed to walk out the other side.

The details Shade shared were usually generalized and watered down. It used to make her mad, but over the years, she'd realized it wasn't because Shade didn't think she could handle it; it was that Sunny internalized the emotions and it took her days to recover, even with her mother's and Tiffany's healing. Shade buffered the evil so it couldn't scar Sunny's light spirit.

Shade's grimace was clear on the night vision camera. "What's happening?" Sunny asked.

"He's raping her. He's convinced himself she's loving it and enjoying it thoroughly. Fucking prick." Shade paused, then suddenly she began to laugh, and chills danced on Sunny's spine.

Tiffany's hand tightened around Sunny's. "Maybe we should—"

"No, I'm good." Shade held up a hand to stop their advance. "She has a knife."

Sunny perceived a brief flash of metal.

"I can see it now," said Tiffany. "There's blood on the floor. I think I'm standing in it."

Sunny's pulse sped up. Francine's terror bubbled in the room along with the desperation she felt over the horrific circumstance.

She was prepared this time and mentally slammed the gate

around her mind, instantly shutting the feelings off before they affected her own.

"I can see them on the bed," Tiffany said. "Oh, how horrible!"

"She cut his throat before he snapped her neck," Shade said evenly. "Enough. We know what happened." She stood and cracked her knuckles.

"There's blood everywhere," Tiffany said. She started to tremble slightly.

"Okay, Tiff. Let's go. Time for a break." Sunny pulled her toward the door. "We'll come back, Francine. I promise."

Shade picked up the equipment before leaving the room, and Sunny shut the door behind them. "That was exhausting. Poor Francine." She didn't spare a thought for the man who was killed; in fact, she felt a small thrill that he got what he deserved.

The sound of running boots on the floor below them caught the breath in her throat. They turned in unison to the stairs. "Everyone hears that, right?"

A beam of light made crazy patterns on the walls, dancing as it came closer.

"Sunny?"

"Jordan." Sunny shoved her camera to Tiffany, and hurried toward the sound of Jordan's frantic voice. "Here. I'm coming."

Before she got to the head of the stairs, Jordan reached her and dropped onto a stair, out of breath. Sunny sat next to her. Shade and Tiffany sat behind them.

"Are you okay? Look at me, Jordan." Sunny was glad to see that her eyes were clear and focused. She also realized that it was the first time Jordan had run *to* her. Jordan nodded, and Sunny was glad to see some of the tension leave her shoulders.

"Let's fill in our notes and take that break."

Together, they returned to the lobby. Sunny handed out bottles of water, and they all plopped into seats in front of various pieces of technology.

Sunny looked over at Jordan and Shade huddled in front of the equipment with their heads bent over the keyboards. Apparently, they'd reached an uneasy truce after Jordan offered Shade a lukewarm apology.

Tiffany rested in a chair with her eyes closed. Sunny didn't want to interrupt her because she knew she was meditating after the gruesome scene she'd witnessed in that room. The owners hadn't mentioned anything about a double murder in the hotel, so she doubted they even knew about it. In the early nineteenth century, it would have been easy to sweep something like that under the rug. All you needed was money to grease the right palms and you could make anything go away.

She was just about to join Jordan when something darted across the room just outside the circle of light that the lamp provided.

Sunny stood and took a few steps toward the direction the shadow disappeared. "Hello," she called before clicking her recorder on. "Where did you go?"

"See something?" Shade asked, looking up from the desk.

"Shadow at two o'clock. Mark the time, please." Sunny was all business again but startled when Jordan touched her elbow. She hadn't heard her approach, but welcomed the body heat that warmed her back.

"Who are you?" Tiffany stood then crossed to the old wooden banister to place her hand on it. "Oh, I see a party." She smiled. "One of those grand ones, you know? Where the women all wear frilly dresses and the men are in suits with tails. There's dancing, waiters are passing out finger food and fancy glasses of champagne."

"How does she do that? I can't see or hear anything," Jordan whispered so as not to distract Tiffany.

No automatic denial, thought Sunny. No disbelief pouring out of Jordan. She was asking questions, not shutting down. The realization made her happy and she kissed her quickly.

"What was that for?"

"For believing." *For running to me.*

"Working here," Shade said. "That's on tape."

"Sorry." Sunny reluctantly stepped away and smiled at Jordan before focusing on the room again. Even after her terrifying experience in the basement, Jordan found herself becoming fascinated with the investigation process. She had dozens of questions but didn't know which one to ask first.

"If you're going to follow Sunny around for the rest of the night, make yourself useful," Shade said.

Jordan crossed to the desk and took the camera in Shade's hand.

"Thanks, *Lacey*." Jordan smirked, and then turned her back when Shade hissed at her. That felt good. She felt like a part of the team. After taking a few minutes to familiarize herself with the equipment, Jordan focused the lens on Sunny, who was standing next to Tiffany and speaking into the recorder.

"Elderly man in a black top hat, showing me a name. Gerald? Jerry? No, Gerald. Yes? Thank you. He says it's his hotel and he's showing me a clock with the hands spinning round and round." She looked at Jordan. "That's my sign for the passing of a long time. Now I see a lot of people going in and out the front door with boxes and crates."

"Several owners?" asked Jordan.

"Yes, exactly that. Very good."

Jordan was ridiculously pleased with Sunny's approving tone.

"The ball is over," Tiffany said. "He's sitting alone on the stairs with his face in his hands."

Sunny picked up where Tiffany left off. "Gerald is tired, so very tired of watching his beloved hotel go to rot."

"But they're restoring it," Jordan said. She tried not to cringe at how inane it seemed for her to try to reassure a ghost.

"There are men with tools running out the door."

"You can see all that just by touching the wood?"

"Tiffany can see the past and pick up the energy left behind in the environment," Sunny explained. "Everyone leaves an imprint, a physical trace of where they've been, and what they've experienced. The intensity of the emotions they felt during the situation is what determines how powerful the energy is that remains after they're gone. That's why Tiffany felt the party first. The larger the crowd, the stronger the imprint is in the area."

That made sense. Now that she thought about it, Jordan could recall many times she'd been to a crime scene, and before she'd even seen what carnage had been left behind, or smelled the blood, the location *felt* different. She had always thought it was experience, a cop's intuition.

A breeze lifted her hair a second before Sunny announced that Gerald had disappeared. Tiffany drew her hand back and swore.

"What?" Jordan asked.

"Do you feel how cold it's getting?"

Her chest felt a little heavy, and Jordan was finding it difficult to catch her breath. Was it her imagination or did it get darker in the room? No, that's stupid, she told herself. It was already dark. A loud screech rent the air. It appeared to be coming from nowhere, but echoing everywhere. She was instantly on the balls of her feet, ready. Ready for what, Jordan wasn't sure, but she pulled Sunny behind her anyway. "Please tell me you heard that."

"We heard it."

"Thank God. Where is it coming from?"

"Basement." Shade pushed away from the desk and headed for the door.

"Shit." Jordan's fledgling sense of fun and adventure flew right out the window. She had to grudgingly admit she admired the hell out of Shade's bravery.

Sunny followed Shade, keeping ahead of Jordan even as she continually tried to walk in front of her. "Stop that!"

"Can't help it. Habit, sorry." *My job.*

Shade stopped suddenly and Jordan ran into her.

"Not your job here, cop. Not to piss you off or anything, but it's ours."

"It's really creepy, Lacey, how you read my mind."

"Don't call me that," Shade said between clenched teeth.

"Quit it, you two," Tiffany said. "You can have your pissing contest later. I just want to finish the job and go home, okay?"

Since Shade again took the lead, Jordan dropped to the rear and followed the group. "Eww," Sunny said. "This stench wasn't here earlier. Mark that."

"What do you mean, mark that?" Jordan asked.

"For the report. When we listen to playback, we'll add it to our findings for the owners."

They reached the bottom of the staircase, and Jordan wondered what they were waiting for. Her muscles tensed with anticipation and adrenaline began pumping faster through her bloodstream until she thought she might scream.

*Help!*

"Disembodied voice heard," Sunny said into the recorder. "Did you hear it?"

"Are you fucking kidding me? Of course I heard it." Jordan heard it loud and clear but stood frozen in place. Two weeks ago, she wouldn't have believed any of this or would have had rational explanations handy for it if she had. How the hell was she supposed to switch gears so quickly? Her stomach churned with the effort.

The women fanned in front of her, holding out various pieces of equipment and walking toward the voice. Jordan sure as hell didn't want to be left behind. She forced her feet to move. She hated feeling scared and uncertain. It pissed her off and made her cranky. "Can't we turn on the goddamn lights?"

Tiffany laughed. "I'm all for it. I hate the basements. We always do investigations in the dark. It's usually when places are more paranormally active."

Jordan tried to get used to looking through the viewfinder of the camera to see where she was going.

"Nasty man ahead." Shade stopped.

"Where? I don't see anyone."

"You should be thankful. Half his head is blown away."

Jordan swept the hall with the camera.

"Sunny, don't even talk to him. He's just a distraction; a sideshow to keep us from going in there. And, Tiffany? Don't touch anything yet."

"Does anyone else hear growling?"

"Ignore it. Scare tactics. Here. Put your camera down for a second."

Jordan dropped her arm and stared into the dark. Ignore it? How did one ignore a rabid ghost? Was there some sort of trick to it she needed to learn? Shade rustled in her backpack and Jordan yelped when something sprayed in her face. She swung her fist, hitting only air when Shade jumped back.

"It's just holy water." Shade laughed.

"Again with the water in the face. What's wrong with you?"

"Shade," Sunny said. "You could have warned her."

"I thought you guys weren't religious."

Sunny kept a gentle but restraining arm around her waist. "We're not. But chances are"—she pointed down the hallway—"*they* are. It doesn't matter what we believe. When we're dealing with spirits, it matters what they believe will hurt them that's important."

Jordan's head was swimming and water dripped from her face into her collar. "What if *they* don't believe?"

"Then we have a problem." Shade sprayed Sunny and Tiffany. "Ready?"

"No," Jordan muttered but continued her pace at the rear of the line.

They entered the dark area and stopped. Sunny turned on her flashlight, shining it into corners and along the beams. Aside from broken drywall and a few stray boards, it was empty. A hallway lined with doors led to the right off the main room.

"This must have been the sitting room," Tiffany said. "There's a couple of those big stuffed chairs and a table over there." She pointed to an empty corner. "There's a large desk here. It's very dreary, actually."

"Tiffany. Take your hand off the wall, now." Shade tried to stop her, but it was too late.

"But—oh."

Jordan followed her voice with the camera and saw Tiffany bend over and start retching; Sunny came into the viewfinder as she hurried over to help.

"What is it?" Jordan asked.

"Murders," Shade said grimly.

"I'm sorry. Did you just say murders, as in plural?"

"Yes."

"How do you know?"

Shade looked at her, her eyes cold and empty through the little camera window. "I can see them."

"Tiffany, honey, do you want to leave?" Sunny helped her take off the backpack and removed her own so she could sit with her. "We can go if you need to."

"No, this is important." Tiffany closed her eyes and took a couple of deep breaths. "Let's get on with it. And I'm going to want a really strong drink when this is over."

Sunny was proud of Tiffany. She hadn't always been able to face her fears. She felt some apprehension of her own but cut it off. She'd never had any problems with investigations or spirits attacking her until recently. She ground her teeth against the doubt and forced herself to let it go completely. "Shade?"

The metal click of a lighter sounded incredibly loud in the silence, but she welcomed the small light as Shade lit three white candles and settled across from them. "Jordan?"

"What are we doing?"

"Here, sit down, please. We're going to attempt to find out what happened here."

"What about the camera?"

"We have one in the corner over there that we set up earlier." Sunny felt *other* tap the top of her head. "But you can still film from here if you like."

Once Jordan settled next to her, Sunny welcomed the warmth of her legs alongside her own. "Once we start, keep still, okay?"

"All right."

"And no screaming," Shade said.

Jordan snorted. "As if. What are we going to do, solve a hundred-year-old massacre?"

Sunny heard the sarcasm in her voice but told herself it would take baby steps. At least Jordan hadn't run or completely shut out the possibilities.

"Not old," Tiffany said. "Recent. I can tell by the way they're dressed."

Jordan's leg stiffened and Sunny knew that the answer poked at her cop's instincts. Okay, she thought, time to go to work. "We know you're here. Can you tell us why?" Silence thundered in her ears before she heard a faint murmuring. It was too low; she was finding it difficult to decipher what they were saying. "Something is holding them back, keeping them from talking to me."

"Them?" Jordan twitched again.

Shade rested her hands on her knees and closed her eyes. Her features looked serene, but Sunny knew that inside, she was bracing herself to wrestle with whatever bad entity was here. It was her gift, the ability to physically interact on the spiritual plane. She would find and attempt to distract and hold back the entity that was interfering and blocking the other spirits from communicating with Sunny.

Sunny knew when Shade connected with the entity because the candlelight flickered, and shadows danced along the walls in the windowless room. She reached into her own bag for her lighter, just in case, and handed it to Jordan. "Light them again if they go out." Jordan's eyes were wide with surprise, but she looked more curious than truly afraid. Good.

Sunny felt a trace of the psychic barrier between them slip to the side, and a trace of Jordan's emotions slipped out and over to Sunny. Her heart lightened. Having Jordan's confidence and trust, rather than her fear and skepticism, would help tremendously.

"Got him," Shade snarled. "Asshole."

Three separate spirits, two female and one male, rushed forward, all talking very fast and bombarding Sunny with their stories. "One at a time."

"Could you give us a sign for the recorders, please?" Tiffany asked. "How many are here with us?"

Three distinct knocks sounded from the wall behind Sunny. Jordan's body jerked, but to her credit, she didn't say anything. "Thank you. If you can, or want to, you can also talk to the red light in front of me."

An image of a young girl began to take form behind her eyes. "Okay," Sunny said. "She's young. Sixteen, seventeen? Blond hair, blue eyes. Seventeen, she says. The letter *B*. Barbie? Really? Is that your given name? She's nodding."

"I see her now," Tiffany said. "Blue shirt and short black skirt that she's wearing with cowboy boots."

"Hold it there. Two more are coming forward. One is a young man, and the other is jumping up and down, waving her arms in the air. It's okay. We're going to talk to all of you."

"Three?" Jordan asked.

"Yes. And I hear the name Ray, very clearly. He's indicating that he's the same age as the girl next to him. Is that correct? And that they knew each other in life." Sunny paused. "Tiffany?"

"He's about five foot seven maybe, wearing ripped jeans and some kind of mesh tank top."

"Christ!" Jordan said.

"What?"

"Something just poked me in the shoulder."

There was an audible sigh from the center of the circle followed by a fierce growling. "Not today, prick," Shade said. "You have no power here tonight."

"Sunny? What's going on?"

"Um, Jordan? I don't want to scare you, but the third spirit is right next to you. She seems very excited to see you."

Jordan's head ached. There was something nagging at her, like she should be remembering something important. This whole night had been surreal, to say the least. Maybe she'd lost her mind after all and she'd be waking up in the hospital and finding that the last eighteen months had all been a dream or illusion while she was in a coma.

Sunny's arm draped over her shoulders. No, thought Jordan, she wasn't crazy. Sunny's warmth surrounded her, and Jordan's jitters let up slightly. What had Sunny just said to her? She laughed nervously. "I'm sorry. I thought I just heard you say that this ghost knows me."

"I did."

"Crap, it's not my mother again, is it?"

"Nope."

The hair on her body prickled, chilling her, and Jordan

swallowed. If she could handle perps with guns, she could handle this paranormal shit, right? "Okay." She winced when she heard her voice crack.

"Ready?" asked Sunny. "This girl says she knows you. She's showing me the image of you in your uniform. She's, uh, very attracted to you."

"Excuse me?"

"She's very attractive, but young. She's jealous of me," Sunny said. "And she says you had lousy taste in your previous relationships."

"Who *is* it?" And how bizarre could this be, being chastised by a ghost?

"Okay, sorry. I'll ask. Sometimes they don't always answer. Oh no, no, honey, don't cry. She saying she's cold, so cold. She's confused now. Could you help us with your name, sweetie?"

Sunny called to Shade. "She's really scared. I can't get a clear image of her, and she keeps fading in and out."

Shade's eyebrows drew together in concentration. "He's snapping at me. He doesn't want her to talk, especially her, because she's the favorite." She paused. "It's okay. He's not as strong as he thinks he is. I'm not even breaking a sweat over here."

Footsteps shuffled along the cement corridor. Shade chuckled. "He's thinking he's going to distract me enough to let go."

"What is Shade doing? What does she mean by that?"

*Kill the fucking cop.* The voice that bellowed out of Shade's throat was not her own. It was a deep, raucous sound that chilled her to the bone.

"What did you just say?"

"Oooh, Jordan." Shade's voice returned. "He does not like you."

"Enough!" Jordan snapped. "What the fuck is going on?" She tried grappling with all the vague half explanations she was being given, and her instincts were screaming that she was missing something. The nasty comment did manage to pierce her confusion. Jordan switched to logic, looking for facts now instead of innuendo.

"Don't let him get a rise out of you, Jordan," Sunny said. "It's what he wants."

"Who—it—what—wants? Can't we cut to the chase here?"

"If you can calm down, I'll try and find out," Sunny said under her breath. "See? Now the spirits are upset. They're all chattering at once again and giving me a headache." She held a hand to her forehead. "Shh."

A gust of wind blew out the candles, and Jordan heard Tiffany's sharp intake of breath. She ignored the chill between her shoulder blades and relit them. She'd felt goose bumps so many times tonight she was getting used to them.

"Right, okay," Sunny said. "The younger one is coming forward again."

Jordan tried to relax the stiffness in her body, but her mind was racing. Still, she had the feeling she was missing something vital, a crucial, essential clue that kept slipping away before she could grasp it. Jordan waited for Sunny to continue, though she was sorry when she took her arm back and shifted on the cement to get more comfortable.

"She's losing energy. We only have a few minutes. From what she's showing me, she has straight brown hair, brown eyes, and—"

"But that's not what I see," Tiffany interrupted. "I see very short dark hair, dyed jet-black, and lots of piercings. Ouch, didn't those hurt?"

Jordan's heart skipped a beat and something clicked. Was this for real or some kind of cruel joke? "What is she wearing?" She tried to keep her anger in check while she pulled up the mental file from her memory.

"Some kind of short dress, with a long zipper up the front, torn stockings, and knee-high boots, you know, the clunky kind?"

"She's showing me the letter *G*, then a star. Come on, sweetheart, give me a little more here. Gina? Or Star?" Sunny asked.

"Both," Jordan said. The flames leaned sideways and Jordan jumped to her feet. "That's impossible!" she yelled. "Did you read my files?"

"Either sit down or go back upstairs, Jordan," Sunny said

quietly. "This isn't about you. It's about these three kids. I don't have the time or energy to fight with you right now."

Sunny cut off her own anger at Jordan's outburst to keep from feeding the negative entity that Shade was holding on to in the astral plane. But she knew that Jordan's explosive reaction fed it a great deal of power, and she knew she was right when Shade swore and slumped forward.

"I tried to hold him, but he slipped out."

"Are you okay?" Sunny went to Shade and felt the muscles in her back tremble slightly. Tiffany crawled over and laid her hands next to Sunny's. In a matter of seconds, Sunny felt the shaking subside, then stop.

Jordan stood a few feet away with her back against the wall. They all jumped when a door slammed violently down the hall.

Shade gained her feet and grabbed a camera and recorder. Tiffany turned on her flashlight and followed, blowing the candles out on her way. "Let's go see what that was." The two of them turned right out of the doorway, and the light in the room faded as they moved further away, leaving Sunny to deal with Jordan.

She was still trying not to be angry with her. She loved everything about her, except this one thing. But the one thing was so important, she might have to walk away after all. "Jordan," she began in a calm voice.

"No. God, Sunny. I'm so sorry. It was reflex."

Well, now, she wasn't expecting to hear that, and she understood that the habits of a lifetime were hard to break. Jordan's voice was sincere in the dark, even if she choked on the apology. She got the feeling that Jordan didn't do it very often, and it must have cost her something. She tried talking again. "Nobody read your files, Jordan."

"I'm trying here, Sunny. But you don't understand. These kids you're describing are the missing street kids I told you about. I could recite in my sleep what they were all wearing the last time they were seen. I looked for them for months, but it's as if they disappeared off the face of the earth. And to sit here and hear those details while I'm sitting in the dark during some kind of psychic orgy, well, it threw me off."

"Psychic orgy? Should I be insulted?"

"No, it just slipped out. I'm only digging myself deeper here."

"They all died here," Sunny said softly. "The murderer is dead as well. That's the entity that Shade was fighting."

"Who is it? Was it?" she corrected herself.

"I don't know. They're gone. They disappeared when Shade lost her hold on the murderer." Sunny felt Jordan's tentative hand touch her shoulder.

"Again, I'm sorry, really. Beliefs don't change overnight, do they? Can we do it again? I'll be quiet this time."

"I don't think we have it in us to repeat this tonight." When Jordan's arms came around her, they were gentle and comforting, and Sunny let herself melt into the embrace for a moment. "We'll talk later, okay?"

Jordan let go of her and dropped her arms to her sides. She reminded herself that Jordan's awakening would take time. Sunny had never been in that position, but she respected the honesty and emotional effort Jordan had just shown her. She understood how hard that would be for someone as rigid as Jordan. "Everything is fine. Let's go help the others."

## CHAPTER FIFTEEN

Jordan had just taken Sunny's hand to lead her into the hall when another scream pierced the darkness.

"Tiffany." Sunny ran down the hall. Jordan turned on her flashlight and chased her, but she filled with dread when she saw the door to the boiler room standing open.

How could her experience in that room when she'd arrived have slipped from her mind for even a second? In that instant, Jordan understood the power of denial. How a mind could build barriers to see only what it chose to, regardless of the evidence. There was power in admitting she couldn't control or explain everything. There was freedom in that understanding. Her legs felt weak and she sat next to Tiffany in the dank room.

"Why did you scream?" Sunny asked.

"Sorry, guys. I don't usually fall apart like this all the time," she said to Jordan. "But the energy in this building is so damn strong, it's keeping me off balance."

"Tell me about it," Jordan mumbled.

"I saw him."

"Who?" Sunny asked.

"The man who murdered those kids."

"Where?" Jordan looked around the room.

"Here." Tiffany pointed to her forehead.

Jordan was dizzy but curious. "Do you all see him the same?"

"No," they answered in unison.

"Then how do you know which is real?"

"I'll go," Shade said. "Sunny sees spirits the way they want to be seen. Tiffany perceives them as they actually were."

"And you?" asked Jordan.

"I see them how they looked at the moment of death."

Jordan let that sink in. Shade's whole personality made more sense to her. "So you're all correct in one way or another."

"Yes."

Jordan's analytical mind raced. How come the department didn't use people who had these abilities to solve more crimes?

"Because they see like you," Shade said.

"And you can read minds."

Shade smirked. "Most of the time, but not always. But you're wide open right now."

"Tiffany? Is the recorder running?" Sunny asked.

"Yes."

"Describe him, please." Sunny searched for the presence of *other,* but whoever he was, he couldn't or wouldn't show himself. She knew Tiffany was picking up the residual imprint.

"He's creepy." Tiffany shuddered. "Tall, skinny, stringy hair, bad complexion. He's wearing a stained gray sweatshirt, black cargo pants. He's muttering to himself and laughing. Oh, the stains are blood, I think, but I don't think it's his. He's fumbling with something behind the furnace." Tiffany paused and tilted her head to the left. "Gross! Pervert." She pulled her hand off the wall. "Eww."

"Shade," Sunny called. "Do you see anything?"

"No, and I doubt I will. He was pretty shocked that I was able to hold him. He's afraid of me."

"How did you do that?" Jordan asked.

"We'll explain that later." Sunny stood and inched her way to the furnace in the corner.

"He's taking off the sweatshirt and trying to clean himself up."

"Is all of this what you call residual?"

"Yes."

"So it can't hurt anyone?"

"Not when it's place memory."

"Jordan, could you shine your light over here? Your flashlight has more power than mine."

"Okay," Tiffany continued. "He's pulling something out of a bag. It looks like a red shirt and some kind of baseball hat."

Something clicked in Jordan's memory, and her blood turned to ice in her veins. She turned the beam into Tiffany's face.

"Hey! You're blinding me."

"Sorry." Jordan immediately lowered her arm. "Tiffany, this is really important. Can you see what color shoes he's wearing?"

"They're really dirty. I can't tell. No, wait. Really, dude? They're some kind of weird neon turquoise? I think."

Jordan felt a sense of foreboding, and she pulled the memory closer. Could it really be true? No one here could have known the color of that man's shoes. What were the odds?

"Jordan?" Sunny lay a hand on her arm. "What is it?"

"Just a second. I need to hear what else he does."

"He's digging something up from behind there." She pointed. "One of those green army duffel bags. You know the kind?"

Yes, she did. And she knew what was in it. "Can you see any patches or identifying marks?"

"A stained smiley face? How did you know?"

Jordan took a breath and closed her eyes. "Because I killed him."

"Dude." Shade shook her head.

"Can we turn the lights on now? I need to see behind the furnace."

"Of course. Tiff, could you flip the switch?" Sunny was concerned over the implication of recent murders being attached to Jordan.

They all blinked their eyes to adjust to the brightness after so many hours in the dark. Jordan disappeared behind the metal giant.

"Can you tell us what happened?" Sunny knew Jordan had been shot after she killed a man near here, but she didn't know the details of how this might all tie together yet. No wonder she had negative energy woven as tightly as a basket around her. "The dirt looks off to me. Shade, can you help me?"

There wasn't room for all of them, so Sunny and Tiffany stood to the side.

"There has to be a shovel lying around here somewhere."

"I'll find one," Tiffany said. "I'll be right back."

"Jordan? Gina is here." Tears filled Sunny's eyes. "She says she always knew you would find her."

The overhead light went off then turned back on. "Asshole is back, and he's quite pissed off you found his hidey hole," Shade said, looking over Jordan's shoulder.

Tiffany ran back in and handed the shovel to Sunny, who gave it to Jordan. She met her gaze and nodded once.

"I'll hold him, but it's really not necessary. He's losing power fast," Shade said before Sunny distinctly heard the sound of digging.

"Oh, fuck me," Jordan said.

The smell of death filled the room. "Are those what I think they are under that old tarp?"

"Yes," Jordan answered. "C'mon, we have to go."

"Aren't we going to—"

"No. It's a crime scene now."

❖

Sunny looked over and saw Jordan framed in the doorway of Eric and Frank's apartment. Her gaze darted around the room before she saw her, and Sunny saw the relief soften the hard lines around her eyes.

"Can we leave yet?" Shade asked. "No offense," she added to Frank, who looked shell-shocked in the chair across from them.

"They'll call up when we can go." Jordan sat down and Sunny took her hand before leaning against her and dropping her head on her shoulder.

Eric came in with a tray and poured more coffee. "What are we going to do?" He was clearly upset. "Who's going to want to come and stay here after this publicity?"

"We've borrowed a fortune, and our life savings have gone into the hotel." Frank's hands shook, but he steadied them to gulp his coffee.

"You'd be surprised," Shade said. "Ghost fanatics, the curious, and the thrill seekers. Sad, but true. Haunted castles and shit like that make a fortune in England too."

Sunny let her eyes close while the conversation went on around her. The police had been downstairs for three hours, and gray morning light filtered through the apartment windows.

Jordan shifted and put an arm around her, holding her closer. Sunny was proud of the way Jordan had handled herself and the situation. After she went out to talk to the security officer in charge and they called homicide, the place had been swarmed with people in less than half an hour.

Jordan had to step back from the process because not only was she currently on suspension, it was also tied to a case that she was personally involved in.

Sunny recalled the way Jordan's eyes had flashed fire when she got in the face of a detective who was first on the scene. He had been condescending and rude to the women when he heard why they were there. He made Jordan leave and separated the team, but once Jordan had gotten him alone, his tone seemed more respectful when he next questioned Sunny for her version of events.

Sunny could have told Jordan that she was quite capable of taking care of herself, but she found she didn't want to. It felt good to let her take charge of the situation. She felt protected.

After they were questioned two more times, they were allowed to congregate in the owners' apartment, where Sunny called her mother and asked her to clear the schedule for a few days. She only had to argue with her for ten minutes to convince her to stay home. It was getting easier, this thing called setting boundaries.

"Who are we going to get for the construction work now?" Frank's voice threatened to break.

"You're going to have to wait until they clear the building for use again. It could take a while for them to process the crime scene and evidence."

"I can help you there." Shade leaned back. "I know a crew out of Bremerton that would be happy for the work, and they come with excellent references."

"But what about the ghosts?"

"It won't bother them a bit." Shade chuckled. "It's an all-female crew. Not only will you get better attention to detail, but my friends are made of pretty stern stuff. I'll also come back and clear the place of the darker energy. It's kind of like dealing with bullies. Once you stand up to them, they run."

"See, honey?" Eric said to Frank. "I told you calling these girls was the best thing to do."

Sunny felt Shade bristle at the "girl" remark, but she didn't say anything. Tiffany was sound asleep in the armchair, and Sunny hoped she was having sweet dreams, not reliving the horror in the basement. She sent out her senses to check and was relieved to find Tiffany's energy was calm.

She was unbelievably tired, but at the same time she was aware of every inch of her body that came into contact with Jordan's.

"What else did you find?" Frank asked. "I'm almost afraid to know, but I can't help but be curious."

Sunny roused herself to answer him. "I'm sorry, guys. The detectives confiscated our evidence."

"It could take months to get it back," Jordan said. "And I'm sure I'll never live it down."

Sunny heard the sadness in her voice and squeezed her hand. There would be time to talk later.

"Lawson."

"Sir."

"You can go now." The detective turned to Eric and Frank. "Is there somewhere you can stay for a few days?"

"Hawaii," Eric said quickly and pointed to Eric. "We're taking a vacation right now."

The detective nodded and turned to Jordan. "You know the drill, blah, blah."

"You'll let me know when forensics is finished, right?"

"Clearly, I'm not obliged to let you know, as you're on suspension." He paused and Jordan's mouth tightened into a straight line. "But," he added, "I'll still extend the professional courtesy. That all right with you, Lawson?"

Jordan nodded. "Thank you."

"Now go on. Get out of here and let us do our job."

❖

Jordan helped load the equipment that hadn't been seized and ignored the veiled insults she heard from the uniforms. What was worse was realizing that until tonight, she'd sounded just as ignorant and close-minded as they currently did. She would be standing there doing the same exact thing if Sunny hadn't blasted through her wall of denial. God, had she sounded so sanctimonious and self-righteous? Had she been so willing to ridicule what she didn't understand?

She was ashamed to admit she had. No wonder Sunny had walked away in the face of her scorn. It felt horrible. The night's crazy events and Sunny had changed something inside her, and she knew her life would never be the same.

Sunny put an arm around her waist. "Can I ride with you?"

"Of course." Jordan smiled down at her, sorry to see the dark circles under her eyes and the worry lines etched in her beautiful face. She knew she looked much worse, with her own battered cheek and filthy clothes.

"We need to talk."

Jordan's gut tightened. "Sunny—"

"In our room at the Hilton that the boys just gave me."

Jordan nearly swayed with relief. "Hot tub?"

Sunny flashed the key card and grinned. "Hot tub."

❖

Sunny was tempted to fall face-first into the lake-size bed and sleep for a week, but she was disciplined enough in her craft to know she wouldn't or couldn't rest until she was clean of the night's energy.

Jordan leaned against her almost wearily. Sunny realized she must have been up for over twenty-four hours at this point.

Even after the grueling night, Sunny was struck at how comfortable being with Jordan felt. She wasn't craving the solitude that was required after an investigation to unwind.

The night felt like the passing of a week's time, and it wasn't over yet. Jordan's energy was finally wide-open to Sunny, and she could feel every nuance of her anxiety and the loneliness echoing in her soul.

These were things she could and would heal for her. Sunny turned to hold her. Sorrow, blue and heavy, swam into Sunny's consciousness. Jordan was grieving.

"Let's get cleaned up, then we'll talk, okay?"

"We don't have clean clothes," Jordan said.

"Says you. I gave the concierge a list on the way in. They'll be up soon."

"You don't have my sizes."

"Hello? Psychic here. Go on. Into the shower with you. You'll be better for it."

"Come with me?"

"I have some things to take care of first. Hurry up and join me in the hot tub when you're done."

Jordan tried not to be disappointed when she shut the door. The pure opulence of the bathroom, hell, the whole building, made her feel especially dirty. She'd never been in such a nice place, and she felt like an imposter. Two fluffy white robes hung on a hook next to the shower that would comfortably hold six people. Rich marble gleamed under a crystal chandelier. She was so damn tired that even lifting her shirt took great effort.

She caught sight of her reflection in the large, gold-framed mirror. Christ, she'd looked better after being shot. No wonder Sunny didn't want to come in with her.

Jordan turned her gaze away from the image, then sat to take off her boots. She tried to hear what Sunny was doing in the other room but gave up. Moving her muscles at all felt like swimming through mud. All she wanted to do was close her eyes.

The water pressure was awesome, and Jordan stood under the stream of hot water, letting it pour over her head before positioning herself so the stream pulsated between her shoulder blades. The dirt washed away in black pools, and as it did, she felt lighter, more awake.

The fancy shampoo smelled a little girly for her taste, but she didn't have much of a choice. Jordan tried not to think about anything at all except removing the filth of the basement from her skin.

What about the weight of emotional dirt? Her chest and mind felt heavy with regret over the horrible way those kids had died. Most disturbing of all was the burning of unshed tears behind her eyelids and the tightness in her throat.

❖

Sunny took a psychic shower first. Closing her eyes, she pictured the white light gathering strength in the palms of her hands, growing brighter until her scalp tingled. Starting at the top of her head, with each sweep of her hands, she pushed the lingering negative energy down her legs, then imagined it draining out the soles of her feet. A discreet knock on the door diverted her from her path to the bathroom to join Jordan. The concierge himself stood on the other side with several bags, and a waiter behind him pushed a serving cart into the room.

She smiled inwardly, giving them credit for their discretion training. Neither of them blinked at her bedraggled appearance.

"Thank you. I'll leave the cart outside when we're done. Could you please make sure we're not disturbed?"

"Of course."

Sunny signed the credit slip, leaving a generous tip. "Keep my card. I'd like to stay an additional night, please."

"As you wish. I'll take care of it."

Sunny gave him her best dimpled smile before ushering them

out. She looked longingly at the closed bathroom door. She could hear the water running and wanted nothing more than to go to Jordan. But she knew it wasn't quite time for that yet.

They still had one more ghost to deal with.

Instead, she turned on the hot tub and generously sprinkled salt into the frothy water.

❖

Jordan stepped out of the bathroom in time to see Sunny slip under the water in the hot tub. The rich smell of coffee drew her to the cart, but she kept her eyes on the rolling water.

Sunny's scent of honeysuckle and roses whispered to her senses and brought an awareness of yearning that made her knees weak. When Sunny came up for air, water streaming over her beautiful skin, the night's horror slipped away.

She wondered if this was what other people felt when they went to church, this wonder and need to worship something good and beautiful, longing to connect with something greater than themselves. Jordan wanted this more than anything she'd ever desired in her life, and she was afraid to even hope that she might have a place here, that she was worthy. That she deserved love.

Could she do this? Jordan took a shaky step toward Sunny then another.

Jordan's heart hammered in her chest, and she lowered herself carefully into the water next to Sunny.

Sunny's eyes were clear and bright as she smiled at her, mysterious and soft. She moved close enough to touch her face and kissed her forehead, each eyelid, her cheeks, the tip of her nose, her lips caressing Jordan's face before stopping to press against her mouth.

Jordan felt weightless in the water. The only sensation was this kiss and her connection to Sunny. She was afraid to breathe, scared to death that if she moved, the moment would slip away and she would never, ever get it back.

Sunny moved closer until she straddled Jordan's lap and wrapped her arms around her, bringing their chests together. Jordan tentatively laid her head on Sunny's shoulder.

Was this what home felt like? Jordan wondered. She felt light but complete when their hearts and breath shifted into tandem beats. With nothing to prove or justify to herself, Jordan relaxed for the first time in longer than she could remember. If ever.

"Let me love you," Sunny whispered.

Jordan's breath caught in the lump that formed in her throat before she tightened her embrace around Sunny. "You can't."

"Hasn't anyone ever loved you, Jordan?"

"No."

"The fact that you can answer that so quickly and with one word breaks my heart, but I can show you what it feels like, and how wonderful it really can be."

"I don't know how." Jordan shook her head. "You're too good for me."

"What does that mean exactly? Who gets to define your worth?"

Jordan didn't respond right away. "I've killed people, Sunny. It doesn't matter if they deserved it or not. I killed that man, and I know I would do it all over again for what he did to those kids. And hear this clearly—I would enjoy it."

"Don't you think that I might have that thought as well?"

"Your heart is so pure, Sunny. You don't have it in you, and I don't want to taint that. I just can't."

"Jordan, what you have or have not done in your life does *not* reflect who you are." She paused and placed her right hand over Jordan's heart. "It's not who you are in here."

"But—"

"Shh. Listen. Those things are physical acts that color the way that you look at the world. Your soul *is*—it's everything positive that you could ever imagine. Spirit is the essence of you, a Divine light that's eternal and doesn't have any boundaries. The light loves and accepts you just the way you are. The only limits you think you have are those that your mind and beliefs impose on you."

Jordan heard the words and even felt some weird recognition. She couldn't remember a time in her adult life that she'd felt so vulnerable. She was tired on a soul level, the kind that made you want to go to sleep because you didn't have the energy to deal with one more minute of life.

"Let's get out," Sunny said.

Jordan let Sunny help her to the side of the bed and dry her off, but other than that, she seemed incapable of mustering any energy. She sank into the soft mattress and had just closed her eyes when Sunny climbed in next to her and sat cross-legged.

"Honey?"

"Mmm."

"Your mother's here."

Jordan closed her eyes. "Sunny, please." She felt a little desperate. "I can't take any more tonight." The lump reappeared in her throat and her eyes began to sting.

"Do you trust me?"

"Yes." Jordan was momentarily surprised at her quick answer, but realized that she did have faith in her. Trust was a luxury she hadn't had since she was old enough to know her life was different and not everyone's mother hated their children. She swallowed the rising heartache that threatened to explode in a shower of tears she hadn't shed since she was a child.

"She's says she's so very sorry."

Jordan's temper spiked. "Now, that just pisses me off. *Sorry?* For what exactly? Is it for the hateful remarks, or is it for every slap and kick she gave me? Maybe it's for every occasion she locked me in my room because I was in the way. How about for every time I went hungry so she could buy dope? Or is she sorry that she made me feel unwanted and unloved for every second of my life before she killed herself and left me alone? Sorry? She should be."

"I'm sorry this hurts you, Jordan. But let her say what she needs to say, and then we can let her go, okay? And if you want to talk about it, just you and I, someday, we will. Okay?"

Jordan nodded, too weary to argue, and wrapped an arm around Sunny's waist, drawing strength from her.

"She says she didn't mean to hurt you, that it wasn't until she was on the other side where it was shown to her what she did that she realized how horrible her actions toward you were." Sunny stared at a space next to Jordan. "Oh, she's showing me. Oh, God. Don't you know you didn't deserve that? She says none of it was your fault. There was something broken inside her, something in her soul that made her incapable of seeing, really seeing you." Sunny stopped and squeezed Jordan's hand, kissing her cheek before going on. "Jordan, she didn't know any different. She's not blaming anyone but herself, and she wants you to know she didn't know any other way. She's showing me her childhood, and it's horrible. Her father drank and did unspeakable things to her."

Jordan felt as if her life was uncoiling from beneath her. She nodded to show she was listening.

"Now she's telling me that at first, the drugs took away the pain."

"What pain?" Jordan asked.

"The pain of simply being and breathing in and out."

"I know the feeling."

"She says she would take it all back if she could. She would undo every moment and fill you with love. She would take every opportunity to tell you how precious you were and never waste one second or hesitate to show you how proud she is of you. She's showing me an image of a rolling trash can? Is it in an alley? I can't see it very well."

Jordan jerked next to her. "The night I was shot. If I hadn't tripped over that trash can, I would have been killed." She shuddered. "My mother did that?"

"Apparently. She's fading back a little but wants to remind you of the day on the beach. She says it was the best day in her life too. She's blowing kisses and says be happy. She loves you."

Jordan began to tremble, which then turned into full-scale shaking. She held on to Sunny like a life preserver as the dam burst, threatening to drown her in grief.

"Let it go, Jordan. I'm here. Let it out. It's okay."

The effort it took to try to hold back was too much. Emotional agony built momentum starting in her feet, traveling through her body to her head, crushing her and pushing her thoughts to the side until all she could feel was the pain. She struggled to breathe and almost panicked when she couldn't draw any air into her lungs.

"Shh," Sunny soothed her. "Let it all go."

How on earth did she let all the pain go? It was going to kill her. Jordan's chest hitched as if separate from her will.

The tears came in body-racking torrents, and Jordan cried for the first time since her mother died doing a junkie's dance and left her alone. She cried for the little girl she'd been and the lonely adult she was. She cried for the kids on the streets and the murdered teenagers in the basement.

She cried until she had no more tears, her chest hiccupping with sobs. Through it all, she was aware of the soothing noises and light that was Sunny. For the first time, Jordan knew what love felt like, not just an imagined concept of what she thought it to be. It wasn't anything that could be put into words, it just was. Love was Sunny wrapped around her in the darkness.

# CHAPTER SIXTEEN

Sunny sat at the rich wood table by the window and reflected on the last few weeks, glad Jordan had finally fallen into an exhausted sleep. Sunny had curled against her, wanting her, needing her. Her life had changed since she met Jordan. She'd changed. Something inside was stronger, yet immeasurably lighter at the same time.

And it all came down to Jordan.

Sunny recalled the night she stood in her father's turret and sensed change on the wind. She hadn't been unhappy before Jordan; she loved her life, family, and friends. But it was almost as if she hadn't known she was missing something vital until she found it.

The experience of knowing how she felt rather than riding the emotional currents of others was intimidating, but she knew she would get better at it. It would leave her better equipped to handle the dark forces when they came up. Trial by fire taught her she could walk through it and come out unscathed on the other side. She no longer had to hide behind others.

Jordan's phone rang again, and Sunny glanced at the caller ID. Katerina Volchosky, for the third time. Who the hell was that? A woman who wanted Jordan's attention? Someone from her past?

*Oh, hell no. Not without a fight.*

At that moment, Jordan stirred and ran a hand over her face. Sunny crossed to her with a cup of coffee. "Good morning. How did you sleep?"

"Time izzit?" Jordan's voice was hoarse.

"Nine."

"P.M.?"

"No, sweetheart, a.m. You've slept for almost twenty-four hours."

"What?"

"You needed it. Sleep is healing."

"Hold that thought." Jordan beelined for the bathroom.

A scream from behind the door had Sunny rushing to her side. "What's wrong?"

"I look like a Dr. Seuss character! Look at my face."

Sunny chuckled and ran cold water onto a washcloth. Jordan's eyes were puffy from crying, and the bruising from her altercation at work did make her look fairly cartoonish.

"Are you laughing at me?" Jordan looked horrified. "This isn't funny."

"No, but your reaction is." Sunny tried dabbing Jordan's face, then gave up and handed the cloth to her. "Here. Hold this over it. It will help."

"I need a shower," Jordan said.

Sunny knew she had to leave before she burst into laughter, and she knew she shouldn't be amused at Jordan's predicament. But the Dr. Seuss character reference was so spot on, she was having a hard time keeping it in. Sparing Jordan's pride, she excused herself and ran out of the bathroom.

She waited for five minutes, then went back in. "Can I join you?"

"Yes."

"Want to talk about it?"

"Nope. Don't want to talk." Jordan drew her under the water with her and closed her mouth softly over her lips. Her kiss was soft, so soft, and deliciously hot.

Sunny put her arms around Jordan, holding her as she'd held her during her tears and through their sleep. "Good," she whispered. "I don't want to talk either."

"Wait," Jordan said. "Let's make it to the bed this time."

Sunny smiled. "Okay." She turned off the water and led her into the other room.

"I'm going to love you." She reached to cup Jordan's face and kissed her softly. She searched her eyes while water dropped from Sunny's hair and sparkled on Jordan's face before slipping to soak into the sheets below her.

She knew Jordan had acquiesced when her body relaxed a fraction of a second before Sunny felt her emotional assent and saw her shy, hesitant smile.

Sunny straddled her stomach and started slow and easy with whisper kisses on her face and neck. Sunny took her time. There was no clock, no world, just sensation and the need to make love to Jordan, the desire to elicit another sigh, just like the first one. Sunny kissed the hand covering Jordan's bullet scar. "I want to love you. All of you, you're so beautiful to me."

Jordan's hand trembled slightly before she moved it. Sunny studied the scar, the raised red circle of skin, twisting and forming a crazy volcano peak around a pink crater.

"It's ugly. Don't look at it."

Sunny perceived the gray swirls of Jordan's insecurity and answered the statement by pressing her lips against the scar, then caressing it with her cheek in a soft motion interspersed with butterfly kisses until Jordan relaxed again and, following an exhalation, she yielded.

Sunny trailed her hair along Jordan's thighs, delighted to see her respond by shivering at the contact.

"I love you," Jordan said.

"I know," Sunny answered. And she did. Jordan's aura swam with beautiful colors of passion and grew more vivid with each whisper.

❖

*Seattle Times*
GHOST HUNTERS SOLVE MISSING PERSONS CASE
By Katerina Volchosky

The bones found last Friday by a team of paranormal investigators were found to be the human remains of three long-missing teenagers. Sisters of Spirits, based out of Bremerton, uncovered the gruesome find while doing an investigation in a downtown hotel undergoing extensive renovations.

The owners, Eric Whitman and Frank Story, couldn't be reached for comment. The names of the deceased are being withheld pending DNA analysis.

Inside sources suspect that the bones are those of three missing teenagers from the downtown Seattle area. A press conference is to be scheduled later this week.

# EPILOGUE

*One year later*

Jordan looked at the crowd gathering and reflected on how much her life had changed in the last year. When she'd shut the door to that hotel room, she began the long process of healing.

The first thing she did was resign from the department. While making that decision was easy, letting go of her identity as a police officer hadn't been without its difficulties. She had to learn *she* was more than the job she believed defined her as a person.

After she quit, Jordan went on her first vacation. It was there, on the other side of the country, on a white sandy beach in Florida, that she buried her childhood trauma alongside her sorrow and watched the sky blaze with orange and red fire while she sat next to Sunny.

Jordan's heart swelled with the memory. How had she ever breathed without her? Sunny taught her how to laugh, and she showed her how to love. She helped her believe and trust in a power greater than herself.

The journey hadn't been without bumps in the road. Jordan still dug her heels in once in a while when things got too strange. She discovered quickly that kindness wasn't weakness, and Sunny's temper could match Jordan's own on any day of the week when crossed.

Jordan had gradually come to a truce with Ash and Isis. Just this morning, she woke to find them curled on her side of the bed.

She'd never displayed any more telekinetic abilities, and for that, she was grateful.

Mazie still hid her truck keys and scared her silly with her antics more often than not. Jordan smiled to herself.

Living with Sunny was an adventure. Jordan became a part of the S.O.S. team and went on investigations. But it hadn't been enough. She wanted to work and still felt the need to make a difference.

An idea had formed and grew wings. Jordan had been surprised and grateful that so many people wanted to help.

And here they were to help her celebrate this day.

The sun heated the sidewalk and mist rose from the cracks as the moisture from the night's rain steamed.

Sunny stood to the side of the small crowd that included the mayor and held Jordan's hand. The emotions she felt from the gathering were mixed. Her mother stood on her other side, glowing with pride and joy. Tiffany and Shade were inside finishing setting up the refreshment tables for the reception.

"Thank you all for coming," the mayor said. "To celebrate the opening of this much-needed community resource created by Jordan Lawson, and generously donated and funded by the Skye Trust, we are happy to present to you the Gina Brayden Safe Haven Center."

The mayor handed the large golden scissors to a diminutive woman next to her, who, together with her husband, cut the blue ribbon in front of the door. A cheer went up from the crowd.

"It was generous of you to let the Braydens do the honors."

"I hope it gives them some small measure of closure and comfort."

"It does," Sunny said. "It's sad that the other parents couldn't make it." She thought of the brass plates etched with the other teenagers' names hanging in the entry hall.

"Honey, sometimes the kids have very good reasons to run away."

People were entering the downtown building they had bought and renovated. "Shade's friend's company did such a good job with the place." Sunny searched the smiling faces until she found the contractor shaking hands with the mayor. "Come on, then. Let's go celebrate." She kissed Jordan before tugging her toward the entrance.

Agnes and Steve stood by the reception desk reading the poem Gina had given Jordan so long ago.

Sunny tugged Jordan away, so happy she thought her heart might burst.

"Hey, Lawson!" Katerina called from the hallway outside the kitchen. When Sunny had met her in person, she had to laugh at the first impression she'd drawn of her. Ms. Volchosky was very far from the fragile ballerina she had pictured.

Kat stood taller than Jordan, topping six feet. Oh, she had blond hair, but it was short and spiked. She might possibly be the most handsome woman Sunny had ever met. Perfect features appeared almost chiseled from a Renaissance artist's palette. Her wide, dark eyes constantly moved, never missing a detail. She strode over to them, and the double-breasted suit looked as if it were custom made for her wide shoulders, tapered hips, and long legs. Gold hoops that marched up the side of her ear flashed with her arrival, along with the diamond stud in the side of her nose.

A uniformed officer entered and Jordan excused herself to go talk to her former partner.

Sunny felt Kat's power tickle her skin. The first time she met Kat, the woman's energy surprised her. It felt ancient, and it was definitely not one that she had any experience with. But when she asked her about it, Kat remained enigmatic about the source, preferring instead to remain mysterious.

"Do you miss working at home?"

"A little, but I'm really enjoying the time off. I've been doing this for so long, I've almost forgotten what it feels like to rest. Jordan thought that moving the offices here to the Haven would be the best thing. She suggested it after one of Shade's clients left one day, and the spirit she called up hung around and then scared her to death when she was in the bathroom."

Kat laughed. "I'll bet she did." She gestured to the door. "Do you think she misses it? Being a police officer?"

"Nope. She said she was tired of the dark side. This center for runaways was all her idea, and you can quote me on it."

"We got some great pictures earlier." She pulled out a slip of paper from her pocket. "Here's a list of names of teenagers currently living on the streets downtown."

"So many?" Sunny was sad at the number of them.

"Those are just the ones who were willing to talk to me. I handed out Safe Haven's business cards. Some will come, I promise."

"I hope so. We certainly have the room. When do you think—"

Sunny realized Kat's attention shifted.

Tiffany was laughing at something Shade said to her as they got out of the elevator, but she stopped sharply and turned to meet Kat's stare across the room.

Sunny felt every muscle in Kat's body go taut next to her and then a whisper of her odd energy rose up in the space between them.

She looked at Tiffany, then back at Kat, two frozen statues aware of nothing but each other.

"Uh-oh."

## About the Author

Yvonne Heidt, was born a fourth-generation San Franciscan, but lived half of her life in the Puget Sound area of Washington state. She is currently living with her partner of eleven years, Sandy, and their four dogs in Texas, where she plays at being a rock star on Friday nights.

# Books Available From Bold Strokes Books

**Sea Glass Inn** by Karis Walsh. When Melinda Andrews commissions a series of mosaics by Pamela Whitford for her new inn, she doesn't expect to be more captivated by the artist than by the paintings. (978-1-60282-771-4)

**The Awakening: A Sisters of Spirits novel** by Yvonne Heidt. Sunny Skye has interacted with spirits her entire life, but when she runs into Officer Jordan Lawson during a ghost investigation, she discovers more than just facts in a missing girl's cold case file. (978-1-60282-772-1)

**Murphy's Law** by Yolanda Wallace. No matter how high you climb, you can't escape your past. (978-1-60282-773-8)

**Blacker Than Blue** by Rebekah Weatherspoon. Threatened with losing her first love to a powerful demon, vampire Cleo Jones is willing to break the ultimate law of the undead to rebuild the family she has lost. (978-1-60282-774-5)

**Another 365 Days** by KE Payne. Clemmie Atkins is back, and her life is more complicated than ever! Still madly in love with her girlfriend, Clemmie suddenly finds her life turned upside down with distractions, confessions, and the return of a familiar face… (978-1-60282-775-2)

**Tricks of the Trade: Magical Gay Erotica**, edited by Jerry L. Wheeler. Today's hottest erotica writers take you inside the sultry, seductive world of magicians and their tricks—professional and otherwise. (978-1-60282-781-3)

**Straight Boy Roommate** by Kevin Troughton. Tom isn't expecting much from his first term at University, but a chance encounter with straight boy Dan catapults him into an extraordinary, wild weekend of sex and self-discovery, which turns his life upside down, and leads him into his first love affair. (978-1-60282-782-0)

**Silver Collar** by Gill McKnight. Werewolf Luc Garoul is outlawed and out of control, but can her family track her down before a sinister predator gets there first? Fourth in the Garoul series. (978-1-60282-764-6)

**The Dragon Tree Legacy** by Ali Vali. For Aubrey Tarver time hasn't dulled the pain of losing her first love Wiley Gremillion, but she has to set that aside when her choices put her life and her family's lives in real danger. (978-1-60282-765-3)

**The Midnight Room** by Ronica Black. After a chance encounter with the mysterious and brooding Lillian Gray in the "midnight room" of The Griffin, a local lesbian bar, confident and gorgeous Audrey McCarthy learns that her bad-girl behavior isn't bulletproof. (978-1-60282-766-0)

**Dirty Sex** by Ashley Bartlett. Vivian Cooper and twins Reese and Ryan DiGiovanni stole a lot of money and the guy they took it from wants it back. Like now. (978-1-60282-767-7)

**Raising Hell: Demonic Gay Erotica**, edited by Todd Gregory. Hot stories of gay erotica featuring demons. (978-1-60282-768-4)

**Pursued** by Joel Gomez-Dossi. Openly gay college student Jamie Bradford becomes romantically involved with two men at the same time, and his hell begins when one of his boyfriends becomes intent on killing him. (978-1-60282-769-1)

**The Storm** by Shelley Thrasher. Rural East Texas. 1918. War-weary Jaq Bergeron and marriage-scarred musician Molly Russell try to salvage love from the devastation of the war abroad and natural disasters at home. (978-1-60282-780-6)

**Crossroads** by Radclyffe. Dr. Hollis Monroe specializes in short-term relationships but when she meets pregnant mother-to-be Annie Colfax, fate brings them together at a crossroads that will change their lives forever. (978-1-60282-756-1)